WITHDRAWN

Praise for Walter Mosley

'A pacey, gutsy thriller with an intriguing cast of cold killers and hot women' *Mail on Sunday*

'[A] powerful crime novel' *Sunday Times*

'Executed in the deft, cool prose that is Mosley's trademark'
Guardian

'Above all he demonstrates once again his wizardry with dialogue, matched only by that other great master Elmore Leonard'
The Times

'Mosley's wry streetwise humour is what keeps the fans coming back for more' *Daily Mail*

'His compact dialogue continues to sparkle and his scene-setting is as skilful as ever . . . if it looks easy, it's probably not'
Scotsman

'This is taut, tense thriller-writing at its best' *Telegraph & Argus*

'Elegant, laconic, complex and thought-provoking, *All I Did Was Shoot My Man* is one of the most intriguing crime fiction novels of the year so far' *Irish Sunday Independent*

'Hard-hitting, fast, masterful' *Waterstone's Books Quarterly*

Walter Mosley, recipient of the PEN USA Lifetime Achievement Award, is the *New York Times* bestselling author of thirty-six critically acclaimed novels, including the now classic Easy Rawlins mystery series. His books have been translated into twenty-one languages and have sold more than three million copies to date. He lives in New York. For more information visit www.waltermosley.com

By Walter Mosley

ALL I DID WAS SHOOT MY MAN

WALTER MOSLEY

PHOENIX

A PHOENIX PAPERBACK

First published in Great Britain in 2012
by Weidenfeld & Nicolson
This paperback edition published in 2013
by Phoenix,
an imprint of Orion Books Ltd,
Orion House, 5 Upper St Martin's Lane,
London WC2H 9EA

An Hachette UK company

1 3 5 7 9 10 8 6 4 2

Originally published in the USA in 2012 by the Penguin Group

A CIP catalogue record for this book
is available from the British Library.

ISBN 978-1-7802-2096-3

Printed and bound in Great Britain by
Clays Ltd, St Ives plc

The Orion Publishing Group's policy is to use papers
that are natural, renewable and recyclable products and
made from wood grown in sustainable forests. The logging
and manufacturing processes are expected to conform to
the environmental regulations of the country of origin.

www.orionbooks.co.uk

In memory of Elsie B. Washington,
a quintessential New Yorker and a literary light

1

I'D BEEN RUNNING a low-grade fever for nearly a week. It wasn't debilitating; more like consciousness-altering. My senses were affected. Sometimes the world looked fuzzy and at other times sounds became muffled, then intense. I could feel myself moving through the heavy atmosphere with the full weight of my one hundred and eighty-three pounds pressing down on the soles of my feet.

Aspirin usually dispelled these symptoms, but I'd left the little plastic box on my desk and couldn't leave the urine-smelling corner I was in because I was there to meet a client—of sorts.

The lower level of the Port Authority Bus Station at Forty-second Street was populated by young hopefuls on the way to colleges and new lovers on the way to life. Mixed in with the optimists moved also-rans headed anywhere but where they found themselves. Sprinkled in among the civilians were crackheads, along with various policemen, Port Authority employees, and freelance crooks.

A middle-aged man wearing horn-rimmed glasses and toting a clipboard was standing outside a women's bathroom asking the ladies as they came out if they had any complaints about the facilities. Some were polite, others ignored him, and still others stopped to chat about leaks and smells and the quality or lack of paper products.

The bus was five minutes late, but there weren't many of us there waiting. Other than myself there were three older women and a younger one. All of us were black but that needn't have been the case.

Two young men, one black and the other white, started making up rhymes to an imagined beat as they leaned against the red-lacquered tile wall across the way. The plain young black woman, waiting for the same bus I was, stole glances at them.

The rhyming young men were dirty, probably high, and likely homeless—but they were singing and moving to an imagined beat that men had been keeping alive in their breasts longer than there were any buildings or buses—or prisons.

"Excuse me, mistah?" a woman said.

She had amber skin with pecan brown freckles, burnt orange eyes, and an expression that had been spawned when she needed a doting parent to indulge her fears. The fact that she was near sixty had not extinguished the fears haunting her worried inner child.

"Yes?" I said, happy to be distracted from my fevered perceptions.

"Is this the bus from Albion prison?"

"It will be when it gets here."

She smiled, recognizing the skeptical forecast given by our common poor and working-class ancestors.

"My cousin's child Missy got out this morning. I figured that if I met her here and bought her a sandwich or a dress or sumpin' she'd know that some'un cared about her and maybe she'd feel bettah about her chances of stayin' out."

"I think you might be right about that," I said. I wanted to say "ma'am" but she was only a few years older than I.

"You got family you meetin'?" she asked, now that we were temporary friends.

"Um . . . no. Not really. I'm here on a job."

The nameless cousin of the just-released Missy reared back a little and then turned away. I had transformed from a new friend to a potential foe in just a few words.

That was all right with me. The fever had already latched onto her question and was reeling out a story of its own.

ZELLA GRISHAM had tried to kill her boyfriend—shot him three times. But that's not why she had done eight years of hard time on a sixteen-year sentence.

Some people just had bad luck; in the end, I supposed, all people did.

Hers was a perfectly executed heist, and mine, though I didn't know it at the time, was her release.

"MISTAH?" another woman said.

She was a third the age of Missy's cousin, white and pretty in the garish light of the bus depot. With stark white skin, and hair bleached so completely that it blended in with it, she looked like a beautiful ghost looking for souls in that limbo of the Port Authority.

"Yeah?" I said.

"You want a date?"

"I gave up rutting in public corners when I dropped out of

high school the second time. That was back before your mother was out of diapers."

"I got a key to a janitor's closet upstairs," she replied, unperturbed. "You can't lie down, but there's a chair, and a chain to make sure we're not interrupted."

"How'd you get that?" I asked—professional curiosity.

"I keep the janitor happy and pay him thirty dollars a day. It cost you twenty-five for a blow job."

The fever had many facets. It was a fount of revelations but also violent. A depth charge went off in the sea of my mind when that child said the words indicating the act she was willing to perform. The muscles in my abdomen twisted and I sneered with anticipated satisfaction.

"I could see you interested," she said in that knowing way of youthful power.

I took in a breath, searching for the right words.

"I got a condom you could wear if you afraid'a disease," she added.

I rarely go to prostitutes, but I hadn't had sex in months. My wife had other interests, and my girlfriend let me go for the sake of her sanity.

"I'm, I'm waiting for someone," I said, smiling at the rare stammer in my voice.

"They could wait," the ghoul hissed.

The fever had associated itself, at that moment, with my soul; the soul I didn't believe in. It felt as if she, this ethereal denizen of the bus station, could suck the fever and the spirit right out of me. It sounded like relief so profound that for a moment I considered following her up to the janitor's closet.

"Missy, girl! You look healthy, child."

The words entered my head in an abstract way, this because the young prostitute was looking directly into my eyes. Hers were ice blue, unforgiving and yet laser-like in their wordless understanding of my needs.

Man is an animal, Trot, my old man used to say, *never forget that.*

"Alyssa!" a woman cried out.

"Mama!" another woman shouted in a husky voice.

"You want it?" the young prostitute whispered.

I was ready to go with her, at least I wanted to be ready, but then I saw the woman I'd talked to earlier walking away with a young dark-skinned woman wearing jeans and a bright green T-shirt two sizes too large.

I looked around and saw that the bus had arrived and disgorged at least part of its complement. Young and not so young women were walking toward the upward-leading stairs, elevators, and escalator. Only the ones met by loved ones were smiling.

I turned my back on the white woman to look at the door to the bus port.

She was coming through, sporting red hair and an orange rayon pantsuit. The rucksack she carried was drab green and the look on her face was sour.

"Zella!" I shouted.

I raised my heavy mitt to wave her toward me. She reared back as Missy's cousin had done and then cautiously leaned in my direction.

I turned then to apologize to the young white woman. But she was gone. I looked up to see where to, but it was as if she had evaporated in the few seconds that had elapsed.

It was then that I worried that there was more to the fever

than I had believed. Could I have hallucinated the whole encounter? Were my desires and distractions driving me mad?

That question would have to wait for the moment, however.

I had a job to do and she was standing a few feet away, glowering at me like so many others in my long life of misdeeds.

2

"**DO I KNOW YOU?**" Zella asked as I approached her. Her coarse red hair was combed back but otherwise untamed. It wanted to stand up like porcupine quills or an angry cat's back.

There was an unmistakable ripple of violence in her body language—no doubt learned at her previous stint in the women's maximum security prison at Bedford Hills, before her transfer to the milder setting of the Albion facility.

This is Zella Grisham, Gert Longman's words rang in my ears from nine years before.

It was a photograph taken to fit in a wallet. I had already seen her on the front pages of the *Post* and the *Daily News*. That face had adorned the upper half of the front page of the B section of the *Times* too.

"No," I said in answer to Zella's question. "I was sent here by Breland Lewis. He asked me to meet your bus to—"

"Lewis? That's that lawyer, right?"

"Yes. He asked me to—"

"Tall black guy," she said.

"White," I said, "and short. Even shorter than I am, with no bulk either."

Zella was thirty-six and no longer pretty as she had been before her incarceration. There were three strands of gray that I could see. She took that moment to tie the mane back with a black elastic designed for that task.

"And he sent you?" It was more an accusation than a question.

"He had a court case today but wanted somebody to meet you when you got in." It sounded like a lie, even to me.

"He didn't say that he was going to send anybody," she said, "or come himself, for that matter."

I wanted to answer but there was really nothing to say. I was standing right there, obviously to meet her.

"I don't even know why he's helping me," she added in a tone that undercut her words. "I mean, he was right. I didn't belong in prison. All I did was shoot my man when I found him with his dick in my best friend, in my bed, under the quilt that my Aunt Edna made for me.

"But even so there's a lotta women locked away when they shouldn't be. A lotta women separated from their family . . . their children . . ."

She stopped at that point. I knew why. If we had been friends I would have put a comforting hand on her shoulder.

"Breland didn't tell me anything but to come and meet you here," I said—the words echoing in the chambers of my fevered mind.

"Okay," she said. "You've met me. Now what?"

"Uh, well, Breland, Mr. Lewis, has, um, found you a place to stay, and a job too. He wanted me to take you to those places and make sure you got settled in."

I didn't want to be there. I didn't want to talk to or look at Zella Grisham but there are times when you have to do things that eat at you.

"What's your name?" she asked.

"Leonid McGill."

"And do you work for Mr. Lewis or does he work for you?"

"I . . . I don't know what you mean, Miss Grisham."

"It's a simple question. Here you know me by my face. A nigger in a cheap blue suit at Port Authority waiting at the door like a fox at my grandmother's henhouse."

I resented her calling my suit cheap. It was sturdy, well crafted, a suit that had three identical blue brothers between my office and bedroom closet. It's true that it cost less than two hundred dollars, but it was sewn by a professional tailor in Chinatown. The price tag doesn't necessarily speak to quality—not always.

As far as the other things she said I made allowances for her being from rural Georgia and having just gotten out of prison after eight years. Socially and politically, American prisons are broken down according to race: black, white, Hispanic and the subdivisions therein—each one demanding complete identification with one group attended by antipathy toward all others.

"I'm working for Lewis," I said. "I thought that would be obvious by me being here and knowing your name."

"Listen, man," she said with all the force her hundred-and-ten-pound frame could muster. "I don't know anything about any millions of dollars. I don't know how the money got in my storage unit. I do know that Madison Avenue lawyers don't donate their time to white trash like me, getting them out of prison and sending apes like you to meet them. I also know that I'm not going anywhere with you."

I was stymied there for a brief moment. Zella was understandably suspicious. I should have expected as much. After a cheating man, a duplicitous best friend, then being framed for the biggest heist ever in Wall Street's history, sent to prison for attempted murder, but only because she refused to give up confederates she never had, and finally, when someone really wants to help her, she becomes suspicious.

For all her bad timing—I couldn't blame her.

"Listen, lady," I said. "I don't know anything about all that. Lewis paid my daily nut to get down here to meet you and take you where he said to go. If you say no, that's fine with me. I'll just give you the information he gave me and you can make up your mind from there."

I took one of two envelopes from my breast pocket and handed it to her. She hesitated a moment and then took the letter from me.

"There's an address in the Garment District for a woman needs an assistant and another one for a rooming house in the east thirties. You don't have to go to either one if you don't want. It's just my job to tell you about them."

While she was looking at the information I continued: "Breland also said that he wanted you to call him and check in if you had any questions. He said that you already had his number."

If anything, Zella was getting angrier. The fact that I could keep her attention worried her, made her feel that she was being trapped somehow.

"Would you like me to wait until you've spoken to your lawyer?" I asked.

"No, I wouldn't. What I'd like is for you to leave."

"You know I'm really not trying to trick you, Miss Grisham."

"I don't give a fuck what you're trying to do or what you want," she said. "I'd send your ass away if you were a white man with a red ribbon tied around your dick."

Sex. It's the bottom line of human relations. Eight years in prison and it blends in with every emotion—hate, fear, loneliness.

"There's one more thing," I said.

"What?" She hefted the strap of her rucksack and actually took a step away.

I took the second, thicker envelope from my pocket.

"He wanted me to give you this at the end of the day. I guess this is the end so . . ."

She was even more hesitant the second time. I stood there, holding the envelope toward her.

"There's money in it," I said. "Twenty-five hundred dollars. Just ask Breland if you think I stole any of it."

Her fingers lanced forward and snagged the packet.

"What's it for?" she asked without looking inside.

"Like I said, lady, I'm just the errand boy, a private detective who's taking any work he can get during the economic downturn."

She had nothing to say about my rendition of current events so I took a business card from my wallet and handed it to her.

"I know you're suspicious of me, Miss Grisham, but here's my card anyway. If you should ever find that you need assistance, and I haven't earned my day's wages yet, call me and I'll do what I can."

Zella shoved the envelopes and card into her rucksack and moved toward the escalator. I stayed where I was while she rode up toward the main floor, looking back now and then to make sure I wasn't following.

3

I WAS STANDING at the empty bus queue, listening to the young men rhyme. The man in the horn-rimmed glasses that had been questioning the ladies on the state of their toilet was now speaking to a very tall, older white man wearing blue overalls with a nametag declaring PETE over the left breast. Pete was leaning on a long-handled push broom.

"Not again, Pete," the women's toilet interlocutor said.

"No, Joe, it's not like that," the towering white man replied. "You know I do any work that they give me. It's just that these idiots are tryin' to make me the scapegoat for their mistakes."

Joe said something but I didn't hear it because I had slipped into what can only be called a reverie.

GERT LONGMAN was dark-skinned and heavy the way old-time movie stars used to be. Her mother's parents had come from the Dominican Republic but she didn't know from Hispaniola. Gert was born and raised on the island of Manhattan. With no accent, and no pretense to history, she had been my lover for six weeks before she found out about Katrina—my wife.

I hadn't lied to her—not really. I just never thought to mention my circumstances. I mean, Katrina and I hadn't been intimate or jealous of each other's lives in years. We had three children but two of them had nothing to do with my DNA. Katrina said they were mine and I went along with the sham because they were in my house and Katrina maintained that house. She also made the best food I ever ate in my life.

But Gert didn't see things the way I did. She had been hearing wedding bells on those long nights in her SoHo studio.

She cut off our physical relationship but kept contact for the sake of our business.

That enterprise was the perfect blend of our talents and resources.

When I first met her Gert was an office worker in the downtown parole office in Manhattan. That post gave her access to files all over the city. I worked for organized crime and other professional bad men finding patsies for those that felt law enforcement closing in.

Gert would find the right fit and I'd plant false evidence, alter phone records, and forge documents to prove that some other poor slob at least might have been the perpetrator. Sometimes the men I framed went to prison, but, more often than not, there was just enough doubt cast for the District Attorney to call off proceedings against my client.

I kept working with Gert because she was a great resource and because I hoped that one day she would forgive me.

It was only after she kicked me out of her bed that I realized that I felt something akin to love for her.

Gert was my partner in crime but she was also the reason I went straight. That's because the daughter of one of the men whose life I destroyed grew up. Her name was Karmen Brown

and she was as single-minded as any wartime general, child molester, or great film director. She discovered my perfidy, had Gert
killed to hurt me, and then, after seducing me, had a man come
into her house and choke her to death, intending to frame me for
her rape and murder.

I managed to get out from under it, but after that I went
straight; at least as straight as a man can get after a lifetime of
being bent.

I USUALLY BROUGHT work to Gert, but after a while working
with me she developed contacts of her own.

Nine years before, a man named Stumpy Brown, a gambler by
trade, came to her with a proposition. Someone had robbed the
vault of Rutgers Assurance Corporation, a unique organization
that took in capital to insure short-term transactions conducted
outside the borders of the country. Rutgers held anything of
value—paintings, jewelry, or cash. They then used these resources
to float short-term loans and investments at outrageous interest rates.

Back then they had been holding a sum of fifty-eight million dollars to assure that an oilman in Galveston received a certain portion of a Saudi Arabian tanker's load when it landed
in port.

It was an illegal deal, and the parties were later censured and
fined, but the money was stolen, one of the five guards protecting
the vault was murdered execution style, and no one knew who
had gotten away with the money.

It was assumed that the guard, Clay Thorn, was the inside
man, but he was dead and left no leads.

Stumpy had gotten his hands on fifty thousand dollars from the heist. He wanted Gert to use her magic to further implicate some hapless criminal who no doubt deserved the attention.

It was Zella's bad luck as much as anything else that made her Gert's target.

Six days before the robbery Zella Grisham had a serious bout of nausea just before lunch. She was working for real estate lawyers whose offices were down the block from the Rutgers compound. Her kindly boss sent her home, where she found her lover, Harry Tangelo, in bed with her friend Minnie Lesser.

Zella told the police, and later the courts, that she didn't remember what happened after that. She didn't remember going to the dresser, pulling out her daddy's .32 caliber pistol, or shooting the errant boyfriend in the right shoulder, left ankle, and hip. She never denied it; she just didn't remember it.

The DA wasn't hell-bent against her. Public opinion was, she should have killed the bastard. After all, Harry and Minnie had apartments of their own. Many wondered why she hadn't shot Minnie too.

Two weeks later Gert called me.

She had procured, from Stumpy, a picture of Zella, the key to her storage unit, and the money wrapped in Rutgers bands. One stack had a drop of the dead guard's blood on it.

"It's the perfect frame," Gert said. "And she's going to prison anyway."

Even back then, before I'd developed a conscience, I had qualms. It had been discovered that Zella's nausea came from an unexpected pregnancy. Framing a pregnant woman felt wrong.

But there was a lot of money involved, enough to pay many months' rent and children's doctor bills. On top of that, Gert had asked for my help and I still had hopes that she might forgive me one day.

But still, I hesitated. I remember the exact moment, sitting there in Gert's apartment, looking down on the quaint SoHo street.

And then Gert touched my left hand.

"Do this for me, LT," she said.

And so I disguised myself as well as I could, took a storage unit on Zella's floor, and cut off her lock, placing a trunk inside her space. I altered the evidence somewhat because there seemed to be something wrong about the whole deal. I hadn't talked to Stumpy, nor had Gert told him that I was her operative. The money was good, but I felt that I needed, and that Gert needed, some protection.

After that I made an anonymous phone call to the police, telling them Zella Grisham had a journal in her storage unit where she detailed the assault on Harry Tangelo. They cracked the space and found the evidence linking her with the robbery.

THE DA, who might have let the shooting slide on diminished capacity, came down on Zella with everything but the Patriot Act. He demanded that she give up her confederates.

There was a brief window of time where I might have been able to get back with Gert but I felt bad at what I'd done—even way back then when backstabbing was a way of life for me.

ALL THESE YEARS later I got a windfall from a grateful client. I took the money and rolled a story for Breland Lewis about padlocks and faulty police work, about false money wrappers and blood that didn't belong to Clay Thorn, the slaughtered guard.

And now I was standing in the lower level of the Port Authority at Forty-second Street still feeling like a louse.

"**EXCUSE ME?**" a man said.

I ignored it. People were always asking for handouts at the station. I'd given all that I could for one day.

Zella, if she knew the truth, would have hated me. Knowing that, I harbored a little hatred for myself—and my fellow man.

"Sir?" The voice was more assertive than the usual denizen.

I turned to see that it was a policeman, a white guy maybe five-ten—four and a half inches taller than I.

"Yes?" I said.

"Do I know you?"

"Is that a trick question or are you hitting on me?"

"What?"

I angled myself toward the escalator and walked away before the cop could figure out the ordinance that I'd broken.

4

I TOOK THE STAIRS up to the main floor of the transportation hub. The station was alive with activity. Hundreds of travelers were coming in and going out, waiting patiently for their time to leave or talking on cell phones. Some were conversing with their travel companions. Tourists and homeless persons, businessmen and businesswomen, prostitutes and policemen, all there together, proving that the melting pot was not only a reality but sometimes a nightmare.

It was Monday, late morning, and now that Zella had cut me loose I had things to do.

My blood son, Dimitri, was moving out of our apartment that day. And I had a fever to assuage.

At a news kiosk I bought a little packet that contained two aspirin for fifty cents and a bottle of water for two ninety-five. I stood there, a squat man amid the throngs of citizens and denizens, swallowing my medicine and feeling low.

"Leonid," a man said.

It was like the public building was hosting a private party with all my old and new friends invited.

He walked up to me. A slender man, tall and light brown, wearing a dark yellow suit with a navy dress shirt.

"Lemon," I said with insincere emphasis. "How are you, man?"

"Walkin' the streets with no day in court on the horizon," he said. "I had a good breakfast and still got a twenty-dollar bill in my back pocket."

There was something unusual about his choice of words and images, but I didn't care.

"How are you, LT?" Sweet Lemon Charles asked.

"Fever's goin' down."

"You been sick?"

"For quite a while."

"Nuthin' serious, I hope."

"Nothing that death won't settle."

"Wow, man. That sounds bad."

Sweet Lemon was around fifty but he had a boyish look to him. He must have had a given name but no one knew what it was. He was a grifter who dealt in information about the goings-on on the street, kind of like a low-level version of Luke Nye, the pool shark, who knew almost everything going on around the shady side of New York and its national, and international, environs.

Lemon had a cheery disposition. You imagined him smiling through a hurricane.

A pair of cops about thirty feet away noticed us. One of them pointed in our direction and the other one glared.

"What you doin' here?" I asked the street-level answer man.

"Makin' the rent and dreamin' about better days up ahead." Again his words were peculiar—askew.

"Mistah?" a woman said.

It was the pale child from downstairs. I was somewhat relieved that she really existed.

"We've already done this dance, girl."

"Hey, Charlene," Lemon said.

"Hi, Sweetie. What's news?"

"They found Mick Brawn down around City Hall. He had an awl wedged in the back of his neck."

"An awl?"

"Yeah. I guess they don't sell ice picks too much anymore."

"Mickey, huh?" the prostitute lamented. "And he was so nice too, gentle as a lamb."

"When he wasn't on a job," Lemon added. "I hear that he was enforcement on some pretty big ones."

"Man can't help what he has to do for his family," Charlene said. I was sure she said those words often.

"Well, he's dead now. His cousin Willoughby caught it last week in Jersey City. Seems to be goin' around."

"Uh-huh," Charlene said. She was looking off to her right, where a chubby man in a faded gray business suit was stopping to drink from a bottle of Coke Zero.

"Excuse me?" Charlene said as she drifted toward the half-hearted dieter.

"She's a real trooper," Lemon said as we watched her go.

The police still had eyes on us.

"What you up to, Lemon?" I asked. The fever was just beginning to abate. For the moment I was enjoying standing there among my fellows.

"Poetry," the con man replied.

"Say what?"

"I'm studying poetry."

"Reading it?"

"No . . . I mean, yeah, but writing it too."

"You're a poet now?"

"Not exactly."

"What's that supposed to mean, not exactly?"

"I'm what my teacher calls a literary conduit."

"Am I supposed to understand that?"

"It's not too complex. You see my auntie, Lenore Goodwoman, raised me along with twelve other children in a shack next to a tobacco plantation down South Carolina. Every word she ever spoke seemed like it came from on high. She believed in God and nature and what she called the bottomless wells of the earth. She'd sit us kids down and lecture us on the deep meanings of every cloud and breeze, scent and tragedy.

"All I do is remember what she said or the way she said things and write it down and bring it to my poetry workshop. They eat that shit up like it was tapioca puddin'."

"So it's some kinda scam?" I asked, my strength returning.

"Life is a scam, LT. From the president to the prisoner, they all got the wool to pull over our eyes."

I saw Charlene and the chubby businessman headed for the up escalator, probably going to the janitor's hopper room, and thought that Lemon might be making sense.

"I got poems published in three different literary quarterlies," Lemon was saying, "and a twenty-nine-year-old girlfriend that keeps me writing and even got me doin' public readings here and there."

"No shit?"

"I think I done found my callin', man."

"Well, good for you, Mr. Charles. I wish you the best."

I was ready to leave. The fever was on its way down, my mind clearing with the cooler head. I was still guilty but maybe an inch or so closer to the light.

"Hold up, Leonid," Lemon said then.

"What?"

"I heard from Luke Nye that you lookin' for a dude name of William Williams."

I became as still as a Mohawk scout who hears a branch crack in the woods after midnight.

"Is that true?" Lemon asked.

"You better have something to say, Lemon. This is not a joke with me."

"Shit. I know better than to fool with Leonid Trotter McGill. You a serious mothahfuckah—we all know that. It's just that Luke mentioned Williams, and I was talkin' to somebody about it, and Morgan said that there was a famous twentieth-century poet named William Carlos Williams. So I figure that if Willy is usin' that particular fake name, maybe he's into poetry or sumpin', and I could look around to see if somebody on the poetry circuit fits the bill, so to speak."

"So what are you tellin' me, man? Did you find somebody?"

The fever was coming back. Lemon became very aware that I was leaning toward him.

"No, no, no, LT. I just heard it from Luke when I was by there droppin' off these books he wanted. Then when I seen you I remembered what he told me. I'm just askin' if you want me to ask around."

"Sure." I said the word as if it were a threat.

"How old is he?"

"Old."

"And if I find him does he know you?"

"Oh yeah." Tolstoy knew me all right.

5

TOLSTOY MCGILL. In my life he had been God, gone for good, and then seemingly resurrected. He didn't enroll my brother Nikita and me in public school, electing to educate us at home. He took that job seriously. Instead of Dick and Jane we learned about the Paris Commune. Georg Hegel and Karl Marx replaced Lincoln and Washington. Goldman and Bakunin were the heroes we were to pattern ourselves after.

My father was an anarchist who thought himself a Communist; a fool no matter what way you looked at it. He would have been number one on the hit list if the Revolution he worked for was ever successful.

As it was, he left our family to go off and fight in the Revolution when I was twelve. My mother died of a broken heart, and Nikita and I were separated by the so-called child welfare system. Word came to me that my father was dead when I was sixteen, but I already knew . . .

And then one day, within the last year, it turned out that he was alive, that he survived the South American guerrilla wars and had returned to New York decades ago without ever telling his sons.

Nikita was in prison for robbing an armored car, and I was so bad that the law hadn't caught up with me—yet.

Since I found that Tolstoy was alive, going by the name William Williams, I'd sent out a few feelers but my attempts had been halfhearted at best. I didn't know if I wanted to kiss or kill my father; find or forget him.

For a long moment I was off in the ether of passionate ambivalence. Tolstoy was the joker in the deck stacked against me. I hated him for existing. Hated him.

AND THEN I was back in the Port Authority again, with Sweet Lemon looking at me, waiting for an answer.

"Who's this Morgan guy?" I asked as if I were standing there with him rather than reliving an entire life of spite.

"That's my girlfriend, Morgan Lefevre. She's from this rich Boston family. They been here since before the Revolution."

"So have our families, most probably," I said, ever a good student of my father's rants.

"But these folks got the papers to prove it."

"You meet 'em?"

"Stayed at her aunt's house up in Concord, Mass."

"They know about you?"

"What's there to know?"

"Three felony convictions that I know of, more misdemeanors than a savant could count, and twelve years' hard time. And then there's the things that you were never caught for."

"I'm straight now, LT."

"You still talkin' to Luke," I suggested.

"That's just information. I don't get involved no more."

I had to hand it to him, as much pressure as I brought to bear, he was still smiling and nonchalant.

But the proof was there, in the fact that our language had taken on the quality of the street. That's how close we both were to dropping the pretense to a straight life.

"What about you bein' here?" I asked.

"Where?"

"Here. Port Authority." I waved around indicating the impossibly high ceilings of the main hall.

"What about it?"

"Ain't this where you did that bag switch con for so many years? Ain't that why the cops watchin' us right now?"

"They watchin' you, Mr. McGill. They know the only reason I'm here is to push the NYLT."

"The what?"

Lemon reached into his jacket and came out with a professional-looking, triple-folded brochure. The image on the front was a daytime scene on Broadway around Times Square. Famous writers were superimposed here and there among the crowd. I recognized Mark Twain and Langston Hughes. There were others, though, mostly in black and white, among the four-color mob of tourists.

Hollowed-out letters over the pictures said THE NEW YORK LITERARY TOUR.

"We go from Djuna Barnes's old place on Patchin Place down in the Village to Langston's brownstone up in Harlem. We cover the whole city, talkin' about poets, essayists, playwrights, and novelists. You know, it takes three full days just to show everybody everything. We hit all five boroughs. It's not just literary; we give a full account of New York—past and present."

"You do all this?" I asked, finally impressed.

"No, not me alone, LT," Lemon said with his patented grin.

"Morgan, along with her exes, Lucian and Cindy, they lead the tours. I drive the van on Tuesday through Thursday and hand out these brochures on the days I get off. I also advertise readings that they put on."

"Lucian and Cindy?"

"Morgan's what you call a, a, a bisexual. You know. She loves who she loves no mattah who or what."

"Damn, Lemon. How long have you been out of prison?"

"I haven't even been arrested in three years. You know Morgan was teachin' a prison class in poetry and I took it 'cause they said how pretty she was. I already knew how to read and she the one figured out my conduit thing. I come to see her the day I got out and we been together since that night. She put it right out there that if I wanted to keep on gettin' that sweet sugar that I had to give up my criminal ways.

"Now, what man in his right mind gonna argue with that?"

I was grinning broadly. Lemon Charles was like a magic trick that enchanted me with its unexpected transformation. The hapless crook had disappeared and a new man stood in his place. The prestidigitation made sense but was impossible, still and all.

"Mr. McGill?" someone said.

I turned to see that the police had performed a magic trick of their own—they had multiplied from two to three uniformed officers.

"You can go," the new cop, Asian and female, told Lemon.

For the first time Lemon's smile faded; it didn't evaporate, just weakened as the light waning at day's end.

"You go on, Mr. Charles," I said. "I wouldn't want to be the reason you got that sugar knocked off your rind."

He looked me directly in the eye and nodded, took in the cops as if to say that he saw what had happened here, and then backed away.

As I watched him go I saw Charlene coming down the escalator. She had in her hand a bottle of what looked like Coke Zero.

"What are you doing here?" a tall milk chocolate–colored cop was asking.

"Came to meet the nine forty-seven bus in from Albion. It didn't get in till almost ten though."

"What for?" his partner asked. That cop was white, a bit shorter, and broad of shoulders and chest.

"Somebody told me that women coming in from the prison are open to persuasion . . . if you know what I mean."

"You don't seem to have that sort of company," the lady policeman commented.

"I was misinformed."

"What are you doing here?" the black cop asked.

"Talking to you, my friend."

"I'm not your friend."

"No," I agreed.

"What do you have in your pockets?" the white cop bid.

"Whatever the Constitution says I can carry."

"This isn't a game." The white cop had brown hair and eyes the same hue but a little darker. He had a stripe on his shoulder and three freckles over his left cheek.

I turned to my left and walked away. That was the only option I had outside of assault.

They could have come after me.

They didn't though.

I wondered why.

6

I WAS USED to being stopped by the police. My face and name were well known among the law enforcement crowd. They suspected me of everything from contract murder to armed robbery, from kidnapping to white slavery. I had been rousted, arrested, and thrown before more courts than Sweet Lemon Charles knew existed.

Before last year I had my own private cop—Carson Kitteridge. He dropped in on me once a month or so and made sly innuendos. If anyone would ever cause my downfall, it was Carson. But he had stopped contacting me, and police all over the city, even though they still gave me a hard time, seemed to be holding back.

I didn't know what had happened or why, but I had decided to accept it as a temporary gift from the Patron Saint of Thieves, whoever he or she was.

MORE IMPORTANT to me, as I ambled up Tenth Avenue, was Lemon Charles. He had taken the life of a habitual criminal and turned it around, if only for a brief span of time. He wrote poetry, dealt in it, slept with a poet at night, and was asked politely to leave by cops that saw him as a tourist guide rather than a petty con.

This was cause for hope.

I wondered if I could just drop the role I carried like a mantle of a dethroned prince. Maybe I could become a poet or a fifth-grade math teacher . . .

This notion tickled me. The humor caught me by surprise and I laughed so hard that two young women, who were walking in the opposite direction, actually veered out into the street to avoid me. I felt bad about it. I wanted to apologize to them for the outburst. But just the idea of apologizing for my humor sent me on another jag of hilarity.

Finally I went out into the street myself and hailed a yellow cab. The avenues were not safe for young women and poets—not while a laughing hyena like me was on the prowl.

I HAD THE CAB bring me to my building on the Upper West Side, not a block away from Riverside Drive. Parked out front was a small U-Haul truck. The man sitting in the driver's seat was a murderer and I was his only friend.

I walked up to the street-side car window, intending to greet Hush, but he was in the middle of a sentence.

". . . I don't think that it matters what you do," he was saying. "I mean, it matters, but it's more the way you do it and your attention to detail . . ."

"Hey, man," I said. It wouldn't do to eavesdrop on Hush for too long. He was a stickler for his privacy.

"Leonid," he said.

I moved around to see that he was talking to Twill, my youngest and favorite child. We might not have been related by blood, but Twilliam, at the tender age of eighteen, had committed more crimes, and more lucrative ones, than most hoodlums and thieves. I had him in tow as a detective-in-training at my offices, but it was a toss-up if I could save him from his own brilliant, if bent, ways.

"Hey, Pops," Twill said.

He was wearing faded jeans and a graying but still white T-shirt, the appropriate attire for a young man helping his older brother move out of the house. Twill was always appropriately dressed for any occasion.

"What's up, boy?" I asked.

"Everybody's up there workin'," he said. "Bulldog and Taty, Shelly, and even Mardi dropped by. Moms ain't too happy about it though."

"Her baby's moving out," I explained.

"I think it's more than that."

"What do you mean?"

"She's drinkin' pretty hard."

I sighed. That had been Katrina's MO for some time. At first it was just when she'd sneak out with one of her boyfriends—once or twice a week. She'd come home a little tipsy, happy not sloppy. But lately she'd been drinking every day.

"Why'ont you go upstairs and help your brother, Twill? I'll be there in a minute."

"You got it," the young man said. He hopped out of the passenger's seat and headed for the front door to our building.

"That's some kid you got there," Hush said.

"He'll be a helluva man if he survives his own criminal genius."

"I wouldn't want to be the one who stood in his way."

Twill had called Hush to come help in the move. He had the number from an emergency list I'd given him, because, despite his criminal proclivities, he was the most trustworthy member of the family.

Hush had told Twill that he had to check his schedule and then called me to make sure it was okay. He knew that I might be uncomfortable having New York's most successful assassin (albeit retired) carrying my son's boxes from the eleventh floor to a moving van.

I would have said yes anyway. Twill's friendliness and generosity could not be suppressed.

And I had an ulterior motive.

"So?" I asked the killer.

"She's the kinda woman take your life and still you'd have a smile on your face." He was talking about Tatyana Baranovich, the woman Dimitri was moving out to live with. She was from Belarus and would give Twill a run for his money when it came to working the system while avoiding the consequences.

"Tell me something I don't know," I said.

"Until the end of the season all aphids are born female and pregnant."

"Something pertinent."

"She cares about your boy."

"You think she's into anything?" I asked.

Hush was deft and perceptive; he had to be. An assassin deals in absolutes rendered in shades of gray. One slight error could mean his demise.

"I don't know if she is right now," he said, "but she will be. No question about that."

"Yeah," I said with another world-weary sigh. "I know."

"You want me to kill her?" It was a joke. But if I had said yes, Tatyana wouldn't have seen another week.

"I'll get back to you on that," I said.

I patted the murderer's shoulder and headed for the front door.

7

KATRINA AND I had lived in that apartment for more than twenty years. Most days I walked the ten flights to the eleventh floor. That was both my Buddhist and boxing training.

The Buddhists tell you that you have to be mindful of every act, and acquiescence, in your life. They say that life, everything you do and don't do, is an action that must be brought into the light of consciousness.

For the boxer it's simpler—all you have to do is keep in shape.

So I rushed up the hundred and forty steps, looking around at nooks and crannies that I did and did not recognize while concentrating on the increased intensity of my only slightly fevered breathing.

THE DOOR to our apartment was ajar. I had installed one of the world's most sophisticated locking systems on the titanium-reinforced portal. The lock was both mechanical and electronic. When the door closed a metal rod was anchored in a slot in the floor below. Only the signal from the family's keys, or turning the inside knob, would release that bolt.

But what use was it if the door was left open?

I entered the small foyer, closing the door behind me. There were half a dozen boxes stacked in the corner, with a pile of rumpled dirty clothes dumped on top.

The clothes belonged to Dimitri. The fact that they were unwashed and not folded spoke volumes about the drama that I could hear playing out all over the large prewar apartment.

From down the hallway where the bedrooms were I could hear the deep bark of Dimitri's voice. He was talking to someone; you could tell that by the silences between his rants. He was angry, shouting. This was odd because the only time my blood son ever raised his voice was against me, usually in defense of his mother.

Not that I ever attacked Katrina. It's just that there was a tight bond between the young man and his mother—a bond much stronger than she and I ever had.

From the dining room came the sounds of argument and shushing. I recognized the contestants by their voices and was about to intrude when Mardi Bitterman came out of the bedroom hallway. She was wearing a dress whose hem came down to her ankles; a faded violet shmata, loose and threadbare—the young woman's version of Twill's T-shirt and jeans.

Mardi was five-seven, with pale hair, skin, and eyes. She was slight but had a will tougher than most. There was a midsized cardboard box cradled in her arms.

"Hi, Mr. McGill." The wan smile she gave me represented greater hilarity than I had guffawing down on Tenth Avenue.

"Mardi. What's goin' on?"

My office receptionist and general passe-partout put down the box and sighed. You couldn't hear the exhalation, only see it in her expression.

"Mrs. McGill is upset that Dimitri's moving out. I don't think she likes Tatyana. And Dimitri is mad at his mother, saying all kinds of terrible things down in his room. Twill and I have been doing most of the packing but that's okay."

For Mardi, whose parents sold her to a child molester before she even had the defense of language, the war between mother and son must have seemed like happiness.

"What about Shelly?" I asked.

"She's spent most of her time trying to calm Mrs. McGill down."

"Really? What kinda miracle is that?"

Mardi smiled. She never spoke unless she had something to say—a rare quality among Americans of any age.

I headed for the dining room as Mardi made her way back toward the ruckus my eldest child was making.

I stopped at the doorway and listened before entering.

Old habits die hard.

"THAT BITCH has stolen my son's soul," Katrina wailed.

"Don't say that, Mom," Shelly, ever the middle child, said. "D's twenty-three years old. It's time for him to move out."

"My whole life is shit. Dimitri is, and you are too. Sluts and bastards, is all you are."

"Mom," Shelly pleaded. "You just had too much to drink, that's all. Dimitri loves you. I do too."

I never thought I'd hear Michelle say those words to her mother again. When Katrina left me for an Austrian/Argentinian banker Shelly wrote her off. Things had to be really bad for her to find forgiveness now.

"Bullshit," Katrina was saying. "Bullshit. You're just like your father. He sent that monster to help so nobody could stop my baby from leaving."

"Twill called Mr. Arnold, not Daddy."

Arnold was not Hush's real name but one of his many aliases. What's in a name anyway?

"He's a piece-of-shit killer, and your father is too."

"Daddy didn't do anything, Mom."

I walked in then. Regardless of the rancor between Katrina and me I didn't want to see Shelly punished over accusations that were closer to the truth than a loving daughter could ever believe.

Katrina was sitting at the large hickory dining table, my private crystal decanter of fifty-year-old cognac unstoppered before her. I didn't see a glass.

My wife of twenty-four years had passed the half-century mark but maintained a good deal of the beauty of her Scandinavian youth. That beauty was marred by the sour sneer on her face. Her hair was the blond of a young girl and her eyes blue like the North Sea. It was no wonder that Katrina had so many young lovers.

Shelly was dark-skinned in the way people from Southeast Asia are. Her eyes were Asian also but modified by her mother's bloodline. Her father had been killed in a natural disaster before Katrina got the chance to leave me for him.

My daughter was on her knees next to her mother.

"What's going on in here?" I said in a strong voice.

Both women looked up, startled by a genetic memory.

Shelly smiled and stood up.

Katrina's left nostril lifted. "Fuck you," she said.

"Mo-om," Shelly complained.

"Why don't you go help your brother, baby," I said to my daughter. "I'll take over here."

"Yes, you little slut. Move out with him. See if I care."

Near tears, my little girl ran from the room. The fever flashed back and I clenched my hands into fists.

"Are you going to hit me?" Katrina asked, putting her hands up in false fright.

She was surprised when I took two steps forward and grabbed her by both wrists.

"Wha?" she cried.

"Calm down now, Katrina. You know I'm not happy with D movin' out and dropping out of school. But he's a man now and there's no way to stop him."

"As if you cared," she said, a little cowed by my speed, strength, and uncommon willingness to use them.

I let her go and pulled a chair up next to her. I then offered my hands for her to hold. She didn't take up the offer, but at least her belligerence ebbed a bit.

"What's wrong, baby?" I asked.

After decades of marriage it took only a few words for a sermon's worth of communication. I never called Katrina baby. The fact that I did meant I was ready to do whatever I could to assuage her pain.

But she was still angry.

"What do you want me to say?" she spat. "That not one dream I ever had came true? That my children are all disappointments and you were never there when I needed you? And after all that even my own body betrays me and there's nothing left, no one left."

"D's only movin' six blocks from here," I said. "And Shelly's a good girl."

"Huh," Katrina grunted. "Ask Seldon Arvinil about that."

"Who?"

At that moment the dam broke and she reached out for my proffered hands.

"Oh, Leonid."

I leaned over and picked her up, lifting her into my lap.

She put her arms around my head and squeezed.

"I've lost everything," she whispered, "everything."

"Not me. You still got your bad penny."

She patted my bald head and hummed. I could smell the brandy on her breath—it was good stuff.

She put her cheek against mine and exhaled in the way I knew foretold sleep.

"Your skin is hot," she said and then nodded off.

8

". . . THAT BITCH is always tellin' me that she wants me to be happy and she wants me to be a man, but the first thing I do on my own and she's actin' like the world's comin' to an end and, and, and . . ."

These words came from Dimitri through the closed door of his room.

I was carrying his mother down the hall to our bedroom.

Negotiating the doorway without banging her head, I put her down on the bed as gently as possible. We have a big bed, custommade, one hundred inches square. I considered undressing her, but that might prove a problem if she woke up and came running down the hall to yell some more.

So instead I put a pillow under her head and sat next to her a while, trying to understand how I came to that moment, that place.

As I considered, Katrina's breathing deepened.

She was a beautiful woman, and brilliant in her own way. For many years she searched for a man who would take her and Dimitri away from me and the other kids. It wasn't that she didn't love Twill and Shelly but that they loved me too much.

We didn't love each other, at least not like man and wife, but we were tied together by a knot of blood, children, and history.

When she began snoring I knew that Kat would be unconscious for hours. I shifted her so that she was sleeping on her stomach, to make sure she didn't drown in her drunken repose. After that I headed out the bedroom door and back down the hall.

". . . I MEAN, what have I ever done to her?" Dimitri was saying as I walked in. He looked at me, hesitated, and then went on. "Taty has only tried to be nice with her. And Mama won't even say a word if she's in the room. She just stands there with that look on her face."

Dimitri had a child's baseball mitt in his hand. I wondered if he intended to take it to the new apartment. Tatyana, the svelte former prostitute, was on her knees, rolling socks, while Mardi and Twill picked around in the mass of detritus that filled D's deep closet.

Shelly was sweeping the floor.

"Why you doin' that?" Dimitri asked his sister.

"I'm cleaning up so Mom doesn't have to after you're gone."

"Why? You don't even like her."

"She's our moms, Bulldog," Twill said. "Only mother you ever gonna have."

"I wish she was dead," Dimitri said.

"D!" Shelly cried.

Tatyana kept rolling socks.

"That bitch just wants to—"

"Stop," I said in a voice that I hadn't used in fifteen years.

Dimitri, cut off in midsentence, stared at me.

"Come on out in the hall," I said to my only true son.

I turned to leave the room. He had no choice but to follow in my wake.

WE STOOD there face-to-face, but Dimitri was looking down at my shoes. D snorted now and then, his shoulders hunched—waiting for the attack.

"I want to ask you something, son," I said.

"What?"

"Why do you think your mother is so upset?"

"Because she doesn't want me to grow up and be my own man, that's why."

"It's because she's afraid."

Dimitri lifted his head to look me in the eye.

"Afraid of what?" he asked.

I didn't have to answer.

"That was a long time ago," he complained.

"Two years isn't all that long. And she was living with that gunrunner in Russia less than a year ago."

"She didn't know."

"That's why your mother's afraid," I said. "Because Tatyana has lived an outlaw's life. But you're so in love with her that you deny the truth."

Dimitri and I look a lot alike. Our faces were not made to express powerful emotions. Our people carried heavy loads and looked into the wind. But right then there was unbridled passion in his eyes and a quiver coming up from his neck.

"So what are you sayin', Pops? You don't want me to go?"

"That would be like me tellin' a gosling not to migrate down south his first mature season. You got to go. Got to. There's gonna be snakes and foxes, and in your case, with Taty, there might even be men with guns. All I need you to do is think about that."

"So you agree with me moving?"

"Honey, I know what that girl means to you. I look at her and even my blood pressure gets dangerous. Just understand that your mother can only do what a mother can do, like you doin' what you need."

"And you understand why I dropped out of school for a while?"

"She's got a good gig at that Columbia program. It's the man in you workin' to help her make her way through. But what you got to remember, D, is that it's a gift, not an investment. Tatyana is not a bankbook."

That last bit of wisdom put a new wrinkle in my son's brooding brow. It was one of the longest talks we'd had in a dozen years and carried more meaning than anything we'd discussed since he passed puberty.

There was a question brewing behind his furrowed eyebrows. He even took in a breath to expel the words.

"Hey, Bulldog," Twill said at just the wrong moment.

"Wha?"

"Come help us bring all these boxes downstairs."

Twill, Mardi, and Shelly all came out, carrying boxes. From long experience they all knew how touchy things were between me and Dimitri. I was sure that they meant to help, to get him working, so that I didn't lose my temper and knock him to the floor.

"Okay," the man/boy said.

He stomped back into the room, grabbed three boxes, then followed his siblings and Mardi down the hall.

I went into the room to see Tatyana, sitting comfortably on the floor, working with D's clothes and smaller items. She was wearing thin cotton pants the color of beached coral and a sky blue blouse that was loose and yet still somehow appreciative of her figure.

I hunkered down easily, part of the boxer's side of my daily training, and looked at her.

"Not a very pleasant induction into the family," I said.

"She loves him," Tatyana Baranovich explained, shrugging her left shoulder.

"Even still, it must not feel too good."

"It is not my business about what happens between a son and his mother. I can only be here for him if he wants me."

She was working with the socks and watches, cuff links that D had never used and scraps of paper that he was always making notes and little drawings on.

"He's been making those little doodles since he was a child," I said.

"He has great talent."

She stopped working then and looked straight at me. There seemed to be an accusation in the words.

I remembered again what a formidable character Dimitri's girlfriend was.

"Did you meet my friend Mr. Arnold?" I asked.

There was more than one intention behind the question. Immediately I wanted to derail her insinuation that I dismissed my son's talents and abilities. I believed in D but he purposely kept me out of his life.

On the other hand, I didn't only want to know what Hush thought about Tatyana; I was also interested in how she saw the ex-assassin.

"Yes," she said, shaking out a pair of black-yellow-and-green argyle socks.

"What did you think of him?"

She rolled the socks, placed them in a box, and selected another pair from a pile on the floor.

"Well?" I prompted.

"He has dead eyes," she said to the floor.

"What do you mean?"

"He is one of those men my babushka used to tell me about."

"What men?"

"The tightrope walkers who have their death on one side and yours on the other."

9

KATRINA'S SNORING could be heard throughout the apartment. She sawed on while the kids packed and carried, ate sandwiches and cleaned. Dimitri spent half an hour whispering with Tatyana in a corner of the kitchen. After that he calmed down. He stopped talking about his mother and woes and concentrated on preparing for his new life with the Mata Hari of the Upper West Side.

After they had all gone, ferried by Hush to the new place, the only sound was Katrina's rough breathing.

I stayed home out of duty to my wife. She was in pain, more than she ever had been in our long years together—and apart. I suppose I was worried about her.

But the sound of her snoring, for some reason, unsettled me. Soon after the kids were gone I went into the dining room and closed the door. There I took a crystal whiskey glass from the cabinet and poured myself a drink from the decanter.

The snoring was diminished but not extinguished. It sounded like recurring susurration from a storm the other side of thick stone walls.

The cognac didn't help. Rather than providing bliss it exaggerated my habit of going over and over facts that I knew and could not change.

BRELAND LEWIS had to call in a lot of favors to get Zella's case back in the courts. He used every bit of his talent and guile to persuade the female convict to let him represent her. Then he had to present new evidence that had to seem to have been derived from *a priori* investigation and not from actual knowledge concerning the facts in the case.

I had replaced the wrappers on the cash with fakes and used blood from a Lower East Side donor named Rainbow Bill to replace the blood I had been presented with. For ten dollars and a quart of wine I got six good drops.

The lock they snipped off her storage space wouldn't have opened with the key they'd taken from her. For anyone willing to look closely enough it was obvious that she'd been framed.

I'd gone through those elaborate precautions because the job had been brought to me by Gert and I was worried that Stumpy Brown might have put her in jeopardy somewhere up the line.

Getting my preparations together in front of a sympathetic judge cost money—a lot of it.

Thinking about Zella while listening to Katrina's faraway exsufflations I remembered the last time I happened upon hard breathing.

IT WAS in an apartment in Queens, not too far from LeFrak City. At three-seventeen on a Thursday morning I entered the building through a side entrance and made it up the stairs without being noticed. The door to apartment 3G was ajar.

Upon entering the dark apartment I heard her ragged breath. Flipping the light switch revealed the young woman, naked and on her haunches, in the corner. There was a hypodermic needle, with a red rubber bulb at the end, lying on the floor between her thighs. She was swaying from side to side, mumbling to herself and breathing like a Greco-Roman wrestler.

In the center of the floor, on a stained white sheet, lay the body of a white man who carried an extra thirty pounds. I knew he was dead by the permanent crease in his left temple; that and the white ceramic box stained with his blood on the sheet next to him. He was on his back. His only article of clothing was a dark green condom.

The girl was cinnamon colored in the way of Native America after it had been raped by Europe. I got on my knees next to her and she looked up suddenly.

"Velvet?" I said.

Her fright turned to hazy curiosity.

"Did he attack you?"

"My throat," she whispered.

She lifted her head and I could see the bluish bruises that told of the fingers strangling her.

"And you hit him with that box?" I asked.

She looked at the body and nodded. This motion pushed her off balance. I moved into half lotus and let her fall into my lap. There she put her arms around my head, as Katrina was wont to do in our rare moments of intimacy.

Just that quickly Velvet was asleep. I wondered if she would die too. That would have made things much easier.

I didn't need to talk to Velvet Reyes. I had already been informed about her situation—more or less.

"LEONID?" Breland Lewis said on the phone an hour or so
earlier.

"Late for you, isn't it, Bre?" I said lightly, knowing that the
weight would soon be coming down.

He explained that a wealthy client of his had a live-in maid
who had a daughter with a drug problem. This young woman,
Velvet, had called her mother a while before—hysterical. She told
about a man inviting her to his apartment and then trying to kill
her. She fought him off but now she didn't know what to do.

Velvet didn't have to say that the invitation included a mon-
etary transaction or that the john promised some good aitch to
sweeten the pot—so to speak.

The facts pretty much spoke for themselves. Maybe he was
really going to kill Velvet, maybe not. But he probably said that
that was his intention. The bruises proved that he was squeezing
hard enough to kill. She grabbed for anything to fight him off
with and found the porcelain box. He fell over and she called
her mother. Her mother told the rich man, he called Breland,
Breland called me, and in the meanwhile Velvet found the dead
man's stash. She used this to blunt the trauma of near death
and murder.

With the child (I knew from Breland that she'd just turned
twenty) on my lap I fished the cell phone out of my blue jacket
pocket and pressed three digits.

"Leonid," Breland said before I heard a ring.

I explained the situation, and asked, "So what is it exactly that you want from me?"

"I want you to fix it."

"You know I'm straight now, man. And even when I was bent I didn't take on jobs like this."

"Come on, LT. This is for a very important client of mine. And you told me yourself that it looks like self-defense."

"Then why not call the cops and defend her yourself?"

"It's complicated."

I could have pressed him, maybe even talked him out of what he was asking for. But Breland was not only my lawyer, he was a friend. He had been there for me when any other sane man would have walked away.

"I'll call you back."

SITTING AT the hickory table, listening to Katrina's snoring in the distance, I thought about the ugly apartment with the dead man and the ravaged young woman. I had been in many rooms like that over the years. That tableau could have been a painting representing my whole previous life when I still hated my father and believed that dealing in darkness was the only way I could survive.

"YEAH?" Hush said on the second ring. It was past three on that Thursday morning. Velvet was still asleep and the nameless corpse was still dead.

"I got a situation here."

"Where?"

———

"YEAH, LEONID?" Breland said.

"You got two choices," I told my lawyer. "Either I call the cops for nothing or you come up with fifty thousand, cash."

"I can double that and have it in your hands by noon."

What could I say? I needed that much to get Zella out of hock. I'd lose ten thousand points on my bid for redemption, but no boxer ever won a match without getting hit—except maybe Willie Pep.

"I got somebody on the way," I said. "It'll all be cleaned up in an hour."

IT WAS a sour memory, even more so when I thought of Zella's response to my offer of help.

That's when I remembered my advice to Dimitri—*It's a gift, not an investment* . . .

I smiled at my own blind insight, and at just that moment my cell phone sang.

10

IT WAS CLOSE to midnight, and the caller registered as unknown.

"Hello?" The only reason I answered is because I believed any distraction would be better than the memories threading through my brain.

"Mr. McGill?"

"Zella?"

"Yes. Can you talk?"

"Sure. Talk."

"I mean, in person."

"Okay. Come to my office tomorrow at ten. That's in the Tesla—"

"I meant now."

"It's eleven fifty-seven."

"You don't sound asleep."

Recently released convicts don't live in the workaday world, not at first. They've been locked up in a box, and the shock of freedom breaks all rules. Zella had a problem and a phone, so why not call the only man she knew?

"There's a place in the East Village called Leviathan . . ." I said.

I gave her the address and a few special instructions. She made me repeat the directions and agreed to meet there in an hour's time.

I took a three-minute cold shower, donned a blue suit identical to the one I wore that day, and checked to see that Katrina was still on her belly. After all that I skipped down the ten flights to the street, feeling like a kid having received a reprieve from summer school.

LEVIATHAN WAS one of the most secret late-night bars in Manhattan. Three floors underground, it was reputed to be a Mafia bomb shelter in the mid-fifties. The bartender/owner was named Leviticus Bowles, though his mother had christened him Eugene.

Leviticus was a born-again ex-con who acquired the deed and keys from a cell mate, Jimmy Teppi, at Attica before that prison was world-renowned. Legend has it that young Leviticus had had Jimmy's back during some hard times and the mobster was grateful.

Jimmy died not long after the uprising. Mr. Bowles took this as a sign to make a life that kept him away from wardens and prison yards, rancid breath and unrestrained manhood.

Leviathan was beneath a Chinese restaurant equipment store on Bowery. The upper floors of the building were apartments. There was a locked door, with various buttons for the residents. One of these buttons had the name *L. Bowles* scrawled next to it.

I pressed the button and few moments later a voice said, "Yes?"

"Jimmy T," I said clearly.

The lock clicked open, and I walked down a narrow hallway, past the stairs that led to the upper-floor apartments, to a doorway that had an electric eye above it.

I looked up at the lens, and the door came open. Three steps in and I found myself at the precipice of one hundred and seventy-two stairs that coiled down into darkness. This spiral was dank and ominous. You knew that you were leaving the world of city-granted licenses and state-enforced regulations.

The vestibule at the bottom of the stairs presented a bright green door that opened immediately.

I was assailed by Sinatra and cigarette smoke, careless laughter and bright lights.

"Mr. McGill," Tyrell Moss said in greeting.

Tyrell was a tall multi-racial man. Hispanic and black, Asian and some form of Caucasian—he was powerfully built and forever young. He was maybe forty, maybe older, but his smile was that of the God of Youth on some faraway island that had yet to hear of either electricity or clinical depression.

"Moss, man," I said.

Behind him was a large room with ceilings at least twenty-five feet high. There were small pale yellow tables everywhere and at least eighty patrons. At Leviathan you could smoke cigarettes or cigars, drink absinthe, and it was even rumored that there was an opium den in a back room somewhere.

It was like stepping into an earlier day that never existed.

"I got her set up against the back wall," Tyrell was saying. "You *did* invite her, right?"

"Zella?"

"That's her."

WALKING ACROSS the dazzling expanse of Leviathan, I saw many notables. There were no politicians, but their handlers came there to meet and relax; there was a pop star or two; and there were half a dozen bad men with whom I'd done business in the old days.

Zella was wearing the same rayon suit, so I supposed she wouldn't insult my threads again. She was drinking an amber-colored fluid out of a shot glass. That must have given her great solace after eight years of locked doors and stale water.

"Hey," I said as I pulled out the chair across from her at the crescent-shaped table.

"What's that supposed to mean?" she replied.

"It means that you're out of prison, Miss Grisham, and that people don't use codes or special greetings. It means hello."

"Then why don't you say hello?"

I stood up again.

"The drinks are on me, lady. Be my guest. But don't call again." I was ready to leave. No use in wasting time on someone who didn't know how to act on the street, or under it.

"Wait," she said.

"What?"

"I don't know you, Mr. McGill, but Breland Lewis says that I should trust you. The problem is that I don't know him either . . . but I need, I need to talk to somebody."

It was a start.

I sat down again.

"What can I do to allay your suspicions?" I asked.

"Do you think I had anything to do with the Rutgers heist?"

"No."

"What about Lewis?"

"What about him?"

"Is he after that money?"

"I can't say for sure, but I imagine that someone who knew about framing you had a change of heart and paid him to set you out."

"Who?"

"I have no idea," I mouthed.

Zella suspected that I was lying but what could she do? She stared for a dozen seconds or so, and said, "It doesn't matter. It doesn't matter what you think or him either. It doesn't because I don't know anything about any money."

"Is that why you wanted to meet? To tell me that?"

Distrust and doubt are the first lessons you learn in lockdown. Smiles and kind words mean nothing. Promises and even love are less substantial than toilet paper. Zella couldn't bring herself to confide in me even though that's why she'd come to that underground club.

"Hey, Leonid," a man said.

"Leviticus," I hailed.

He was maybe five-eight, with the shoulders of a much taller man. His bald head was a pale dome over a shelf-like brow and deep dark eyes. His features were angry, but I'd never seen the bar owner lose his temper.

"Haven't seen you in years," he said, looking at me but taking Zella in too.

"It's a big city and I got commitments in every borough."

Bowles was wearing an expensive midnight blue silk suit. He looked like a butcher wearing clothes a young mistress bought for him. From his breast pocket he drew out a pack of cigarettes. Before taking one he offered one to Zella. She took the filterless Camel greedily. He waved the pack at me but I shook my head.

Then Bowles took one and lit up both himself and my reluctant client.

He took in a deep, grateful breath.

"You're not here to cause trouble, now are you, LT?" he said before exhaling a cloud of smoke.

"No, sir."

He smiled and nodded to Zella. Then he walked away, having delivered his message.

"Trouble?" she asked.

"I'm known as a rough-and-tumble kind of guy," I said. "People like Leviticus try to keep the breakage down to a minimum."

"Then why let you in in the first place?"

"The kind of trouble I cause can't be kept out with a locked door."

"Are you going to be trouble for me?"

"Depends on what you have to ask."

11

DEAN MARTIN was singing "Amore" and there was laughter from a table of young black gangster wannabes. Zella was halfway through her cigarette and working on a second shot of whiskey. We hadn't gotten to anything pertinent yet but we'd cleared a few hurdles.

I wasn't trying to be her friend. It was enough to seem like I wasn't an enemy. Her cigarette and whiskey helped toward that end. And the fact that I was willing to walk away meant that I had hard feelings of my own. Putting that all together, Zella almost felt almost comfortable enough to speak.

"You hungry?" I asked.

"Always. You know I haven't had a decent meal in almost ten years."

"Leviathan has great steaks."

"You know what I thought about every day since they sent me up to Bedford Hills?"

I shook my head, wishing that I could have a cigarette too.

"Two things," she said. "The most important is that I regret giving up my baby. I delivered her and relinquished all my rights because I thought that I'd be in prison until she grew to be a woman and I didn't want her to spend her whole childhood waiting for a mother who would never come. I was wrong, and now I want to see her more than anything.

"Can you find my daughter for me, Mr. McGill?"

"Why?" I asked, serious as a judge at the Inquisition.

"I just told you."

"Wherever this child is now, she's with the only parents she's ever known. I can find her, but not if you want to rush in without a meeting with the people who took her in after you gave her up."

"Yes. Yes, I understand that."

Zella's previous beauty was returning. There was color in her face, and the beginning of a certain poise that prison wouldn't have allowed.

"What's the second thing?" I asked.

"Harry."

"Tangelo?"

She nodded, lowering her head as she did so.

"What? You sorry you didn't kill him?"

"I don't even remember shooting him in the first place," she said, raising her head defiantly. "The doctors call it selective amnesia. The trauma of shooting him wiped the memory from my head. The first thing I knew, I was in the police station being questioned by a woman named Ana Craig. She told me what happened."

"But you must've been mad at what he'd done."

"He didn't deserve being shot and scared like that. Harry's a weak man. I can only imagine how he felt when I kept on shooting at him. I'm actually glad that Minnie hit me . . . stopped me from killing him."

"That's not what you said at the bus station this morning."

"All I meant was that I was crazy. I didn't know what I was

doing. If somebody hadn't framed me for that heist, the DA would have let me out on diminished capacity."

"So what do you want to do about Harry Tangelo?"

"I want to apologize to him," she said. "I want to look him in the eye and say I'm sorry."

If she was just some prospective client that walked in my office, I would have turned her away. Mothers and guilty lovers, they use private detectives like paper towels in a public toilet.

But Zella wasn't a stranger. If she was a runaway train, I was guilty of switching the tracks.

"I can probably find out who your child was adopted by," I said, "but I can't promise that they will agree to meet you. I can also locate Harry Tangelo, but the same holds true for him."

Zella brought out the envelope of cash that I'd given her that morning. This she placed on the crescent table.

"I spent a little more than sixty-seven dollars of it but you can have the rest."

"You get what you pay for," I said, leaving the white envelope on the pale yellow tabletop.

"What does that mean?"

"You're hiring me to see your child and old boyfriend. I'll probably be able to find them, but the meetings, as I said, might prove to be a little more tricky. You hold on to the money until I come back with some answers."

"You don't want the money?"

"Not until I know that I can earn it. I wouldn't want a hot-blooded mama like you to think I had cheated."

That was the first time I'd seen her smile.

It was a nice smile. Very nice.

"So what now?" she asked.

"I buy you another drink, put you in a cab, and tomorrow I start the job you gave me."

"That's all?"

"Unless you need me to find somebody else."

"No."

"And you don't plan to shoot Tangelo anymore, right?"

She smiled again. "No, Mr. McGill, and . . ." She paused, looking at me directly.

"What?"

"I wanted to apologize for what I said to you at the bus station this morning. I was raised better than that."

"Hey. If you can't lose your temper after eight years being locked up for a crime you didn't commit and another one you weren't responsible for, then this would be a harder world than anyone could bear."

"That's very kind of you, Mr. McGill. It has been hard. Maybe I'll take you up on that drink."

NEAR TWO in the morning I put a slightly tipsy Zella Grisham into a yellow cab, paid her fare up front, and even kissed her on the cheek. The way she leaned into that kiss I could probably have climbed in with her. But I try my best to maintain a certain decorum with my clients.

ON THE STREET I considered taking the subway uptown. I think pretty well surrounded by the rumble of the underground rails.

"Leonid," a man called.

I was unarmed and on an empty street. That could have been

the moment of my death. Could have been. Probably would be one day. But not that night. It wasn't my assassin but Carson Kitteridge, recently promoted to captain on the NYPD. His was an at-large position that allowed him to work wherever he was needed.

Carson was even shorter than I, five-five—no more. Pale white, he had less hair than I did. His suit was light-colored and well worn.

"Kit," I said. "I thought they reassigned you after the promotion."

He strolled up next to me with no expression that I could read.

I'm a burly guy, in excess of one-eighty in my boxers. Kit isn't even a lightweight, but there's a gravity to him that makes bad guys think twice. For many years his main goal was putting me in prison. Possibly my greatest single achievement was denying this brilliant cop that aspiration.

"What you up to, LT?"

"Headed home. That is, unless you wanted to grab a drink. You on duty?"

"What you up to, LT?" he said again.

"Why don't you tell me?"

"What do you have to do with Zella Grisham?"

"I was hired to meet her at the bus station. She liked the color of my skin and the cut of my suit and asked me out for a drink."

"What was she talking about?"

"This and that. Nothing special."

"The heist?"

"Claims she didn't do it. I believe her."

"You armed?" he asked.

That was an unexpected question, enough so to make me look

around the dark street. I had a license to carry a concealed pistol. I'd been granted that when I used to have friends in high places.

"No," I said. "Why?"

"Just wondering if you knew what you were getting into," Carson said. "I see you don't."

"What's that supposed to mean?"

A wan smile passed across the policeman's lips and vanished— like a shark's fin.

"See you later, Leonid," he said.

With that he turned and walked away, making the most of his ominous innuendos.

I stood there a few moments more. Again I thought about taking the subway, but when a yellow cab slowed down to see if I needed a ride I jumped in, knowing that Carson Kitteridge never made idle threats.

12

KATRINA WAS STILL snoring so I settled in on the cot in my office. Between the buffers of the traffic from the street and a solid oak door I was able to drift off; not that sleep was any succor.

Freud says that dreams use the content of the past day or so to chum the depths of a timeless unconscious. That's what my father taught me when I was eleven years old, wishing that I could go to a normal school. I wanted to learn about cowboys and steam engine trains, spacemen and naked women—all the things that I was sure other little kids were learning.

In the dream that night my father was lecturing about guilt.

He was wearing a white suit and a brown T-shirt. He was old, but because he was sitting behind an ivory-colored desk I couldn't tell if he was infirm or not.

"A truly guilty man is like a maniac," he was saying (maybe to me). "He doesn't know his disposition because he believes in a set of rules that defy the beliefs of the worker.

"The worker deals in reality and rules. She cannot afford insanity or feel guilt because she is the law and the foundation upon which the law is based.

"You, Leonid," he said, shifting his gaze in such a way that I was the only subject in the world. "You are both insane and guilty of terrible acts performed in the haze of your madness. You don't know it. You don't realize or even remember the crimes you have committed. You believe in the lies of the despot and have therefore sentenced yourself to the ultimate punishment."

This pronouncement tore at my heart. I wanted to speak up, to deny the accusations leveled by my judge, my father. I tried to speak but my voice was gone. I tried to stand but found that I had no legs. My arms ended in stumps. And though I racked my brain I couldn't recall the good things that I'd done.

"You are the living dead," someone said.

I wanted to cry but I had neither breath nor eyes.

I wanted to wake up but instead I fell into a dark cavern of pitiless sleep.

IF A DEAD MAN could shake off that ultimate repose, he would have felt like I did with the sun lancing painfully into my eyes that morning. My body was too heavy to lift, the air so thick that breathing felt liquid, viscous. The thought that I was experiencing a heart attack went through my mind and I sat bolt upright, then laughed.

"A dead man scared to life," I muttered, and smiled again.

KATRINA WAS on her back in the bed, fully clothed. Her eyes might have been open.

"You up?" I asked.

"What happened?" She tried to rise on her left arm, but the elbow slipped out from under her and she fell back on the pillow.

I turned to her and held out my hands.

Pulling her to an upright position, I smiled at the similarities between us that morning.

"Well?" she said.

"Dimitri moved to his new place and you passed out."

"Did I make a fool of myself?" She covered her face with her hands.

"Mothers get a dispensation when it comes to seeing their firstborn go out into the world."

She put down her hands and gazed right through me. At that moment she looked every one of her fifty-three years.

"That woman is no good for him," she said.

"She's a piece'a work," I agreed, "that's for sure. But D's got to find it out on his own. He's never had a woman before. And you know how men are."

"Don't you care?"

"What do you want me to do, Katrina? Try and break his spirit? Make him into a child rather than letting him become a man?"

"She could get him killed. You know that."

"He knows it too."

She let go of my hands and turned away.

I waited a moment and then went to take my cold shower.

An hour later I was leaving the house. Katrina didn't come out to say goodbye.

13

IT WAS SEVEN-THIRTY exactly when I got to my offices on the seventy-second floor of the Tesla Building. There was light coming from under the door so I pressed the buzzer instead of taking out my keys.

The lock clicked and I pushed my way into the reception area.

Mardi stood as I came in. She was wearing a pearl gray dress under a thin white sweater.

"Good morning, Mr. McGill. How are you today?"

"What time did you get in?"

"Seven."

"Any particular reason?"

"I like to get in early in case there were messages from the night before. You get a lot of late-night calls sometimes."

"Did I last night?"

"Mr. Lewis has called you four times since five-fifteen. He says that it's urgent you call him."

I took out my cell phone and noticed that the battery was dead. Breland could have been calling all night. He knew the home number but was aware of my prohibition about business calls on that line.

The only thing in life that truly frightens me is the anticipation of talking to a lawyer. Even good news from my own lawyer brings up bad feelings and insipient dread.

"If he calls again tell him that you don't expect me until ten," I said.

"Okay. Anything else?"

"How'd the rest of the move go?"

"Dimitri was fine after we left your place. Twill took us all to pizza and over to this avant-garde theater in the East Village. They performed a Renaissance play that they modernized some."

"Twill took you to the theater?"

"I think he's dating one of the actresses."

"Did Shelly go too?"

"Uh-uh. She said she was going to meet someone."

There was more to that story, but I wouldn't be getting it from Mardi.

"So," I said, "what do you think about D and Taty?"

She looked up above my head and considered for a moment.

"She loves him," Mardi said at last. "She really does."

"You sound surprised. I mean, they've been together for a while."

"At first I think it was just a convenience for her. Don't get me wrong, she was just using him, Tatyana has had a hard life and she doesn't have a lot of trust in men. But in the last few months something has changed in her. You can tell by the way she looks at D."

"Love," I said.

"You make it sound like a curse."

"You know about Tatyana, right?"

"She's had a hard life," Mardi argued mildly.

"She's dealt one too."

"She can't help what she had to do."

Mardi had once planned to murder her child-molester father. She knew how to cut the deck as well as my son's Belarusian girl-friend.

"That's what I'm sayin', M," I said. "The one you fall in love with brings a lifetime of baggage. In Tatyana's case there's all kinds of sharp edges tucked in with the nighties and toothpaste."

"Dimitri loves her."

"Yes, he does."

"So what can you do?"

"Keep lots of bandages in the medicine cabinet and hope for the best."

BACK IN MY OFFICE, ensconced behind my oversized ebony desk, I called information and asked for Harry Tangelo's phone number. There was no listing.

I had phone books in my closet going back six years. Tangelo wasn't in any of them either.

Lots of people opt not to be in the phone book. If I was Tangelo and tied to a case involving attempted murder and the largest heist in Wall Street history, I might have gotten an unlisted number too. I might have even called on a friend to get me a phone in his name to avoid reporters and cops.

Maybe Tangelo left New York completely.

Failing at normal avenues of research, I signed on to the specially built computer and attendant illegal systems that Bug Bateman had supplied me with.

Bateman was the best hacker in the world, by his own estimation. I have never found reason to argue with that assessment.

The young savant and I had met through his father. The beginning of our relationship had been rocky in that he resented his
old man foisting off another relic on him for his services. But as
the years went by and he met my off-site (and gorgeous) assistant
Zephyra Ximenez, Bug had begun to rely on me to help whip his
three hundred–plus pounds into a kind of shape that Z would
find acceptable.

I signed on to the Persona Search Engine that Bug had lifted
from the State Department. He honed the system down to where
it could be used to find almost anyone almost anywhere in the
world. You entered as much information as possible—age range,
sex, sex preference, race(s), languages spoken, national origin,
height . . . There were even places for DNA codes, photographs
(for a facial-recognition subroutine), and fingerprints. I gave the
program as much information as I could and hit the enter button.

While waiting, on a hunch I tried calling information and
then looking through my phone books for Minnie Lesser—Zella's
supposed good friend and Harry's paramour at the time of his
shooting. She wasn't anywhere to be found either.

There was lots of information on Harry up until nine years
before, a few months after Zella shot him. But the trail went cold
a full ten months before her conviction. He was a sometime car-
penter, housepainter, fiber-optic-wire installer, cook, dishwasher,
and clerk. He was more or less handsome but had weak eyes. As
I looked at the pictures of him I wondered how he managed to
fall so far off the radar.

After noodling on that puzzle for a quarter of an hour, I sicced
Bug's search engine on Minnie Lesser.

She fell from sight at just about the same time Harry did.

Curiouser and curiouser.

If I didn't know for a fact that I was the cause of Zella's incarceration, I would have begun to suspect the boyfriend and his girl.

Perusal of the information provided by Bug's system didn't help me put together a plan to investigate the disappearances. So I picked up the landline and hit a speed dial button.

She answered on the fifth ring.

"Good morning, Mr. McGill," Zephyra Ximenez, my self-defined Telephonic and Computer Personal Assistant, said.

"Z."

"Have you talked to Charles?" That was Bug's given name.

"Not for a week or so."

"Have you seen him for dinner?"

"Only at the gym. He's gotten into good shape."

"Yes . . . he has."

As much as I wondered about Zephyra's interest in Bug's doings, I had bigger problems.

"I'm going to send you two files on people that I can't find anything on in the last nine years," I said. "That's very strange."

"Charles's programs didn't turn up anything?"

"Not an ort."

"Wow. You think they might be dead?"

"If they are nobody buried them—legally. Neither has anyone reported them missing."

"I'll get right on it. And if you see Charles, tell him I said hello."

"You got it."

14

I WAS JUST hanging up with Zephyra when Twill walked into my office. The slender and handsome young man wore silk pants and T-shirt, both black, and a cinnamon-colored jacket with no collar and brass snaps that were not attached. His only flaw was a small scar on his chin—left over from a tumble he took when he was a toddler.

His perfection was very much like that of Achilles.

His skin was actually darker than mine. It was as if Katrina's DNA hadn't affected him at all while his African father completely informed his elegant features and genetic history.

"Hey, Pops," he said. He smiled at me. Twill was usually smiling. As a rule he had everything under control; at least he thought he did.

The reason I'd brought him in as a detective-in-training was because he had gotten into so much trouble in his adolescent years that I feared he'd go too far and end up in prison.

"How's it goin', son?"

"I'm bored," he said, taking one of the chrome-and-cobalt-vinyl visitor's chairs that faced my desk. "You know, listening to your stakeout tapes and readin' old files is good and all but I need to *do* somethin'."

"I know, boy. I know. It's just that the things I been working on don't have a learning curve built into them. Either that or they're very personal jobs that I really need to see through for myself. Can you hold on for a few more weeks?"

"It's been months already, LT. And you know I had problems sittin' at my desk in school every day."

"Speaking of that, have you looked into the high school equivalency test?"

"Me and Mardi go over it two hours every day after lunch, if she's not too busy. I'll probably take it in September."

Since he was five years old he never made a promise that he didn't keep.

"I will get you a job," I said.

For a moment Twill's perpetual smile dimmed, but then the grin broke through again.

"Don't worry 'bout it, Pops. I know you tryin'. And, who knows? If you hadn't roped me in here, I might be sittin' in some jail by now—maybe worse."

Unlike Achilles (at least since his sixteenth birthday), Twill did not suffer from false pride nor did he deceive himself with unrealistic optimism. He was tough and smart. But, most of all, he saw the world for what it was.

I have always loved him without reservation.

"How you been doin'?" Twill asked with a peculiar slant to his gaze.

"Okay. Fine. Why do you ask?"

"I don't know. For the past few days your eyes been kinda glassy. And sometimes you look off into space . . . like, forever."

"Yeah, yeah," I said, feeling as if I was talking to a peer instead of a young man not yet out of his teens. "I've been running a little fever. It's nothing."

Twill's smile evaporated for a moment and he nodded, agreeing with some notion that I had not put forward.

I was about to ask him what he was thinking when the buzzer sounded. Looking at my watch, I saw that it was three minutes after ten. A red light was glaring on my desk phone.

I nodded at Twill and he left with a parting nod.

I took in a deep breath, picked up the receiver, and pressed the clear plastic cube that was imprinted with the number six.

"Hello, Breland."

"I've been calling you since early this morning," the lawyer said, his lack of civility telling me that something was seriously wrong.

"Thanks for helping with Zella," I said, deflecting his urgency. "I picked her up at the bus station. I guess she called you."

"Yes. She was very reserved. Minksy at the Rag Factory said that she came in and will be starting work today. I gave Minks your assurance that there won't be any trouble."

"Thanks again."

Then came the necessary lull when I was supposed to ask why he called.

"My phone died," I explained instead. "That's why I didn't get your call. You know, I usually plug it in. But Dimitri moved out and Katrina tied one on. Between those two fiascoes I guess I was a little thrown off."

"You remember the Mycrofts, don't you?" he asked, no longer able to hold back his business.

I'd never met the billionaire family, but I knew that the Mycrofts' live-in maid was Velvet Reyes's mother.

"What's up with them?" I asked.

"Shelby called me last night. He was very disturbed."

"Oh?"

"It's their son—Kent. They have two children, Kent is the elder. For a while there he was estranged from the family but he's been back for a couple of years—enrolled at NYU."

"College man, huh? He need a math tutor or something?"

"Your kind of math, LT."

"Spell it out, Breland."

"It has come to the attention of Mr. and Mrs. Mycroft that their son has fallen in with a very bad crowd down in the Village. He's an extremely emotional and impressionable young man and they fear for his safety."

It was lawyerspeak. I knew from his elocution that Breland felt pressured.

"What kinda crowd?" I asked.

"We didn't get into specifics."

"No? Are we talkin' about the Little Rascals or the Purple Gang?"

"I'm sure it's nothing you can't handle."

"And what is it exactly that the Mycrofts want me to do?"

"*I* want you to go see them and give them any help you can."

The prospect of visiting a rich man didn't appeal to me. I hadn't adopted my father's political zeal, but I didn't like the company of the upper classes.

Prejudices aside, however, I am a private detective in a downward-spiraling economy. When the country's got a healthy GNP the husband or wife wants to know if a spouse is cheating— they're willing to pay a man like me to find out. But when jobs are scarce that same spouse knows they need the extra paycheck.

"I don't know, Breland."

"You don't know what?"

"These friends of yours seem to have more than their share of trouble."

"They have more than their share of cash too."

"The last time I dealt with them I had to break a promise I'd made to myself."

"It's not like that this time."

"You said you don't know what the problem is."

"He's just a stupid college kid, LT. Any trouble he's in is nothing like the other thing."

"If it's so simple why do you need me?"

"Shelby likes to keep things quiet and confidential. His investment fund caters to blue bloods and old money. The kind of folks that don't appreciate scandal."

"How much money?"

"Half the Reyes thing."

I wasn't worried. I knew that Breland was telling me the truth, that as far as he knew this was a routine job. I wanted him to squirm a bit, however. Having covered up for Velvet still stung.

"It would be a deep favor for me and a good payday for you, Leonid."

"Just a college kid took a bad turn on the way to the john, huh?"

"That's all."

"I'll tell you what, Breland. I'll go talk to these people and see if it's as simple as you say."

"Thank you."

"But you have to do something for me in return."

"What's that?"

"You still got that old girlfriend, the assistant to the director of the department of records?"

"Jeanette? I don't see her anymore, not since Madeline and I renewed our vows."

"But you still know her number, right?"

"What do you need?"

"I want to know the name and address of the family that adopted Zella Grisham's baby."

"I don't know . . ."

"You want me to go talk to these friends'a yours or what?"

"It'll cost something."

"I'll pay it."

"I was asking for a favor, Leonid."

"I did your favor the last time I had dealings with these people."

"You were paid for that."

"Not enough to risk spending twenty years in the joint."

15

TWILL WAS SITTING two desks away from my office door in the long two-sided aisle of sixteen desks. I'd obtained my suite quasi-legally when the previous building manager had a problem that only a guy like me could fix. It involved a fake bank account and re-forged documents. The new owners hired Aura Ullman to get me out, but instead we fell in love.

Aura and I had broken off our liaison; at first because Katrina came back to me after leaving for the Austrian/Argentine banker, Andre Zool, and then because Aura realized that one day I would probably die violently and she didn't think that she could bear that weight.

TWILL WAS WORKING on a sketch with a yellow number two pencil. For years and years I had seen both my sons make little drawings. I never paid much attention. I guess it was because there was so much to worry about with each one, for different reasons, that there wasn't much room for simple pride.

The drawing he was working on was a lovely three-point perspective of the hallway before him. It wasn't angular or forced, a delicate rendition of flowing space—solid and yet suspended like mist.

"Hey, boy."

"What's up, Pops?" He had earbuds on, listening to my boring stakeout logs no doubt.

He turned off the tape machine and looked up from the drawing.

"I might have a case you could help me with, son."

"What's that?"

I explained about the wealthy family with the wayward son, leaving out Velvet and the slaughtered john.

After hearing me out Twill said, "Cool. Just let me go change my shirt."

"I'll meet you out at the front desk."

MARDI WAS WORKING on two computer screens and a scanner, reading in and then moving my various documents from one system to another.

"How's it goin', M?"

"Dimitri called when you were on the phone. He said that he and Tatyana want to invite you over for a housewarming dinner."

"Okay. Anything else?"

"Do you want me to make you a doctor's appointment?"

"What for?"

"Your fever."

"I'll live."

She gave me a mild scowl that I managed to ignore.

"Anything else?" I asked.

"I want to get a water tank in here for drinking," she said. "You know, I was reading this article on drinking water in America and—"

"Fine," I said. "I read the same piece."

Twill came out into the reception area then. He'd switched the black silk T-shirt for a pink cotton dress shirt buttoned up to the neck. I had to admit, it did make him look more professional— and less sinister.

"Where you guys going?"

"Pops might be lettin' me work on a case," Twill told Mardi, who was also his best friend.

"That's great."

"We'll see," I told them.

THE MYCROFTS LIVED in a rococo monstrosity so far over in the eighties that it overlooked the East River. There was a doorman outside the open double copper doors and a deskman visible across the wide green-and-white marble hall.

The doorman was tall and tan, probably mostly Caucasian, with broad shoulders and a sexual leer on his mobile lips.

"Yes?" he asked me.

"Leonid McGill for Shelby Mycroft."

"And?" he asked, nodding once in Twill's direction.

"My associate."

"Are you expected?"

"Yes."

"You sure?"

That question didn't seem to need an answer, so I didn't provide one.

The doorman moved his lips around some, waiting for, maybe even expecting, an answer to his non-question.

When it finally became clear that our conversation was over he said, "Wait here," like a crew boss talking to his minions.

As he walked away I glanced at my son. He didn't seem bothered. I didn't expect he would be.

After some talking and electronic communications the doorman sauntered back across the wide floor. He waited a moment before addressing us.

"Mr. Mycroft is expecting *you*," he said to me, "but no one else."

"If you wish," I said in a bland tone, "you can walk back over there and call him again. Tell him that there are two of us down here and either we're both coming up or nothing."

"What's his name?"

"Fuck you."

The lips froze at that moment and I regretted losing my temper in front of Twill. But sometimes I just get mad at those that take out their life failures on people shorter than them.

"I don't have to let you in," the doorman told me.

"Yeah, you do. You know it and I do too. So hop to it, whatever you're gonna do, and let us be about our business."

"You should have a little respect," the doorman advised.

"I give what I get, brother."

He waited a moment before going back to the deskman. They huddled a few moments, made another call, and then my temporary nemesis came back.

"Go down the hall and take the last set of elevators on your left," he told me. "Floor sixteen."

As I went by he added, "I'd like to meet you on the street one day."

I stopped and turned toward him. This unexpected movement fostered uncertainty; he didn't seem to know what to do with his hands.

"I look forward to that with great anticipation," I told him.

THERE WERE FERNS growing in large ceramic pots along the walls. And six huge tables down the center of the extra-wide walkway. These tables had massive jungle-like floral arrangements on them. Sunlight came into the hallway from a variety of sources, infusing the air with the quality of a natural setting.

When Twill and I got to the mahogany elevator door he pressed the up button.

"Sorry about the way I talked to him, Twill."

"That's all right, Pop. We all know you got a bad temper."

"I try to keep it under control."

"I know you do."

16

THE INTERIOR of the lift was understated, even plain. The walls were unadorned cherrywood and the lights were bare bulbs nestled in mirrored-glass fittings in the four upper corners.

"Sixteen," I told my son.

He pressed the button and I clasped my hands at my back. The fever had returned, and, once again, I'd forgotten the aspirin on my desk.

"You need this?" Twill asked, holding out a little tin of Bayer in his left hand.

"How did you know that?"

"I didn't. Mardi gave it to me. She said that you kept forgetting yours."

I swallowed the coated pills dry before we reached the sixteenth floor.

We exited into a lovely room with a broad green-tinted window that looked down onto the East River and out over Queens. There was only one door. Rich people, in my experience, don't share anything—not even a hallway in a glorified tenement.

Twill was looking for the doorbell when the oversized pale green door swung inward.

The woman standing there wore a utilitarian black dress adorned only by a thin white collar of modest lace. She was in her forties, handsome, with similar skin color as that of Velvet Reyes. We were the same height exactly. As usual, this pleased me.

"Mr. McGill?" she asked with only a hint of Puerto Rico encompassing the last syllable.

I nodded.

"Come in," she said with no smile. "Follow me."

The circular foyer was maybe eighteen feet in diameter; it went up three floors, with no stairs or ornamentation; there was a domed skylight above. The architect was saying with this simple gesture that nature trumped any attempt Man might make to consecrate the portal to a family's domicile.

We followed the maid into a room that had a ceiling only twenty feet high. The centerpiece dominating this chamber was a dark metal sculpture of two wrestlers, almost certainly wrought by Rodin. There were no windows in this room and the walls were charcoal gray. The only lights were yellowy spots that showed highlights of the brilliant forms exhibited by the sculpture.

Left to my own devices I would have dallied for an hour or so before that grandeur, but our guide led us onward.

We came to a sunken living room with a wall of glass that looked over a manicured garden that in turn gazed over the river. It was a big cubical room, with four identical large blue sofas that faced one another across a solid-glass coffee table set upon shiny golden globes. Embedded in the thick plate of crystal was a six-by-eight blue painting of a Negro musician playing a fanciful horn. He was sitting in a chair in a lopsided room. There was a broom leaning sadly in the corner.

This was an unknown Picasso.

"Have a seat," the woman told us. "The Mycrofts will be in in a few minutes."

We settled in side by side on the sofa with its back to the river. I sat forward, elbows on my knees, while Twill reclined.

Despite, or maybe because of, my class consciousness, I was impressed by the oil in glass. A lot of good money went into this monument to wealth.

I was well on my way to hating the Mycrofts and I hadn't even met them.

"Hello," a man said in a modulated tenor.

He was tall (of course) and fit. His mottled tanned skin seemed to come from sportsmanship and not vanity. His trousers were khaki and shirt lime cotton. His feet were moccasined in red-brown leather and his hair was onyx and silver as opposed to the more pedestrian salt-and-pepper.

Behind Shelby Mycroft came a tall thin woman. She was forty-five or -six, a decade less than he, but she looked younger than her years. That was because of the plastic surgery and expensive spa treatments. Her hair tended toward blond, and the metal ball suspended from the impossibly thin chain around her neck was platinum, not silver. Her dress was a luminescent gray that came to mid-calf.

I don't remember the color of her eyes. That's probably because our eyes rarely met.

Twill and I both rose.

"I'm Mr. Shelby Mycroft," he said, extending a hand. "This is my wife, Mrs. Sylvia Mycroft."

The lines were drawn. I smiled at the possibly unconscious class strategy.

I shook hands with the man, Twill nodded, and we both sat back down.

The Mycrofts lowered on the sofa to our right, smiling demurely.

"Can I get you something to drink?" Sylvia asked.

"Water," I said.

"Nothing for me, thank you," Twill added.

She rose and left the room for a moment, returning before her husband started his spiel.

"We were expecting you to come alone, Mr. McGill," Mr. Shelby Mycroft said, the insincere smile delicately etched on his lips.

"When Breland explained the problem I called my associate Mathers here. He, uh, will probably prove useful."

"This is a confidential matter."

I nodded but refrained from showing my temper, or fever.

The maid came into the room carrying a silver platter with two glasses of water on it. She was followed by a greatly transformed Velvet Reyes. The young prostitute/heroin addict was wearing a loose floral dress, and her long black hair was tied up at the back of her head. Behind Velvet came a young girl, maybe three years old. The child had big black eyes that honed in on me. Her mother was taking in my son.

"This is Adonia," Shelby said of the maid, "her daughter Velvet and granddaughter Minolita."

"Hello," I said.

"Hi," the child said and smiled.

"Have I met you?" Velvet asked me.

The question caused Adonia to focus on me.

"I don't think so," I said. "I'd remember you."

Adonia put our glasses down on the priceless painting and hurried her brood from the room.

I picked up my glass and, true to his word, Twill left his where it was placed.

There was a moment of silence in the wake of the servants' departure. Shelby was still a little miffed about Twill's (aka Mathers's) presence.

"We were asked to come here at the last minute, Mr. Mycroft," I said. "I have other appointments to keep."

He didn't like my tone.

That was okay—I didn't like his doorman.

"My . . . our son Kent is studying political science at NYU," he said. "He's twenty-three but young for his age. Recently we've been made aware that he's gotten himself involved with a rough crowd. We're worried that he might get into trouble."

"What kind of trouble?"

"Well . . . we aren't exactly sure."

"Maybe what you heard isn't true," I said, "or an exaggeration of the facts."

"No," Shelby said.

"How do you know?"

"Someone who knows him at school made us aware. Someone that we trust."

"Who's that?"

"What does it matter who told me? I'm telling you."

At that moment the aspirin kicked in. The fever abated, and it was like I was suddenly aware of my circumstances.

I stood up.

"Let's get out of here," I said to Twill.

He stood too.

"I, I, I don't understand," Mr. Shelby Mycroft said, also rising.

"Look, man," I told him. "I'm only here because Breland asked me to come. You got a problem and I'm here to help. But if you don't wanna come clean and tell me what you know, then I don't have the time."

"I've told you what you need to know."

"Come on," I said to Twill.

"It's our daughter, Mr. McGill," Sylvia Mycroft said. "She's the one that told us."

Shelby stood there somehow glowering at both me and his wife at the same time.

"And what did your daughter say exactly?" I asked.

"What I've already told you," Shelby said brusquely.

"I'm going to have to hear it from her."

"No."

"Then I can't help you."

"I'm the one paying for your services, Mr. McGill."

"Not if I don't take the job," I said, looking up into his darkening eyes.

"Shelby," Sylvia said, glaring at his profile.

17

ONCE AGAIN Twill and I were sitting alone in the big sunny room with our backs to the river. We weren't talking because there was nothing to say. I was executing my profession and Twill was learning everything he could. He wasn't impressed by wealth the way I was. Even though he was an accomplished thief by the age of fourteen he didn't really covet money or the things it could buy.

Twill, the son of my heart, was a native of modernity. For him money was a found natural resource like the wind—or dry dung.

LITTLE MINOLITA appeared at the corner of a doorway to the room. Not the door we'd come through. She was staring at me while picking her nose.

"Come here, you little creature," I said, proffering my big boxer's paws.

She opened her mouth, took in a big gulp of air, and then ran at me like a hungry puppy that just saw an unguarded plate.

The ecru-colored child hopped up on my knee and grabbed my index finger.

"Hi," she said.

"Hi yourself."

She'd never heard that phrase, and the newness of the man and the words made her smile.

"I can pick up Miss Sylvia's two-pound weights," she told me.

"I pick up weights too, down at Gordo's Gym."

So many new words and ideas. The child started rocking from side to side.

"Do you ride horses?" she asked, reminded by her own movements.

"Never," I said, shaking my head.

"I do. With Mama."

"Horses are big."

Minolita nodded with such vehement seriousness that both Twill and I smiled. She smiled too, basking in the warmth of our attention.

"Minolita," Velvet said, standing in the same doorway from which her daughter had come.

The child twisted on my knee as if it were her private saddle and said, "Here, Mom."

"Stop bothering Miss Sylvia's guests."

The young woman came into the room with the careless grace of youth. She wasn't over twenty-one, and I was impressed by her recovery from the shape she was in when last we met.

"I'm not bothering them, Mom. He doesn't even ride horses."

Velvet lifted her daughter from my knee and held the child in her arms. She intended to turn away but then stopped.

"I had a dream about you," she said to me.

"That seems like a waste for a beautiful young woman like yourself."

"You were in a big dark place," she said, ignoring the compliment. "Or maybe it was me. Yes. I was in a hole, looking up at the nighttime, and you came and held out your hands. I know that it was you because it was your hands."

"That's some dream," I said. "Or was it a nightmare?"

"When I woke up the sun was shining," she said. "My mother was sitting beside me and I was home."

I wondered how much she really remembered. It didn't much matter. Hush and I had covered up the particulars with the assassin's close attention to detail. Even if the man, Bernard Locke, was missed, his body would never be found.

While I was reassuring myself the Mycrofts returned with another young woman. The new girl was about the same age as Velvet but white and heavier—that's not to say that she was fat.

Velvet heard her mother's employers and whispered to her daughter, "Come on, little one."

As they left the child waved to me. I think that was probably the happiest single moment I had all month.

"This is our daughter," Sylvia Mycroft said, "Mirabelle."

The young woman had longish light brown hair and wore a violet dress that only made it down to the middle of her powerful runner's thighs. Her brown eyes were taking in Twill, who managed to pay just enough attention to her legs.

Sylvia ushered her daughter to the couch on the right. She sat near to her. Shelby stayed on his feet. Maybe he thought this tactic would give him some kind of advantage.

"Hello, Mirabelle," I said.

"Hi." She had a nice smile.

"This here is Mathers."

She smiled at him.

"You have something to tell us about your brother?" I suggested.

Shelby coughed, and then said, "Before we start this I need to set down some ground rules."

"Yes?" I said.

"This is to be a completely confidential conversation. You will not repeat it to anyone, not even Mr. Lewis. I expect you to sign a letter agreeing to that stipulation."

"Sit down, Mr. Mycroft."

If anything, he raised his shoulders up higher.

"Sit down," I said again. "This is not a contest. And furthermore it is not within your sphere of influence. The reason you called me is because you need someone with my particular skills to try and do damage control. I'm not here to have my hands tied. So sit down and let's talk this out."

A beat passed and then another. Shelby Mycroft finally gave in and lowered down on the space next to his wife. This surprised me a little. I expected him to lose his temper and send me away. Maybe that's what I wanted.

The fact that he relented meant that his fears about his son were deep and more troublesome than he let on.

Managing not to smile over my victory, I turned back to Mirabelle. "I was asking about your brother."

She nodded and looked down at the floor.

"You go to NYU with him?"

"No. I attend the New School nearby."

"But you see him a lot?" I asked.

"Not a lot. Maybe every two weeks or so. We usually just run into each other on the street. He calls sometimes though. I mean . . . we're not very close. When I was a sophomore in high school he left home for two years and by the time he got back he was different."

"Different how?"

"I don't see what that has to do with anything," Shelby said.

"He was fun when we were kids," Mirabelle said. "But when he got back he was kind of cold and a little angry."

Like his father.

"So what kind of trouble do you think he's gotten into?" I asked.

Twill laced his fingers under his chin, placed his elbows on his knees, and leaned forward.

"I was at this late-night party in the Meatpacking District last week," she began. "It wasn't the kind of thing I usually go to, but my girlfriends had met this actor and he was going to be there. It was really late but Tonya had a car, so . . ."

"Was your brother there?"

"No." Mirabelle brought her hands together around her bare left knee.

"Then what?" I asked.

"It was a roof party and it was kind of wild," she said, twisting her shoulders to show her discomfort. "There were all kinds of things going on. Drugs. Sex. I wanted to leave, but Tonya had hooked up with that actor guy and so I felt like I had to wait."

The girl was uncomfortable talking around her parents. Her version of the story to them was PG rated. I knew this and waited for the details to come of their own accord.

"I went to sit with this girl I met," she said. "She was African, from Cameroon. We talked for a long time and then this guy I'd never seen before came up to us. He was wearing army fatigues, but I don't think he was a veteran or anything. He asked if I was Kent's sister and I said yes. I guess the girl thought there was something going on with us and so she left, and the guy, his name was Roger Dees, sat down next to me."

Mirabelle shifted in her seat and sat up straight as if trying to throw off the influence of the young man named Roger Dees.

"What did Roger have to say?" I asked.

"He said that Kent better stay away from the Handsome Brothers because they weren't going to have their good looks for very long."

"And what did you think that meant?" I asked.

"I didn't know but it sounded like a threat. I was so upset that I left the party and took a taxi back to my apartment. The next day I went to Kent's place and told him what happened. He begged me not to tell Mom and Dad, but his friends—these Handsome Brothers, Jerry Ott, Loring MacArthur, and a girl named Luscious—had been involved in some kind of disagreement with some drug dealer guys. He said that it was all settled, that it was just a misunderstanding, and that Roger Dees didn't know anything."

"But you didn't believe him?"

"My friend Tate told me that Jerry Ott had been arrested for assault with a deadly weapon and that a lot of kids got their drugs from him. I, I thought that maybe he had been lying to Kent."

Looking over at Shelby I said, "Drugs, huh?"

"It's not Kent," the father said defensively. "He just knows these people."

"If it's not that bad, then why don't you just confront him yourself?"

Shelby's hands turned to fists on his knees. His already serious visage hardened.

"The last time we had a confrontation he left New York and we didn't see him for two years."

"He's going to NYU," I submitted. "I suspect he'd want you to keep on paying his tuition."

"He's got a scholarship. He doesn't take anything from us."

"Nothing?"

I finally sat back on the blue sofa. The cushion was firm. I was pretending to think about the Mycrofts' problem but really I was thinking about my father; about how I wished that he would have taken me down with him to the Revolution, wherever that was. My heart throbbed a bit, and I realized that the fever was coming back already. This inner heat wave had caused my irrational mental connections.

Or was it all that illogical?

Twill was a tough kid and capable of being almost invisible. He'd barely said a word since we entered the room. The value of silence was a lesson most young men never learned.

I turned my attention back to Mirabelle.

"Do you ever socialize with your brother?" I asked.

"Sometimes we get a pizza together or something. He likes to talk about political philosophy—Nietzsche and Lenin mostly."

"Could you get together with him and bring a date?"

"One time he brought that girl Luscious when we had dinner."

"Call him up. Tell him that you have a new boyfriend, Mathers here. Tell him to bring the girl and you'll buy the pizza."

"We're hiring *you*," Shelby said with emphasis.

"You want me to go on a date with your daughter?"

"Certainly not!"

"Then let this happen. Mathers, as you can see, knows how to keep quiet when he should be listening."

18

"JUST GET the lay of the land, Twilliam," I was telling my son in
the cab headed back downtown. "I don't want you to *do* anything.
Find out what's what and report back to me."

"Okay. All right. But what's this Mathers stuff?"

"They don't need to know your name, and I especially don't
want Kent to know."

"Why not?"

"Because even though his parents think that he's an innocent
nerd I have some reservations. I don't want him thinking about
you too closely."

"Lotsa people know me. You know that, Pops. If I use a fake
name and he knows it, that'll be all the worse."

"Just do what I say, Junior."

"Okay, you got it. That Mirabelle's cute anyway."

"This is business, son—not pleasure."

"And I am on the job," he said, exhibiting a boyish smile.

AFTER THAT Twill and I reverted to our roles in the modern
world: we started checking our cell phones for texts, forwarded
e-mails, and voice messages.

I had five voice mails and two texts. They were all from people I knew: Breland Lewis of course, Zella Grisham, Zephyra Ximenez, Carson Kitteridge, and Gordo Tallman—the most important man in my life.

"HEY, LT," Breland said. "I heard from Shelby that you were a little hard on them. He said that some guy named Mathers and their daughter are supposed to get together with his son. He's uncomfortable about getting her too deeply involved, but I told him that you were the best and that you wouldn't put anyone in danger. Don't make me a liar, okay?

"About that other thing—Jeanette looked up the adoption papers for Baby Grisham and found that she was taken in by Sidney and Rhianon Quick of Queens. I've texted you the particulars.

"Zella called the office when I was in a meeting. I haven't talked to her yet, but it sounds like she's in some kind of trouble already."

THE NEXT MESSAGE was from Zella.

"Mr. McGill, I know I keep calling you with my problems but I'm just telling you something this time. I tried Mr. Lewis but he's been in meetings all day, and I thought he'd like to know that this woman, from Rutgers Assurance, came to the place he got me the job and then they told me that they had to let me go. The woman's name was Antoinette Lowry and she told the floor supervisor that the police would be involved.

"When I got home Ms. Deharain told me that Lowry had been

there too. I thought that she'd kick me out, but she told me that you and her went way back and it would take more than a corporation's private security force to scare her.

"That made me wonder. I thought that it was Mr. Lewis who was helping me, Mr. McGill—not you."

WE WERE MOVING through heavy traffic on First Avenue. I put the phone down a moment, worrying about the choices I made while under the influence of the fever.

Mary Deharain was a client from the old days. I'd gotten her husband arrested for a murder that he did commit. Living on her own and lamenting the hard choice she'd made to have her insane husband sent to prison, Mary ran a boardinghouse for folks who liked to live under the radar.

I'd lodged a lot of clients there. But that wasn't such a great idea if I didn't want the client to know that I was looking out for them . . .

". . . **NO HARRY TANGELO**," Zephyra said in her message. "No Minnie Lesser either. Harry disappeared before his wife's trial. He was an orphan so there's no family. The funny thing was that Minnie's mother, Teresa Lesser, was easy to find. She lives in the Bronx. I ran a check on any missing persons reports on both Tangelo and Lesser. Nothing there either. I'll send you a text with Minnie's mother's information and anything else I found."

. . . and curiouser.

"**I NEED** to have a meeting with you, LT," was captain-at-large Carson Kitteridge's single-sentence message.

Kitteridge had studied me over the years. He was my own personal Inspector Javert—intent on making my life miserable. I imagined him rooting around in my trash and going to judges to get wiretapping writs.

Funny thing about a nemesis, however, is that while they're studying you you learn all kinds of things about them. I knew what Kit was looking for by the tone in his voice and words he used.

For instance: Carson only ever used the word *need* when there was a third party involved. He only asked for a meeting when the crime I was suspected of being involved in was more important than putting my ass in stir. If I was in trouble, he'd just tell me to come down to his office—no ifs, ands, or buts.

And so, from that single sentence, I knew that there was some cop or team somewhere investigating the Rutgers heist and they wanted to talk to me.

"**HEY, KID,**" Gordo Tallman, one of the great unsung boxing trainers of this century and the last, said. "I got me a problem that's your fault even though I can't be mad at you for causin' it. Make sure you get down here soon."

I knew Kit because you had to be able to read a predator's signs. But I understood Gordo because I loved him, because he took me into his gym and taught me the right hook/left uppercut combination while everybody else was telling me that I shouldn't be angry for my father abandoning us, leaving my mother to die from a broken heart.

I DISCONNECTED from the voice mail system and noticed that I'd gotten another text while I was listening.

This message was from Aura Ullman.

Before reading what she had to say I sent a text of my own, to Gordo.

I be by in a few hours, G, just have to do one thing first.

CALL ME, was all Aura's message said. Two words that meant more than anything else that had been said that day.

19

A FEW MINUTES LATER the cab pulled up in front of the Tesla Building. I was still thinking about my messages and how they formed the pattern of my day.

"Pops," Twill said.

"You get out of here," I told him. "Go up to the office and tell Mardi to give you two hundred dollars out of petty cash. Use it for the pizza and anything else you might need."

"What about you?"

"I got places to be."

I GAVE THE DRIVER a Wall Street address and sat back while he put up a tactical offense against the midday traffic.

As he struggled silently I thought about Aura.

We hadn't seen much of each other in the last half year. I was pretty sure that she was using a private entrance to the building and taking the freight elevator to avoid running into me.

We loved each other, but I was married and living a life that seemed hell-bent on destruction. Aura could have handled either situation, but dealing with both was just too much for her.

I tried to decipher her message but found that it was beyond my abilities and so I took two more aspirin, sat back, and started counting my breaths until reaching ten, at which point I started the count over again.

"MISTER?" the small brown-skinned cabbie said.

I'd been sound asleep in the back of the cab. It was an animal nap—dreamless and broad.

THE ENTIRE first floor of the block-long office building comprised the Rutgers Assurance security system. First there was a desk where you made your bid for admission.

I started out by asking to speak with Antoinette Lowry. When asked the nature of my business I let it drop that I represented a woman named Zella Grisham. This proposal, along with a state-issued picture ID, caused the visitors' turnstile to unlock. I passed through and walked down a wide pale green hallway that had no doors or other ornamentation. I suspected hidden cameras backed up by computer software and human wetware that studied the travelers there looking for clues to their motives.

By the time I reached the next room, carpeted in deep red and furnished all in mahogany, the receptionist had prepared a badge with my name and picture on it. She was young, possibly Korean, and smiling.

"Go down this hall, Mr. McGill," she said, gesturing in case I was deaf or didn't speak English, "and take the second elevator on your right."

The orange passageway was also spacious and bulged out in

places where there were elevator doors. When I got to my destination I realized that there was no button to push.

All that security and they were still ripped off for fifty-eight million dollars.

I wondered if some member of the security force noted my smile.

THERE WERE more hurdles to pass before I got to the modern antechamber with a solitary, rather aged receptionist and a tan couch. Needless to say I passed every barrier: like a flightless bug making his way into the interior of an insect-eating plant.

There were no magazines or other distractions there, in what seemed like my own private waiting room; no clock or monitors, wall calendars or framed photographs of the gray-headed sentinel's family. She, the hard-eyed receptionist, was white and wrinkled. She wore glasses and had not smiled in years. Behind her desk was a tan door, off center in a bare white wall.

I sat for maybe three minutes before taking out my cell phone.

This action caught my guard's attention.

I had no new messages.

For a few moments I considered calling Aura and finally decided that this wasn't the right environment to talk about lost love. But I had the phone in my hand and so I decided to call my daughter—why not?

I began entering numbers.

"No cell phone usage in the building," the nameless picket said.

I smiled, nodded, and brought the phone to my ear.

"Hi, Dad," she said after the third ring. She sounded a little out of breath.

"Hey, doll."

"How are you?"

"I was worried when you didn't come home last night."

"I stayed at Gillian's house. We had like a slumber party, five of us girls."

"Was it fun?"

"Yeah. Was there anything you needed to talk to me about?"

"I'm sorry about your mother. She's having a tough time."

"I know."

Somebody cleared his throat just then.

I looked up to see a little guy in a light gray suit and a burgundy tie, not silk. He was wisp thin and had a mustache that was once black but had frosted over a bit. The invasion of white hairs was a subtle warning to the thatch on his head.

"Mr. McGill," he said.

I held up a finger and said, "But you don't have to worry about her, baby. I'll make sure that she's okay."

"I know you will, Dad."

"Talk to you later?"

"Okay. Bye."

I folded the phone and pocketed it, stood up and realized that the little guy was still taller than I.

"No cell phone use in the building," he said.

Had the receptionist called him? I didn't hear her. Was there a special button under her desk expressly for cell phone emergencies?

"Sorry," I said.

"I'll have to ask you for your phone," he said, holding out his left hand.

"More than that," I said. "You'll have to take it."

The little white guy had bushy eyebrows that furrowed. There was no gray in them yet.

"You're here to see Miss Lowry?"

So he hadn't come for the phone.

"Yes."

"My name is Alton Plimpton," the man said. "I'm a general manager for Rutgers."

"What's that exactly?"

"All senior receptionists answer to my office," he said proudly.

I could tell that he expected me to be very impressed.

"And Miss Lowry?" I asked.

"She's not here and her supervisor is indisposed, so I came over to see if I could help."

"Miss Lowry doesn't report to you?"

"No."

"Does she work for your boss?"

"Um . . . no."

"Then you can't help."

"But she isn't here."

I sat down.

"I can't think of any place I'd rather wait. What else could you do in a room like this?"

"You can't wait if she's not here."

"If not," I speculated, "then why let me in in the first place?"

"Mr. McGill—"

"Mr. Plimpton, I'm going to sit on this couch and wait until I speak either to Miss Lowry or somebody she reports to. You can go back into your rats' maze and tell the king rat that I said so."

A tremor went through the reception manager's thin frame. He almost said something and then didn't. He turned away and went through the tan door, leaving the dour receptionist to glare at me.

I put my hands, palms up, on my knees and stared vacantly at the doorknob, counting my breaths and emptying my mind of all malice and love.

20

THE ZAZEN PRACTICE calmed me and the aspirin kept back the flood of fever in my blood. Between these two forms of self-medication I drifted over the details of the past few days; my brooding blood son and wild Twill; Zella, my victim and albatross; and Aura . . .

The doorknob turned and out came a solidly built black woman with shoulder-length straightened hair and an ocher suit that was well-tailored, exposing her figure without overaccentuating it.

Even without the heels she would have been an inch taller than I.

"Mr. McGill?"

"Yes?"

"Special Investigator Antoinette Lowry. Will you follow me, please?"

I rose up, feeling the lightness of the meditation, and went through the doorway behind the brisk-moving agent.

We turned here and there into one hall after another, passing many a closed door along the way. Finally we reached the end of the maze at a black door that had my guide's name on it.

She went through, obviously expecting me to follow.

I did.

The first thing you noticed about Antoinette Lowry's office was how small it was; eight feet wide and only a dozen paces from the entrance to the window wall. This window would have given the illusion of space if it didn't look directly into another office building across the way. The street separating Rutgers from its neighbor was small and so it seemed as if the woman sitting at the desk next door could have reached out and touched Antoinette's shoulder if she wanted to. This intimacy added to the closeness of the investigator's work space.

Antoinette's desk was only wide enough to have a top drawer, and there was no other furniture except for a walnut chair that she gestured at while swaying sideways to pass through the narrow space between her desk and the wall.

We both sat and took a moment to regard each other in the coffin-like booth of an office.

Antoinette was in her early thirties. Her face was handsome but hard, the kind of look that had to grow on you. In a certain light, after a good conversation (or a couple of drinks), you might suddenly come to think her fetching. She had skin nearly as dark as mine and intuitive eyes. There was the mild patina of a sneer on her lips. I wondered if this expression was normal or if she brought it out especially for people like me.

"You're here representing Zella Grisham?" Antoinette asked.

"She called to tell me that you got her fired and tried to make her homeless."

"She's a criminal. She should be in prison."

This brazen claim raised my eyebrows.

"I knew corporate America had its own private police force," I said, "but I didn't realize that they now have commoditized the justice system too."

"You get that kind of talk from your Communist father," she replied, "Tolstoy McGill."

If she meant to impress me she succeeded.

"So it's not only Zella you're hounding."

"I'm investigating the robbery of fifty-eight million dollars from my employer," she said. "Fifty-eight million, that's a lot of money."

"Water under the bridge."

"Sheikh al-Tariq gave us that money to assure the delivery of a certain portion of one of his father's oil tankers would reach Houston," she said. "Rutgers had to eat the loss. So if they want me searching down the river and to the sea, that's exactly what I'm going to do. And if you show up on my screen, I will use all the resources at my command to follow you."

"Are you threatening me, Ms. Lowry?"

"Merely telling you what I'm doing and what I intend to do. If, along the way, I find that you're involved in some chicanery or mischief, I will use that knowledge to achieve my ends."

"Chicanery? Where in the South are you from, girl?"

"I will hound Zella Grisham until either she dies or I do. And I will do the same for you, Mr. McGill."

"Unless?"

The sneer morphed into wan complicity.

"If the company's money is restored, the hunt will be over."

"This is a mighty small office to be issuing such large edicts," I said.

"The full weight of Rutgers is behind me."

The woman through her window was white, in her twenties, nearly bald, with dark blue or maybe even black lipstick. This image and Antoinette's words elicited my smile.

"Zella was framed," I said. "The judge was convinced of that; that's why she vacated the sentence."

"Judge Malcolm lifted the sentence because we didn't oppose that decision."

"And you didn't because you felt that on the outside Zella might lead you to her confederates."

"I'm looking at you, Mr. McGill. NYPD files have you involved with everything from embezzlement to armed robbery."

Wow. I wondered if this private cop could succeed where Carson Kitteridge had failed.

"But," Antoinette added, "if you help us retrieve our losses, we can offer a one and a half percent reward on all monies returned."

"That's a lotta money."

"What do you say?"

I sat back and watched the bald white girl laugh at what someone was saying on the phone.

"My father told me one time that corporations have the rights of citizens but that they are not organic creatures. And so Rutgers doesn't have the capability of feeling like it has to protect its biological appendages. That said, Ms. Lowry, do not believe that you are safe from the forces unleashed by this . . . campaign."

I had to throw down that gauntlet. If somebody wants to threaten you, you have to respond in kind; I learned that lesson not from my father but by raising myself on the streets of New York.

The special investigator took it pretty well. She considered my words, weighed them. But she was tough too.

"Is that all?" she asked.

"In your investigation have you looked into Harry Tangelo and Minnie Lesser?"

"They were considered," Antoinette said candidly, "and rejected. We believe that Zella had some connection to Clay Thorn. It's possible that you knew him too."

Thorn was the guard who was executed during the heist.

"Harry and Minnie are missing," I said, "have been since before Zella went to trial. That's strange, don't you think?"

I could see the suspicion rising in Lowry's eyes, also the resentment that I could tell her something she didn't know.

"What's your interest in them?" she asked.

"I work for the lawyer who got Zella out of hock."

"Breland Lewis is your lawyer, Mr. McGill. He's working for you."

That was my cue to stand. Antoinette had come out a point or two ahead in our competition, but I had learned more about her than she had about me.

"I think I'll be leaving now, Special Investigator Lowry. If I don't show up downstairs in a couple of hours, send out a search party. It's a fuckin' rat's nest in here."

21

ON MY WAY uptown on the A train I was thinking about one and a half percent of fifty million. So far Twill was the only operative at my agency bringing in any cash that month.

I was standing in the middle of the crowded car, holding on to a metal pole, when I noticed the blue-and-pink-haired, much tattooed woman standing next to me. She was young and white, flipping through pictures of naked women on her iPad. The moment after I noticed what she was doing she turned her face to me and smiled.

I thought about LeRoi Jones's play *Dutchman* and the bug in the carnivorous plant that I imagined while waiting for Antoinette. I smiled back at the young woman and turned away.

I had to have learned something in all my fifty-five years.

COPPER-SKINNED Iran Shelfly was trying to hurt the heavy bag when I came upon him in Gordo's Gym. He was whaling away on the canvas-covered bale of cotton next to the murky window that looked down on Eighth Avenue.

I watched the thirty-something ex-con throwing body shots

like a real pro. I had wanted Iran to work for me as part of my growing firm but he preferred the ambiance of the gym.

I couldn't blame him.

There were about a dozen men and one woman warming up that afternoon. The formal training sessions would start in an hour.

"Eye," I said.

He stopped and turned to me, sweat pouring off his forehead. He was wearing a tight yellow T-shirt and red trunks. His hands were wrapped but not gloved, and his smile was infectious.

"Mr. McGill. How you doin'?"

"If I complained, somebody might shoot me."

"And that would only make you madder."

"There's a new tenant at your rooming house," I said.

"Zella Grisham. That girl need to learn how to smile."

"You don't like her?"

"She okay. We talked some, but wherever she's from she ain't left there yet."

"I have a special interest in her. I want to make sure that she's safe but I don't want her knowin' what I want."

"Anything you say, Mr. McGill." Iran thought he owed me. When he got out of prison I made sure he had a job, and whenever he found himself in trouble I showed him an exit sign.

Iran was grateful for my help, and I neglected to tell him that I was the one who got him incarcerated in the first place.

"Thanks, Eye. How's the job?"

"I'm so tired every night that I'm asleep 'fore my head hits the pillow. But I always wake up with a smile on my face."

The odds were against an ex-con making it in the straight life, but if he learned the trick, he was the happiest man on the street.

I smiled and went toward the back of the floor-sized room.

Gordo was sitting at his desk in his cubbyhole office, making checks on a long graph-like form. In some arcane way he used these forms to gauge the progress, or decline, of a boxer's talents. Other than the names scrawled in the upper left-hand corner, I could never make sense of these charts.

"Mr. Tallman," I said.

He looked up and then stood.

"LT," he said over an extended hand.

Gordo was my height and red-bronze in color. He was a mixture of all the races America had to offer and was therefore referred to as a black man. He had more hair than I did and was somewhere between the ages of seventy-seven and ninety. He was looking younger though. Beating cancer and falling in love was a fountain of youth for him.

"Sit, sit," the impish trainer said.

His visitor's chair was a boxer's corner stool, where you sat for sixty seconds between rounds, getting yelled at, before your opponent proceeded to beat on you again.

"What's the news, G?" I asked.

Gordo's brows furrowed, his eyes peered into mine. He could see the fever in me. Probably no one ever knows you as well as your trainer.

But I saw something too. There was a hint of sadness in Gordo's gaze; something I'd not seen in a long time.

"What's wrong with you, kid?" he asked.

"You first, old man."

The trainer sagged back in his green-and-gray office chair. His shoulders slumped down and he shook his head slowly.

"I prob'ly shouldn't have called you," he said.

"But you did."

"She might already be gone."

"Who?"

"Elsa."

"Gone? I thought you two were getting married?"

Elsa Koen was the private nurse that Katrina had hired for Gordo when he came to stay with us while being treated for stomach cancer. At the time we thought that he had come to us to die.

The German nurse had fallen in love with the old guy even though she thought he was nearly homeless.

"What happened?" I asked.

"I told her about my properties."

"Plural?"

I had always thought that Gordo rented the fifth-floor gym. There was a property supervisor and everything. It turned out that he owned the entire building; fifteen stories in lower mid-town Manhattan.

"Yeah," he said. "I got two more buildings three blocks up."

"Fully rented?"

"Yep. Skidmore manages them too."

"Damn. So, so you told Elsa about that and she just said she was leavin'?"

"Uh-huh."

"There had to be sumpin' else. You want a prenup or somethin'?"

"No. I told her what's mine is yours."

"Damn."

"Talk to her for me, will ya, LT? Elsa respects you."

The full range of sadness showed on Gordo's face. But it wasn't

the grief that moved me. Gordo never asked anybody for anything. He was a boxer that lived by the philosophy that you didn't
admit defeat—not ever. You might get knocked on your ass, but
even then you used every ounce of strength you had to try and
beat the count.

"Okay," I said.

THE STAIRWAY to Gordo's illegal fifteenth-floor apartment had
a small window at every landing. These looked west on Thirty-
fourth Street toward the Hudson River. I took the steps two at a
time to make up for the exercise I hadn't done in the gym.

Gordo's door was ajar.

I knocked anyway.

There was no answer so I went in.

"Hello?" I said. "Elsa?"

The rabbit warren apartment must have had eleven rooms but
it took up less than twelve hundred square feet. The ceilings were
low, and many rooms didn't have windows.

I found Elsa in a tiny windowless chamber that contained a
dirty cream-colored sofa and a portable TV. There were three
pale blue suitcases sitting in front of her. She'd been crying.

"Elsa."

She looked up at me, letting her head tilt to the side.

"What's wrong, honey?" I asked.

She opened her mouth but words were temporarily un-
available.

The nurse had red hair and pale skin. She wasn't beautiful but
she was fair—in every way.

I sat down next to her and she hugged me.

"Tell me about it," I prompted.

She let go and tried to find something to do with her hands.

"I don't know," she said at last, clasping her palms together tightly between her knees.

She was wearing a plaid skirt and a black T-shirt, no stockings or socks, and white nurse's shoes.

Elsa hadn't been in her forties for very long, and she looked younger still.

"Gordo told you about his property," I said.

"Why?"

"Why what?"

"Why did he lie?"

"He didn't."

"He should have told me before we, we got together."

"Maybe he should have but he couldn't—that's a fact."

The words were said with such certainty that Elsa got suddenly intent.

"Why not?" she asked.

"When you moved away from your parents' house it was already the nineties, right?"

"What does that have to do with anything?"

"When Gordo was born we were in the Great Depression," I continued. "That was back when a black man never owned anything that a white man couldn't take from him. Back when they could put up signs that said 'White Only.'"

"So? It's not like that anymore."

"That's true, things are different today. When young people like you look at the world you see trouble but not like the mess

Gordo's seen. He learned to cover up early on. I didn't know about all of what he owned until a few minutes ago."

"You? But you're his best friend."

"You can leave him, Elsa, but be sure about it. He's a good man and he loves you. You are the only reason he survived that cancer. All three of us know that."

22

I **LEFT ELSA** pondering the pedestrian and impromptu history lesson.

One thing I know, Trot, my father once said. *You can't be in love with a woman and practice Revolution at the same time.*

But don't you love Mama? I asked fearfully.

I do, surely. But not when I'm doin' Revolution.

I don't understand, Daddy.

When I'm with your mother, he said, *she's the only thing in the world. There is no economic infrastructure or class struggle. When it's just me and her it's husband and wife—that's all.*

That was one of the many fragments of conversation that had clattered around in my head for decades. Walking down the stairs, I realized that what I learned from my father was not what he had meant. He wanted to make me a better soldier, but I, slowly and over time, came to believe that men were not only alienated from their labor, and therefore from one another, but they were also, in a similar way, alienated from themselves by the passions they felt pitted against the things they had to do.

I was at the exit door on the first floor before I knew it. I meant to stop by the gym to tell Gordo what had transpired but, at the threshold of the street, I thought that there was really nothing to say. Either Elsa was going to leave or she wasn't. When G went upstairs he'd find out for himself. I'd talked to her like he wanted me to but there was no telling what her decision would be.

I FOUND MYSELF walking east on Thirty-third. I was in trouble but it didn't seem too bad. Rutgers would probably put some pressure on me but I knew how to push back.

The cell phone throbbed against my left thigh. I pulled it out and saw that it was Aura calling. I wanted to flip the phone open but my thumb refused. The vibrations ceased and the little green light of the display faded to black. It felt like watching something die.

I had stopped walking and stood there on the busy thoroughfare, feeling something close to grief over a missed phone call.

Then the screen lit up again.

It was Aura.

"Hello?" I said.

"Why didn't you answer?" she asked.

I tried to find the words to lie but they evaded me.

"What's goin' on, babe?" I asked.

"I miss you calling me baby."

It wasn't just lies that escaped me, I couldn't tell the truth either. I wanted to say how much I loved her, how that love had disappeared like it had with my father when he was being a soldier and not a husband. The feeling struck like an unconscious memory roaring into existence, necessarily unexpected and painful like plague boils erupting from glands deep in the neck.

"Um," I said.

Aura laughed.

"Leonid?"

"Yeah . . . Yes, Aura."

"I know that I've been stringing you along. It isn't, hasn't been fair, but I didn't know what else to do. I was stuck. I love you so much but you scare me."

A horn honked. For some reason that sound made me aware of a woman ranting almost incoherently on the corner a dozen yards away. People were hustling around, moving to the beat of their happenstance lives. This all seemed proper. Life was a cacophony, I'd always known it. Every once in a while there was a piece of beautiful music amid the dissonance, but lucidity was a danger in an irrational world—my father had taught me that too.

Aura made sense. She said that I frightened her.

"Leonid?"

"Yeah."

"Are you going to talk?"

". . . mothahfuckah try an' tell me what to do," the ranting woman cried, "but he don't even have a appendix . . ."

"Sure," I said. "I mean, I want to but I don't know what to say."

"Do you love me?"

"Like seaweed loves the sunlight," I said in free-association mode.

"I love you."

". . . and the niggers was cowboys and all the white men were cryin' . . ."

"What can I do, Aura?" I asked.

"I want you back in my life."

A deep silence set in on me. The people and traffic and crazy woman all stopped making their noises. My mind was like an ovum and her words the impregnating germ. Nothing else could get through. Nothing else mattered.

I forgot where I was going, fought off the desire to sit down on the curb. I wasn't sure what I wanted; instead I had become something else, transformed by a desire I thought had died.

"Leonid."

"Yes, Aura."

"Did you hear me?"

I nodded.

"Leonid."

"Yes, I heard you. I hear you."

"Am I too late?"

"If you had asked me that first, I would have probably said yes."

"Can we try again?"

"I need seventy-two hours to answer that question," I said. I don't know why. "Seventy-two hours and I will tell you what I can do."

"You have seventy-one," she said, bringing a smile to my face.

"I'll call you at . . ."—I looked at my watch—". . . four-seventeen three days from now."

"I love you," she said.

"Talk to you later."

THE PHONE RANG once and he answered, "Kitteridge."

"You called?" I asked.

"LT," he said in way of greeting. "Good to hear from you."

"What's the problem, Captain?"

"There's somebody I want you to talk to."

"Who's that?"

"There's a short street over in Flatbush called Poindexter."

"I know it."

"Twenty-six is the address. All you have to say is Lethford."

"And why am I going there?"

"Because you don't want those kids of yours to be fatherless."

I'd called Kit to snap me out of the daze that talking to Aura cast on me.

It worked.

"Somebody's trying to kill me?" I asked.

"I believe that your name might be on a list somewhere."

"What kind of sense does that make?"

"You think you're so innocent that no one could ever mean you harm?"

"No. What I wonder is why would you care?"

"I'm a cop, LT. It's my job to protect the welfare of even garbage like you."

I disconnected the call. No reason to argue or protest. I was interested at the obvious anger that Kit was feeling. He rarely showed his feelings. I didn't much either. That's why we might have been friends in another life.

23

THOUGH IT WAS early evening the summer sun still shown down on Brooklyn. I reached the address on Poindexter a little after seven. What looked like a homeless man in gray clothes sat in the doorway of the boarded-up brownstone.

I say he looked like a homeless person because, even though he had the clothes and state of dishevelment down pat, he wasn't doing anything; not sleeping or reading, drinking or eating, rifling endlessly through his belongings or engaged in an endless diatribe with some imaginary friend—or enemy. For that matter, he didn't have any belongings—no backpack or grocery cart filled with the necessities and diversions that all humans (homeless or homed) need to survive.

I walked up to the doorway, where the tousled and unkempt black man lounged, and looked down at him.

"Wha?" he said, looking up with eyes both clear and unafraid.

He was in his thirties and fit underneath the loose garments. I could see what was probably the outline of a pistol in his right front pocket.

"Lethford," I said.

His nostrils flared.

"Get the fuck outta here, main," he replied.

"I don't think Captain Kitteridge would like that."

The pile of gray clothes rose up more like a panther than a broken man. He stared hard at me and then stepped aside.

The door seemed to be boarded, but all I had to do was push and it swung open.

The hallway was dark and narrow. At the far end a faint radiance hinted at but did not necessarily promise light. I walked in that direction, running my left hand against the wall. At the end I turned left, finding myself at the foot of what might have been a stairway.

Two silhouettes came from the sides of the barely visible steps. A bright light shone in my face, blinding me.

"Who are you?" a gruff voice demanded.

"McGill for Lethford."

"What for?" the other man, who held the torch, said.

I reached out, pulled the heavy-duty flashlight from his hand, and threw it down on the floor.

"What the fuck?" one of them said.

Another light snapped on up above. I took a step backward so that the two shadow men could not grab me.

They were both in street clothes with badges and holsters at their belts. The man on the left, the one I'd taken the flashlight from, looked quite angry. His close-cut hairline was receding and his blue-gray eyes were sparks looking for an accelerant.

"McGill?" a voice from above said.

"That's me."

A very large dark-skinned man descended halfway down to the first landing of the stairway. Looking up at him, I remembered a time thirty years before when I let Gordo talk me into climbing in the ring with a natural heavyweight.

The guy's name was Biggie Barnes and he had fists like anvils.

Don't let him hit ya was the only advice Gordo gave me at the bell announcing round one.

"Come on up," the big man said.

I followed in the wake of the giant up four flights. It was a dimly lit journey and my fever made it feel like a ride in a rocking boat. These two elements brought a flicker of fear into the center of my chest.

At any other time I would not have gone to some unknown destination just because Kit asked me to. He was my enemy, my opponent, not a friend.

But I was sick, in love, and seeking redemption. I should have been under the care of two doctors and a Zen monk. Instead I was in Brooklyn with no real way out.

On the fifth floor there were three doors. One of these had a thick dark green curtain hanging over it. The big man pushed the fabric aside and went through. I followed . . . coming into a good-sized room that was lit by bright incandescent fixtures. There were six desks, here and there, with no rhyme or reason; each had a monitor on it and a plainclothes cop to study it.

The windows were sealed with thick black paper. I counted a dozen small digital cameras, supported on poles of various heights, attached to the walls. The video feeds were routed to the monitors.

The images on the screens were of a social club on Pox Street, one over from Poindexter. Black men and women, many bearing dreadlocks, were coming in and out of the storefront establishment.

I had passed the club on my way to the meeting because I decided to walk around the block before approaching Number 26.

The members of the street-level society sounded like Jamaicans. They seemed rather tough.

"Drug dealers," the big man said, noticing me staring at a screen.

"You Lethford?"

"Come into my office."

He led me through a real door this time, into a smaller space that had two wooden folding chairs and a peacock blue phone on the pine floor. No carpeting. He shut the door behind us.

"Sit," he said in a tone that was neither friendly nor hostile.

The big black man wore a short-sleeved black shirt, black cotton pants, and black shoes. I could tell by his right ankle that his socks were white.

"So," he said, "do you know why I wanted to see you?"

"Who are you, man?" I replied.

He bit the left side of his lower lip and so refrained from slapping me for my insolence.

The cop had a long face and almost no hair except the few sprouts of white that showed on his chin. He was my age, more or less, and the whites of his eyes were no longer that color.

"Captain Clarence Lethford," he said, "Special Investigations Unit."

"Huh."

"Do you know why I wanted to see you?"

"We're not gonna get anywhere with you treating me like a trainee," I said. "I'm here because Carson Kitteridge asked me to come. Now, if you have something to say, then say it."

Big men throw around their weight from an early age. At some
point they assume this is a God-given right. Every now and then
it's good for a short guy like me to disrupt that surety.

"I expect some civility out of you, McGill."

"Is that it? Because you know absence is the ultimate form of
bein' civil. If I'm not there, I can't insult you." I stood up.

"Sit down."

"Fuck you."

That was the moment we had to get to. He was either going
to hit me, let me leave, or get down to the business at hand.

"I was the chief NYPD liaison officer on the Rutgers heist,"
he said.

I sat down.

"I was working that case," he continued, "until Zella Grisham
was charged with complicity."

"Oh." I crossed my right leg over the left, lacing my blunt fingers around the knee. This made me think of Mirabelle Mycroft
and so I released the joint.

"Yeah," Lethford agreed. "Oh."

I think he expected me to start shaking and confess or something. It would take more than one confrontation to break him
of his big-man complex.

When he saw that I wasn't made of straw he continued. "They
got me to look over the case again when Breland Lewis got her
cut loose. First thing I did was go to the shylock's file. I found a
flag there with your name on it."

"He hired me to help her decompress into civilian life."

"Kit says that Lewis is your boy."

"And that means?"

"It means that maybe you had something to do with the heist,"

Lethford said, holding up his thick left thumb. "It means that even if the brass says to lay off you, I'm gonna crawl up your ass until I see brain. It means that maybe I was wrong about Grisham, that maybe you got her out because she knows something that can make your retirement plan shine."

Every time he said the word *means* he showed another finger—not necessarily in proper order. He put up the pinkie for the retirement plan.

"No, Captain," I said. "The only thing to glean from my involvement and her freedom is that she did not commit the crime and that the real culprits are still out there."

"Why would they fake the money wrappers and make her the patsy?" he asked.

"I have no idea," I said, falsely answering the perfectly sensible question. "My job was to help prove that she didn't have any connection to the heist. I accomplished that end."

"You're dirty, McGill."

"That's the general consensus," I agreed.

"And I'm the one who'll take you down."

"That brings us to the reason I'm here," I said. "Kitteridge said that I might be in some kind of trouble . . . and not necessarily from arrest and conviction."

"Bingo," the big cop replied. It was not the exhortation of victory.

At that moment the door to the little meeting room slammed open.

"Captain!" a young white cop shouted. She seemed both angry and afraid. "They're shooting out there!"

Lethford surged up so violently that his chair fell over. He rushed past me into the observation nerve center.

I followed.

"Get the hell out there!" he shouted. "Hurry up!"

I glanced at the screens as the men and woman gathered what weapons they had and rushed out of the room. Some of the cops were already wearing their bulletproof vests; others lugged theirs along.

On the monitors I could see that a black van had crashed into the storefront social club and a cadre of men had jumped out, using semi-automatic weapons against the residents.

On my journey around the block I had noticed a slender alley that led from Pox to Poindexter. On a monitor I saw a young boy, maybe eight, run down that artery with a skateboard under his arm. A few seconds later a tall man with a pistol in his left hand went the same way . . .

I GOT to the street maybe ninety seconds later. The police had used another route. The guards for the stairway and door were gone. The pretend homeless man/sentry was also absent.

I made it to the alley just in time to see the back of the tall man. He was carrying the boy like a shield in front of him as he backed toward the possible safety of Poindexter.

There was a lot of shouting and gunfire coming from the POX TURF WAR, as the papers called it the next day.

I moved in low and relatively quietly. The man wasn't pointing the gun at the young boy and so I hit him hard in the right kidney and left ear. It was a combination attack, but the punches were so fast as to seem simultaneous.

The boy hit the ground, bounced up, and tore out of there,

leaving the unconscious man, his pistol, and even the rainbow-colored skateboard in the alley.

I picked up and pocketed the gun so that no other child might retrieve it. Mission accomplished, I walked away from the noise and turmoil.

It wasn't my fight, not at all.

24

BINGO HAMAN, aka Mr. Human. I was thinking about him as I walked down Flatbush Avenue.

Bingo was his own impact on any situation. He was famous in the underworld, one of the best heist men in the business. He was compared to people like Cole Younger and Jesse James, Baby Face Nelson and even John Dillinger.

The myth claimed that he'd never been arrested.

Maybe it was true.

I hadn't met the venerable Mr. Human. He was good enough not to require the services of a cleanup man like I used to be. That is, unless Stumpy Brown had represented him on the Rutgers job.

At any rate, his extraordinary luck or smarts abandoned him three months earlier at two-sixteen in the morning when he was cruising down the LIE . . . *on his way from his girlfriend's house back to his wife and kids,* Luke Nye, the pool shark and endless fount of information, had told me.

A car with no license plate sped up to pass and fired three dozen shots into the driver's-side window.

———

BLACK MEN *hating and killing each other,* my crackpot father used to say. *That's the legacy of slavery and capitalism. And you don't have to be black, you don't even have to be a man—but it's black men killin' each other, still and all.*

By the time that memory surfaced I was on the 1 train headed uptown, thinking about the photograph of the pudgy white face alleged to be Bingo Haman. The only dirt the *News* could pick up on him was that he was a suspect in a series of robberies around the country. But he was so much more than that. Bingo was a ruthless and merciless killer. He went out on every job fully armed with each weapon cocked.

They had killed a man on the Rutgers heist, if indeed it was his crew that executed that job and the guard.

And how could I claim innocence when I used my wiles to cover up for him? Was I any better?

I STOPPED moving forward at the corner of Ninety-first and Broadway. The light of day was almost gone but I didn't want to head home yet. So I sat on a bus stop bench and took out my cell phone.

She answered on the fourth ring.

"Hello?"

"Ms. Lesser?"

"Yes?"

"Teresa Lesser?" I added.

"That's me."

"My name is Alton Plimpton," I said easily. "I'm a floor manager at Rutgers Assurance."

"Where?"

"We're kind of like an informal international insurance company."

"I don't need any insurance, Mr. Plimpton. Sorry."

"We don't sell insurance, ma'am. We take in money under short-term conditions to protect the interests of people not covered by international law."

"What does that have to do with me?"

"Ten thousand dollars," I said.

"I don't understand."

"We're running an internal investigation and are willing to pay ten thousand dollars for information leading us to the whereabouts of Mr. Harry Tangelo."

At that point the woman admitting to be Teresa Lesser hung up.

IT WAS very comfortable there in the twilight, on that bench. So much so that it took me a moment to realize that the fever, once again, had caught up to me. I downed the last two aspirin that Twill had given me and made a call.

"Hello?" he said.

"Johnny?"

"LT. How you doing?"

"Good. You?"

"All healed up."

On our last collaboration Johnny Nightly made a slip and got himself shot in the chest by a very accomplished killer. The assassin died and Johnny didn't—that's the most one could have hoped for.

"Luke there?" I asked.

A moment passed, and then, "Hey, Leonid. What's up?"

"I got some issues."

"With me?"

"A thing or two you could help me with."

"Shoot."

"I'm looking for an address and I need you to put up a woman for a week or so. You got any empty rooms upstairs?"

"No problem with the room."

"She should probably stay out of sight and maybe Johnny could look in on her now and then."

"That's easy."

Luke Nye was many things. He'd killed men, dealt in women, even pulled a heist or two in his time. He'd been a regular jack-of-all-trades until deciding on pool as his major and dealing in information as his minor in the ongoing adult education University of Life.

"And then there's Stumpy Brown," I said.

"What about old Stumpy?"

"You got numbers on him?"

"Five hundred a night for the room and a thousand for Stumpy," he said.

"HELLO?" she said on the house phone in the downstairs hall of Mary Deharain's rooming house.

"It's Leonid, Zella."

"Oh . . . What do you want?"

"There's a guy named Iran Shelfly lives there. He's in room three-oh-six."

"I've met him."

"He's a friend of mine. I sent him a text, telling him to drive you out to another friend's in the Bronx. I think you'll be safer there until I figure out this thing with Rutgers."

"What are you up to?" she asked.

"I'm trying to help."

"Why?"

"Because Breland is paying and I need the work."

"I didn't have anything to do with that heist. There's no money you can get out of me."

"I know that, Zella."

It was the closest I would ever come to a confession. It wasn't enough to bring me to justice but I think she heard it; I could tell by her silence. After that I explained what was going to happen to keep her safe. She didn't argue.

"YEAH?" he said.

That particular phone never rang—a fact that had something to do with the security system associated with it. No one could eavesdrop on or trace any call to that number.

"Hush?"

"What's up, LT?"

"Are you working?"

Hush, since retiring from the assassination business, had been employed as a limousine driver. Don't ask me why. He had more money than Gordo.

"Didn't I tell you?" Hush said.

"Tell me what?"

"I bought the company. All twenty-seven cars now drive for me. I just keep my regulars and get to spend more time with Thackery and Tamara."

It was hard to imagine Hush as a family man even though I had been a guest at his house half a dozen times. It seemed both illogical and unfair.

"You want to come get me and take a ride out to the beach?" I asked.

"Okay."

"HELLO?" Katrina said.

"Hey, babe," I said, nearly biting my tongue for saying the same thing to both Katrina and Aura.

"Leonid." There was relief in her voice. "Where are you?"

I was only four blocks away but I said, "In Brooklyn. I'm deposing a witness for Breland."

"Is it safe?"

"Yes . . . very."

"I'll wait up for you."

SEVENTEEN MINUTES LATER Hush drove up in a black Lincoln Town Car. I hopped in next to him. He was wearing dark but not black clothes; chocolate brown jeans and a dusk-colored T-shirt. His dark blue sailor's shoes were made from heavy canvas. His brown hair worked as its own camouflage.

I hadn't told him that we were on serious business—he just knew.

Going down the West Side Highway, I explained about Zella and the complications that had arisen. He listened and nodded and drove.

We went through the tunnel at the bottom of Manhattan and made our way to the Gowanus Expressway, headed south.

"Why don't you just leave well enough alone?" he asked when approaching the Belt Parkway.

"You mean leave Zella to rot in jail for something she didn't do?"

"She shot her man."

"They wouldn't have been so harsh for that alone. I mean, she'd gone crazy."

"It's crazy to get her out of prison."

"Yeah, but . . ."

"But what?"

"I don't know. When I'm in bed early in the morning I wake up sometimes and think about the people I've wronged. Some of them, most of them, were pretty bad to begin with. I can live with that. But people like Zella . . . I mean, what good is life if you can't stand up?"

"That's what boxers do, right?"

"What?"

"They get knocked down and stand up again."

"Yeah. If you've never been knocked down, then you've never been in a fight."

25

THE SUN WAS GONE when Hush parked on a side street five blocks from the address Luke Nye gave me. It was a square, flat-roofed pink stucco house not far from the ocean in a run-down but quiet part of Coney Island.

The doorway was inside a vestibule, so when no one answered our knock I used my tools to pick the lock and go in—we had already donned thin cotton gloves.

The first thing Hush did when we entered was to sniff the stale air.

"Huh," he said.

It was a small, impersonal home. The living room had a couch, standing on short wooden legs, and a tan carpet made from cheap synthetic fiber. It could have been a motel room at the Jersey Shore—in 1957.

The bedroom had an unmade queen-sized bed, a dresser with three drawers, and a maple chair. There were various pants and shirts, shoes and socks strewn on the floor. Dust devils conferred in the corners, and I saw three small roaches rubbing antennae on the barred windowsill.

The kitchen sink was filled with dirty dishes in gray water. The roaches met in greater numbers there.

"Look," Hush said.

At the end of the kitchen counter was a door with two or three plastic garbage bags stuffed into the crack at bottom.

"That's where the smell is coming from," Hush added.

"What smell?"

Instead of answering, the retired professional killer handed me a blue handkerchief he took from his back pocket. He had a yellow one for his mouth and nose.

When he yanked the door open it seemed as if the room was flooded with poison gas.

The roaches froze for a moment and then headed for the smell. We did too.

Between the washer and dryer, tied to a kitchen chair, sat Durleth "Stumpy" Brown. His once pink skin was now gray and his flabby face had hardened into a mask. My eyes stung from the gases his body released.

With three fingers of his left hand Hush touched Stumpy's forehead. Almost immediately a huge gutter roach shot out of the dead man's right nostril. The creature hit the floor and scrambled out between my black shoes. It was then I became aware of the buzzing of flies.

"They tortured him," Hush said.

"They're torturing me."

The killer laughed, he really laughed. It was a jovial, friendly guffaw.

I learned more about Hush in that moment than I ever wanted to know.

"Let's get outta here," I said.

"What did we come for?" he asked, turning to face me.

"What they already have."

26

I GOT HOME at nearly midnight. The house felt empty, but maybe that was just me.

I went to the hall bathroom and got in the shower. Standing in the doorless stall, under the ice-cold spray, I shivered, and castigated myself for doing wrong even when I was trying to do right.

There was a cardinal rule in boxing: You can't win if you don't throw punches, but when you go on the offensive you have to accept the reality that you will most likely get hit. That's why so many fighters are counterpunchers—they wait for their opponent to make the mistake.

I had taken the initiative; moved to get Zella's conviction overturned. Shuddering from the cold, I knew that Stumpy and Bingo had been casualties of my ill-considered quest. Rather than helping, I made things worse—much worse.

"You remember when we used to take showers together?"

Katrina was one of the few people who could sneak up on me. I used to kid her that this stealth explained how she roped me into marriage—the joke wore thin in time.

She was wearing a black lace teddy under a yellow-and-black kimono. Her white skin was perfect, her eyes more engaging than

I had seen them in years. She held a snifter in either hand, each loaded with a triple shot of cognac.

"Yeah," I said. "You told me that you couldn't take the cold."

Katrina's blond hair was piled up on her head rather carelessly. I knew she had been drinking because her slight Swedish accent became more pronounced when she was tipsy—tipsy, but not when she was full-out drunk.

I never understood this foreign inflection, seeing how she was born and raised in Middle America.

"I'm very delicate, Leonid."

"Like white sharks and alabaster."

"Like a voman."

I stepped out of the shower and she handed me a plush red towel, leaning back against the sink as I rubbed and blotted the water from my body.

Katrina is a beautiful woman. Past fifty, she'd done everything to keep her body and face young. And though I'm not handsome I have the body of a fighter—hard and blunt. We both had something to look at, it's just that we were no longer interested in looking.

She handed me a snifter.

If you can't beat them, become them, my father once told me. *That's how the great cultures of the past ultimately tamed and therefore outlasted their conquerors.*

THERE'S A SMALL ROOM on the street side of our apartment. Sometimes we call it the TV room, at others the little front room. There's just enough space for the maroon sofa and the royal blue stuffed chair, facing an old console TV. Katrina led me there and sat next to me. She clinked my glass and we both drank—deeply.

"I vanted to talk vit you, Leonid."

I sat back and away from her saying "talk."

"Sit up," she said and I obeyed.

I was wearing my blue suit pants and a T-shirt that was once white.

"Where are the kids?" I asked.

"Dimitri is vit his whore. Twill—who knows where he goes? He said he vas vorking for you. And Michelle is out somevair sucking on an old married man's cock."

Katrina and I were definitely man and wife. Maybe we were no longer in love but we knew how to get under each other's skin.

"That's something you know a lot about," I said, wanting to attack my daughter's attacker.

I downed the rest of the cognac and Katrina reached back behind the other side of the sofa, producing the new bottle. She poured me another drink.

"I vas looking for love," she said, her blue diamond eyes staring into my brown ones.

To say I felt the stirrings of an erection would be a gross un-derstatement. This biological reaction was shocking to me but not to Katrina. She looked down on the lengthwise tent of my trousers and shifted over, laying her left hand on it.

"I used to kiss yours," she said. "I used to cry out for you."

Her grip tightened and I thought about pushing the hand away. Instead I took another drink.

Katrina started moving her hand up toward my belly button and then down again.

"Do you vant to come like this?" she whispered. "Like a teen-age boy on a date with some fast girl."

"Ummmmmm."

"Or do you vant me to show you what I have done with my lovers? Do you vant me to take you right here on this couch?" Her voice was getting stronger. "Do you vant to get on your knees and suck the pussy?"

"What . . . ?" I said.

"Vat did you say?" she asked me. She leaned over and gave me a wet kiss.

"What did you do?" I asked. "With them."

I already knew. One of her old boyfriends had hired a detective to take pictures of her with the new man. The jilted lover sent the photos to me, expecting that I would exact retribution. He miscalculated. I threatened him and put the pictures in my safe.

But hearing her tell me was better than any pictures. Having her position me and encourage my manhood was exactly what I needed right then.

I don't think that Katrina was trying to help me. She was just angry at life and getting back at the world by seducing me. It made no sense but I wasn't really thinking . . .

"Shouldn't I use a condom?" I remember asking at some point.

"I don't need it anymore," she said into my ear.

IN THE MORNING I woke to find the empty fifth of cognac on the night table next to our bed. Naked, Katrina was on her back, half out from under the covers, and snoring. The erection from the night before reappeared but I was sober enough to ignore it this time.

I lurched from the bed and went down the hall, holding a towel around my waist in case one of our kids had come in during the night.

Another cold shower and I was out the door and down to the street. I felt like a young man with a hangover. My dick was waiting for any excuse, as my mind wandered from here to there with no direction, no reason.

I stopped at a greasy spoon on Seventy-first Street and ordered fried pork chops with an American cheese and garlic omelet. That, with home fries, white toast, and grape jelly, put enough poison in my system to slow down the rampaging hormones awakened by a woman who I now understood was overwhelmed by her change of life.

27

I DO MY best thinking while walking, but sometimes I wonder if I'd be better off with the blinders of an office cubicle around me, facing a monitor with solitaire on it; the only thing on my mind would be the next card to play and if the boss might be walking by.

I didn't feel guilty, not exactly. My emotion was more an uneasiness about having sex with my wife because my ex-girlfriend had asked me to come back. This conundrum seemed petty, childish even.

But I knew the perturbation over the drunken sex orgy with my wife was really just a blind for the murders I'd caused. Stumpy Brown, Bingo Haman, and there might have been more; certainly more was coming.

Walking down Tenth Avenue with artists, businessmen and -women, and the homeless, I tried to imagine that desk job. If the worst thing that happened in my life was getting fired because I was a slacker and replaced by a better-educated Hindu from Mumbai, if that was the cruelest event, then I'd feel that I was blessed.

But instead I was godless, blindfolded, and in line for execution by parties unknown. I did the right thing and got the wrong outcome. I could have been a lyric in the Dr. John song.

My cell phone throbbed somewhere between Thirtieth and Twenty-ninth.

"Boss?" Zephyra said.

"Yeah."

"What's up today?"

"Not much."

"I can see from the GPS of your cell phone that you're headed south. Are you going to see Charles?"

I had to remember to have my tracker disconnected.

"Yeah," I said. "Anything you want me to tell him?"

"No. Just hi."

I WALKED pretty fast, making it down to the intersection of Charles and Hudson Streets in the West Village before nine. A quarter of a block east and seven granite steps down was a shamrock green steel-reinforced door that could stymie a SWAT team or a platoon of advancing Russian militia.

All I had to do was stand in front of that door because a blank white card in my wallet sent out a pulse that made the denizen of the underground bunker aware of my presence.

Thirty seconds after I got there a voice said, "Come on in, LT."

I pressed the door and it opened. I walked through and the mostly steel portal slammed behind.

Everything seemed as it always had; room after room filled with electronic devices used for intelligence gathering, flat-out spying, and, now and then, triggers for more aggressive acts.

Three chambers down I came to a cavernous space that was once the master bedroom of the subterranean apartment. Now the room was lined with computers and air conditioners. In the very center of these frigid electronics was a round Formica table-top with a man-sized hole cut in the middle. Twelve plasma and LCD screens encircled this desk. These monitors flowed with images, texts, and less definable waves of color.

Sitting in the hole was a caramel-colored young Adonis. On top of his head were glasses with one blue and one red lens. These I knew he used to see images represented by colors beyond the range of human sight.

"Hey, Bug," I said.

Tiny "Bug" Bateman (né Charles Bateman) had weighed three hundred pounds when we first met. Somewhere along the way in our dealings he became aware of Zephyra Ximenez. He fell in love with her phone patter and the image he found of her in the virtual world. She told him that he'd have to get in shape if he wanted even a chance with her.

Iran became his trainer and, eighteen months later, he'd lost forty-three percent of his body weight and sixty percent of his fat. Now he ran 10K races and bench-pressed two hundred pounds.

"Leonid," the beautiful young man hailed.

"Bug," I said. "You almost ready for a marathon?"

"Never."

"Why not?"

"Because a guy named Pheidippides, the first man to run what was to become known as the marathon, ran the distance to warn the Greek army about an enemy attack. He was successful but the exertion killed him. I have no death wish."

"Did you get my text?" I asked. On the way down I sent a message to Bug about information I needed.

"Yeah. Let me call it up."

While he was working I thought I'd fill in some gaps.

"Zephyra was asking me about you," I ventured.

"Oh?"

"Yeah. She sounded like she wanted to know what you were up to."

The computer genius smiled.

"What's up, Bug?"

"Z told me when we started going out that she was not an exclusive kinda girl. She said that she had a few men friends and didn't want any of them clinging to her. So we made a deal that we'd get together only once and at most twice a week.

"I called her one time when I guess I shouldn't have and she was obviously with somebody else. After that I started going out myself. I met this woman named Marcia, head of Western Hemisphere computer operations for Euro-Bank. I plugged a leak they had and she took me to Johannesburg for a weeklong vacation."

"That'd do it," I said.

"Here you go," Bug announced. "Teresa Lesser has no regular cell phone but that doesn't mean she might not have a throwaway. She hardly ever makes any outgoing calls from her landline. Up until four years ago she used to call a Margaret Rich once a week on Sundays but then that stopped. Rich is her maiden name. Margaret was probably her mother, probably died.

"For the last nine years she's talked twice a week to various cell phones, all of them belonging to a woman named Claudia Burns." Bug hit a few more keys and then said, "Ms. Burns is the executive assistant for a Johann Brighton at Rutgers Assurance Company."

And curiouser yet.

"Can you pull up an employee flowchart for Rutgers?"

"Sure thing."

While Bug hit keys and clicked around I wondered. What would Minnie Lesser's mother have to do with the heist? I was the one who implicated Minnie's boyfriend's girlfriend. She had nothing to do with it—did she?

"What you need, LT?" Bug asked.

"Are Johann Brighton and Antoinette Lowry along the same chain of command?"

He worked two mouses at once, moving data across a broad screen that hung from a metal stalk attached to the ceiling.

After some study he said, "No. They work in completely different sections. As a matter of fact they are entirely unconnected. He works under the auspices of the CEO, François Dernier, while she reports upward to the president of the company—Pat Rollins."

"Can you get me the name, address, and phone number for this Claudia?"

"It'll be on your phone and computer in under a minute."

Almost as an afterthought I said, "While you're at it will you look up a guy named Seldon Arvinil?"

"Anything special?"

"I hope not. He lives in New York and is over forty—I think."

I took a deep breath and turned to leave the frigid computer room. I hadn't sat down because there was no chair for visitors in Bug's electronic playground.

"Leonid," he said to my back.

"What?"

"There's somebody upstairs in the apartment that I want you to see."

"Somebody for me?"

"Yeah."

"How'd he even know I was gonna be here?"

"All I can say is that you don't have to worry. Take the second door on your left in the second room. That leads to the stairs."

28

I'D NEVER BEFORE taken the stairs from Bug's underground electronic grotto to his first-floor apartment. I knew that Bug owned the apartment above his intelligence laboratory; that he had all mail and deliveries come in and out of there.

I walked up the stairs with sliding panels closing behind me as I went. Finally I came to a slender door. From there I entered into a bright living room that had a large window looking down on Charles Street.

There was a young white woman and an Asian man walking hand in hand on the other side of the block. She wore a pink miniskirt and he blue jeans overalls.

"Leonid," a woman said from behind and to the left.

I turned to see Helen Bancroft, my wife's personal physician for at least twenty-five years.

She was taller than I, but not by much, and gray- instead of raven-haired as she was when we first met. Back then her hair was long and lustrous. Now it was short, more revealing of her face and smile.

"Helen?"

She smiled and said, "Would you come into the kitchen?"

"Maybe if you tell me what you're doing here," I said.

Helen was slender and smart. She wore a gray pantsuit and an orange blouse with a necklace made from leafy and nacreous ceramic charms. Her hands were small and delicate. Her eyes were brown, but one of their ancestors might have been salmon.

"Your wife called me," she said.

"When?"

"Yesterday. She said that you were running a fever and didn't want to take time to see a doctor. She told me that I'd be called by a woman named Zephyra when she knew that you'd be in your office. I had agreed to make a house call. You know, Katrina and I go way back."

"That doesn't explain how you got here."

"This morning, half an hour ago, Zephyra called and told me that you'd be in Mr. Bateman's apartment. She said that she knew my office was only a few blocks away. She's a smart woman.

"Now will you come with me into the kitchen?"

SHE HAD ME strip down to my underwear and sit on a sheet of wax paper that she spread out on the dining table. I sat upright and then laid back, got on my side and let her use her rubber gloves to inspect my prostate. She took my temperature, of course.

"What is it?" I asked.

"One-oh-two-point-one. You should be in bed."

"Not that you're wrong, Doctor," I said, "but bed is the last place I should be."

She looked into my eyes, down my throat, shone a light in my ears, and felt around my abdominal area.

"Does anybody live in this apartment?" she asked toward the end of all those studies.

"Not physically," I said. "What's wrong with me, Doc?"

"It's hard to say. You definitely have a fever. It's either a low-grade virus or infection or, more likely, a virus that has become an infection that settled in an organ or gland. The left side of your neck is a little swollen. You need bed rest."

"Not unless you think the cure is more important than the life of the patient."

This statement brought mild alarm into the doctor's eyes.

"I've brought a new general antibiotic." From her bag she retrieved a little glass bottle filled with tiny purple pills. "If you take one of these three times a day, preferably with meals, that should knock out any infection."

"How many days?"

"Ten, to be safe."

She went to the cabinet and brought out a glass that she filled in the sink.

Bringing the tumbler back to me, she asked, "Have you eaten recently?"

"Not too long ago."

"Then take three of these to start with. It will bring down that fever and keep you going. After that take them three times a day."

"It's been a long time, Helen," I said after downing the Lilliputian tablets.

"Yes, it has."

"What, twenty years?"

"Maybe more."

"How's my wife doing?"

A shadow passed over the physician's intelligent face.

"I'm worried about Katrina," she said.

"Is she sick?"

"I think she's depressed. It's unethical for me to be discussing this with you but the reason I agreed to this unorthodox meeting is partly because I wanted to tell you what I felt."

"She needs medicine?"

"She needs help. A therapist, a psychopharmacologist . . . something."

"Huh." I was pulling up my pants.

"Will you talk to her, Leonid?"

"What do you think it is?"

"Menopause has started. Many times women go through depression at the change. They feel like they are no longer women. Some women believe that there's no place in this man's world for a female who is barren."

Standing there, buttoning my shirt and looking at my wife's friend and doctor, I thought about the barren apartment in which we stood, about the millions of terabytes of secret information that roiled below us—knowledge that could bring down corporations and do more damage to governments than ten thousand daisy cutter bombs.

Then I considered my wife. I felt that I had to be in that room, at that moment, after fever and fear and death. If one of those elements was missing I wouldn't have stumbled onto the words I spoke.

"You know, Katrina doesn't let you in, Helen," I said. "She thinks she does. She gets an idea in her head and she looks at you and imagines that you're thinking the same thing—or that you aren't. But what you think and what you say does not, cannot, mean a thing to her. The idea is already there."

Dr. Bancroft winced as if jabbed with one of her own scalpels. She nodded and said, "But you know her better than anyone, Leonid. You have to try to get through to her."

29

I WALKED HELEN back to her brownstone office on West Twelfth. At the door I reached out to shake her hand but she leaned in and kissed my cheek instead. The good doctor had never kissed me before. She was Katrina's friend and therefore, in some way, always my enemy—or at least in league with my antagonist.

Katrina and I had been on opposing sides for two decades. There had been brief respites; usually when her machinations to find a better life failed and she realized that I was the only one left to help pick up the pieces. This was no trouble because I wasn't faithful or jealous, and I loved all three children even if only one was mine.

Katrina and I didn't hate each other. It's just that our interactions failed to generate love and love was something we both needed.

And so that kiss, from Katrina's friend and physician, spoke of a new era between my wife's world and mine. This was not a truce I was looking for.

Not at all.

———

CROSSING Fourteenth Street, I glanced at my phone to see an e-mail from the new and improved Bug.

Seldon Arvinil was fifty-three, a professor of political science at City College, married, with three children, the youngest of which was nine and the eldest nineteen. His wife's name was Doris Borman-Arvinil. They lived nine and a half blocks from my apartment.

I VEERED to the east on my stroll up to the Tesla Building because Claudia Burns's address was on East Twenty-second. That address turned out to be a package-mailing business that also kept private mailboxes.

I smiled at the subterfuge designed just for a guy like me. And when that grin appeared I realized that the fever had departed, at least temporarily. I missed the subtle rewiring of my mental faculties. In some ways it felt as if I was smarter under the influence of the symptoms provided by the infection.

HEADED BACK toward the west, I tried to use my more mundane thinking processes to understand the problems I faced.

Claudia was connected to the mother of the woman who slept with the man who was subsequently shot by the woman Zella who I falsely framed for the heist.

Zella was the only client I ever had who I knew for a fact was innocent of the offense for which she was charged. This being true—how could her boyfriend and *his* sidetrack girlfriend be implicated in the crime?

There was no answer forthcoming.

I reached my office door on the seventy-second floor without a workable resolution to my problem. I was about to push the buzzer when she called to me.

"Leonid."

Aura was coming down the hall to the right, from the service elevator no doubt. The man at the front desk, Warren Oh, had probably been asked to call her when I arrived. She took the service elevator and made it to my floor just in time.

At least my detecting skills were good for something.

"Hey, honey," I said.

I don't know if anyone else thought that Aura was beautiful. She was certainly good-looking on any scale. But she was unusual because of her Nordic and Togolese heritage. Her skin was the color of darkly burnished gold and her hair was so light brown as to be confused for blond. Her eyes . . . I still don't have a color to define them; certainly not brown or blue or green—there was ocher in there and some gray, but that wasn't all of it.

Aura is taller than I am and solidly built but not heavy.

She walked up to a foot away from me and stopped.

Looking in my eyes, she saw something. For a moment she wondered and then smiled.

"Have the women been after you?" she asked.

"Fallin' from the sky."

She laughed quietly and reached out to touch the knuckle of my left hand.

If I hadn't known that I was still hopelessly in love with her, that touch reminded me. It went all the way down, past where the fever had been.

"I have to go," she said.

I took in a deep breath and nodded.

When she turned away I resisted the urge to follow her.

I stood in the hallway a full three minutes after she had gone.

USUALLY MARDI WAS in competition with the *Mona Lisa* for subtlety in her humor, but not that day. She took one look at me and broke out into a smile, an actual grin.

"What are you so happy about?" I asked.

"Lots of things."

"Like what?"

"Well, for one, I can tell by your eyes that the fever is gone."

"By my eyes? Maybe you should take the back office and I could be out here takin' the calls."

"No," she said, shaking her head with sudden gravitas. "No. I can read things but I can't translate them."

I have never in my life heard a more cogent or succinct understanding of true detective work.

"What else makes you happy, Mardi?"

"You'll see."

Another surprise.

TWILL WAS SITTING at his desk, perusing a dark red hardback book that had no dust cover. He had his feet in an open drawer and his back to the aisle. I stopped behind him. He kept reading and I stood there, waiting.

The standoff didn't last a whole minute.

He turned toward the aisle, kicking the bottom drawer shut to obtain enough momentum in the office chair.

He had on a wheat-colored silk T-shirt and black skinny jeans. His tennis shoes were dark green and he wore no socks.

"Pops," he said with a grin.

I stifled my own smile and took the seat next to his desk.

"Son."

He hadn't been in the office long, but Twill and I had a rapport from before the days when he could talk. All I had to do was look at him and he perceived the drill.

"Me an Em—" he started.

"Em?"

"Mirabelle Mycroft . . . Me and her had a pizza with Kent and Luscious McKenzie last night. The Last Ray of Day, the place is called, over on Ninth Ave.

"I sat next to his girl and he was there next to his sister."

"What was he like?" I asked.

"That's hard to tell, Pops. I mean, he wasn't pushy or nuthin', but he was hard-like. You know, he gave you this look that said *Who the fuck do you think you are to be sittin' here with me?* But he smiled and shit, and asked about what I did.

"Luscious was fine. Mixed white and black, with green eyes and hair like Ms. Ullman. She the kinda girl have men jumpin' outta trees an' shit."

"And Kent?"

"We ate through two pizzas and he excused himself to have a cigarette. While he was gone and Em was trying to talk to Luscious—"

"They didn't get along?" I asked.

"Mirabelle was just nervous. Her brother was too quiet and Luscious said anything come into her head. Anyway . . . Kent was outside and Em went to the bathroom. That's when Luscious slipped her card into my hand. It was real slick-like. She was tellin' me that her moms was from Texas and she was lookin' me in the eye, and then she give me the card.

"So after we finished Kent took us to this rock-and-roll club down on Varick. The kinda music you like, Pops. Him and Luscious run into some'a their friends, and I say that I'm takin' Em home."

"And did you leave her alone like I said?"

"Pretty much."

"What does that mean?"

"She needed a hug 'cause she was so nervous. And it's just a quick turn from there to a kiss. And you know you can't tell how a girl's gonna kiss you. But I told her that I was on the job and I had to go. She understood, for the most part.

"I left her going into her place and called Luscious."

"Hold up a second, Junior. I told you that this was just a fact-gathering mission."

"I know," he said defensively. "I just called to see what she had in mind. I figured if she said she wanted to get together that I could ask how connected she was to Kent and then maybe get a thing or two about him. You know, I could do most'a that on the phone.

"But instead of a hookup she told me that Kent wanted to have a meet with me."

"What?"

"That's what I said, man." Twill even gave a mild expression of surprise. "I mean, she was actin' like one of *his* crew. He'd been checkin' me out while I was checkin' him. That meant his sister and father might'a got it wrong. If anybody's doin' somethin', it's Kent."

"What did the girl say . . . exactly?"

"She said that Kent liked what he saw and wondered if I wanted to get together today."

"What were you talking about to him?"

"Places I go, scams I heard of down around the Village—light shit."

"You think he's trying to protect his sister?"

"Maybe so. But that don't mean he's not in charge."

"What did you tell the girl?"

"That I'd meet Kent at the NYU student center this afternoon at two. And before you start talkin' about gatherin' and not doin' . . . I don't have to go. I could just shine it on and let you take over."

"What's your read on this Kent, Twill?"

"It's hard to say, Pops. I mean, havin' the girl call me for him makes him at least a little bit in charge. But who knows? Maybe he's her connection and this is just a favor. I won't be able to tell until we talk—if we talk."

Twill sat there in his reclining office chair calm as a pensioner on vacation in Bali. He had his hands laced behind his head, the expression on his face free from concern. He was telling me with his posture that the decision was mine and mine alone.

Like hell.

"Broad daylight?" I said.

"In a public place."

"Don't go anywhere with him until you check in with me."

"You got it, Pops."

30

THE FEVER I'd been experiencing had also been a kind of fuel. If I was weakened, I didn't know it, or at least I didn't care. If I was sick, it didn't conflict with my state of mind or sense of well-being. But now that I was on the mend I could feel the exhaustion in my bones. Rising up out of my teenage son's client's chair, I felt twice my weight; like a fighter answering the penultimate bell in a grueling match.

The twenty feet from his desk to my door was like the last mile for a condemned man—I had no idea whether I'd make it under my own power.

I grabbed the doorknob as much to steady myself as to enter my sanctum. I turned the knob, but before I could pull it my cell phone sounded.

Teetering toward my desk, I answered. "Hey, Luke. How's my client?"

"Fine, last time I saw her," the pool shark intoned. "I think she likes Johnny. He's good with ladies just outta prison, opens doors and shit like that. They eat it up."

"Couldn't have a better bodyguard than Johnny Nightly."

"No, sir."

"So do I need to do anything?"

"No."

"Then why'd you call?"

"Sweet Lemon."

The exhaustion increased with that simple two-word declaration. My mind began to wander but my mouth stayed on point.

I took a pill from Helen Bancroft's little bottle and popped it into my mouth.

"What did Lemon want?" I said, thinking randomly about the streets of New York and swallowing hard.

"You okay, LT?"

"Not even in a neighborhood where they know the meaning of the word."

"Lemon says that if you're interested you could meet him at the White Horse Tavern down in the West Village at twelve-fifteen. You know what he's talkin' about?"

"Yeah."

"Lemon a problem?"

The question seemed deep and broad like a mile-wide river that separated whole cultures. Was Lemon a problem? Probably. Probably he was. But I made a living, my whole life, on problems. Time on this earth for me was navigating the Problem River, making it from side to side, connecting contradictory concepts, struggling against the wind and current, the sun, and creatures, both great and small, but all deadly.

"LT?" Luke said.

"No, Luke. Lemon's just fine, just doin' what he does and tryin' not to."

"You take care of yourself now, LT."

I disconnected the call without answering. I knew Luke wouldn't hold it against me.

I **INTENDED** to leave right away but instead I slumped in the chair, leaning backward. My eyes closed of their own accord and something akin to sleep ensued . . .

I was thinking about Stumpy's horrible corpse tied to that chair, besieged by maggots and roaches. Stumpy wasn't a brave man. Under threat he'd fold with four of a kind in his hand. But the professional gambler was cunning and aware of the lay of the land with just a glance. Whoever it was that tortured him planned to kill him anyway, Stumpy knew that. He held out because whatever it was they wanted was also the only thing keeping him alive.

And there were only two possibilities; either the men who brutalized Stumpy were looking for the money or they knew where it was and they were looking to snip loose threads. There were only two such threads that I knew of: Gert Longman, dead six years now, and me.

This realization didn't frighten me. I wasn't worried about becoming a feast for insects in a laundry room somewhere. Understanding that I might be the subject of concern for murderers made me wonder why—not why they were after me but why, or how, I had gotten myself into such a situation.

Why would I ever plant false evidence on a poor woman already going to jail? A woman distraught over her faithless lover and the child in her womb? I tried to remember the state of mind that allowed me to take those actions. I knew the man that did these things intimately, had all of his memories. I could enumerate each and every sin he ever committed. But try as I might I could not bring up the feeling inside that allowed me to do the things I'd done.

Of course men were after me. Of course they wanted to destroy me. Of course they did.

31

I OPENED MY EYES, understanding that I had been in a kind of existential slumber, an intellectual doze. Rather than being in a true state of restful unconsciousness, I could only be described as a philosophical recluse. My spirit had challenged the pretexts and justifications, allowing the truth of my flawed existence to come to the surface.

I felt completely rested and free.

People wanted to kill me. They had valid reasons even if they were not aware of what those reasons were. I wanted to survive because I couldn't make up for my sins if these shadowy men achieved their purpose.

ON THE STREET, walking south, I considered Zella. She was a textbook case of a woman who suffered a severe case of bad luck. From the man she chose to be her lover to the woman she thought of as a friend, she had chosen badly. Having a loaded gun where she could grab it was a bad idea, but the worst thing about Zella's life was completely out of her control—me. I was bad luck, pure undiluted calamity; for Katrina, Aura, Zella Grisham, and one hundred and seven other poor souls who had been blindsided by my machinations. I was Typhoid Mary's meaner older brother, the ire of Moses on the unsuspecting peasants of the Nile Valley. I planted false evidence, sicced the dogs on unsuspecting citizens simply because I didn't like them and was being paid to trap someone, anyone, that would fit the bill. I was a minor, mischievous deity loosed upon naïve humanity for the entertainment of the gods.

Back in the hippie days we would have been seen as Karmic siblings, Zella and I, working out the misdeeds of previous lives. But in 2011 the metaphysical world, as well as the physical universe, was comprised almost completely by corporate plans, prayers, and plagues.

I was so distracted by these useless esoteric reflections that I came up on the White Horse Tavern unawares. It was after one and there were quite a few people at the tables and bar—regulars, tourists, and the odd drop-in.

At a table in the corner, in the front room by the window, a group of nine people were being addressed by a young man wearing black jeans, a dark green sports jacket, and a T-shirt that read GINSBERG FOR RAJAH.

". . . among many of the recognized and lauded lights of the New York poetry scene the allure of Dylan Thomas has faded," the clean-shaven raven-haired young white man proclaimed. "They criticize everything from his depth of linguistic complexity to the obvious melodrama of his most well-known works. But what these poetry pontiffs fail to understand is that Thomas was a people's poet, a man that connected song and meter and the concerns of every human being living their lives and suffering the consequences. His work, in its every repetition, fights for the survival and the lifeblood of a form that most so-called great poets have moved beyond the reach of the common man. . . ."

Not only the tableful of tourists with their pints and bitters were listening to the lecture but people all over the bar were enthralled. The bartender, a red-faced man, was smiling at the effect.

The young man continued, and I found myself taken by his ideas and obvious passion.

Someone tapped my shoulder and I turned to see Sweet Lemon Charles. At the bus station his skin looked olive under the fluorescent lights but in the window, bathed in natural, if murky, sunlight, he was more a wallet brown.

"She's sumpin' else, huh?" he said.

With a twitch of his head he indicated a small white girl with short brown hair, standing behind the lecturer. She was slight, but still with a figure under the maroon dress. She wasn't what you'd call pretty but she had a look that would make a man pass up a dozen comelier girls just to see her smile.

"That's Morgan?" I asked.

"Yep. My girl."

"She could be your daughter, man."

"Every young girl needs a daddy until she has kids of her own."

"That's pretty good, Lemon. You read it somewhere?"

"Auntie Goodwoman," he said, shaking his head.

"Shhh!" a woman seated at the bar near us hissed. She wasn't part of the paying group, but still . . .

"Let's go outside, LT," Lemon suggested.

ON HUDSON in the afternoon there was lots of foot traffic. People walked dogs and toted laptop computers in dull-colored rectangular valises. There was every race, gender, subgender, and age, hoofing it around us.

Lemon lit up a cigarette and I stood close to share the second-hand smoke.

"So this is your new gig?" I asked. It was an obvious question but safer than the ones lurking at the back of my mind.

"Oh yeah," the lifetime thief opined. "I live, breathe, and fuck poetry twenty-four hours a day. Morgan had me go out to Wyoming to this writers' retreat with her. They gave us a cabin out on the prairie. You know one night I saw a coyote not six feet from our front door. A coyote and me!"

"You got any scams?" I asked. I had to.

"They go through my mind," he said with unusual candor. "You know how people get all trustin' when they're excited. They want you to help them lose their money, or at least that's how it seem.

"One night this woman and her husband wanted me to score for them. They would'a paid two hundred dollars for what I could get for fifty. But instead I went back to Morgan's place and wrote a prose poem of what my auntie would say after I had did what would'a been so easy for me to do.

"Now that's what I do every time I'm tempted—by anything. I plan that to be my first book. I call it *Sour Lemons, Sweet Nevermind*."

The grifter was beginning to get to me and that's always a problem. The best con men believe their stories up until the moment they let you down. They're telling you the truth, they're telling you the truth, they're telling you the truth, and then, all of a sudden, they see a different light, take the money and run, before either one of you knows what happened.

"What you call me for, Lemon?" I asked.

The question snapped him out of his reverie of poetry and sex, bad thoughts and the alternative of words never spoken by a woman that died before he went wrong.

"I asked around all over the place, LT," he said. "It was easy enough 'cause I had a name. I was at a readin' last night and there was this woman there that Morgan knows, Tourquois Wynn. Tourquois used to be a adjunct creative writing professor at Hunter College. When she was there, five years ago, she had this older black man student named William Williams. He was in her fiction class."

The chill that flowed into where fever had lain for so many days almost made me shiver. I considered various inappropriate responses: 1) I thought about hitting Lemon with a roundhouse right, knocking him unconscious; 2) I might have taken off, running up the street, back to where there were no answers to unanswerable questions; and, 3) I entertained putting my fingers in my ears and chanting, "Nah, na, na, na naaa, na, na, na, naaaa, na na, na, na na, na."

"This Tourquois still at Hunter?" I pronounced the name as he did—Tur-kwa.

"No. She got a tenure-track job at NYU after her first book of poetry won the Sanders Prize. She told me that Williams said that he named himself after a writer because before, when he was a politico, he said that the movement ground him down until he was just a mirror. He said that when a man becomes simply a reflection that writing is the only honest thing he can do."

That simple explanation meant that the man in the fiction class was my father, Clarence Tolstoy William Williams McGill.

There was no doubt in my mind. I had to clasp my hands to keep them from shaking.

"Did she know how to get in touch with him?"

"Said she hadn't talked to him since that class five years ago. I believed her. But me and Morgan said that the three of us should meet up for a early dinner at the Nook Petit down on Seventh at seven. You could come with. Maybe you got a question she can answer."

"Why you doin' this, Lemon?" I asked. It was a reflex question, like right cross after a left hook to the body.

"Favor."

"I thought you were leavin' my world behind."

"That's right. I stay out of the life. But everybody says that you don't mess wit' gangsters no more, LT. And even if you did, a guy like me might need a friend someday."

"Someday is fine, but how much do you want right now?"

"Nuthin', man. All I ask is that you remember that I gave you this."

32

I'VE ALWAYS LIKED the West Village, through all of its varied incarnations. When I was a kid it was a wasteland, with lots of factories and old Italians, the Meatpacking District, and even a few private homes. As time went on would-be artists, aspiring models, and prostitutes (of various persuasions) moved in. There were late-night clubs where jazz musicians sometimes showed up after their uptown gigs.

Back then it wasn't a tourist destination, with overpriced *trés chic* clothes shops and big hotels; you didn't have to plow through crowds of tourists or the investment bankers who transformed every building into million-dollar plasterboard condos and seven-thousand-dollar-a-month one-bedroom apartments.

The West Village had changed, and changed again, but it still had charm. After a little wander I sat myself down at an outside café on Hudson south of Christopher. There I ordered a café au lait with almond biscotti and waited for inspiration.

I missed the old West Village. I missed my fever too. Both felt like history to me; places where I could hide.

———

"HELLO?" she said.

"It's me."

"Mr. McGill?"

"Yeah."

"Is there something wrong?" Zella Grisham asked.

"No. I'm just sitting here on the street, waiting to meet a friend of my father's."

"Oh. Then why are you calling?"

"This and that. I might have a line on the people who adopted your daughter. I'm going to get in touch with them in a few days, saying that you'd like to meet."

"What are their names?"

"I need to make the first contact, Zella."

"She's my daughter."

"Not in the eyes of the law, and we need to keep the law from looking too hard at you."

She had no words to say about that.

"What else?" she asked. "What else did you have to say?"

"How are they treating you there?"

"Mr. Nightly has been very kind. He's had family that spent time in prison."

"You should keep your head down," I said. "Lotsa people interested in that heist. Some of them still think you might know something."

"What do you mean?"

"I mean, keep your head down. I will find out what's goin' on and tell you when you can come back up for air."

"What about Harry?" she asked quickly before I could disconnect.

"He went missing right before your trial."

"Killed?" There was real distress in her voice.

"I doubt it. Usually when somebody's murdered there's a body or at least a complaint about a missing person. I think he must have moved away. But don't worry, I'm still looking."

"Um."

"What?"

"I don't really understand why you're helping me but Johnny says that you're somebody I can trust . . . so . . . thank you."

"No problem."

WHILE I WAS composing a text message a call was coming through. I sent the text and answered, "Hello, Breland."

"Mycroft called and asked where we were on the case. He wanted your number but I told him that it would probably be better for me to be the go-between."

"Smart."

"Do you have anything?"

"Tell me something, Breland."

"What's that, LT?"

"Is this like the other thing we did with this guy?"

"What do you mean?"

"I mean, do you want me to save an innocent boy or to get a rich kid out of a jam of his own making?"

"You think that Kent isn't just a kid out of his depth?"

"Might not be."

There was silence on the other end of the wireless connection. Breland Lewis had a brilliant mind; a lawyer's mind, but brilliant still and all. It felt good that he was using that intelligence on my question.

"I guess that would just be a case of a silk purse and the sow's ear," he said.

"Glad to hear it," I said, "because you know I'm plum out of spot remover."

"Keep me informed."

TALKING ABOUT the billionaire made me think of my father. As much as I disliked the arrogant Mycroft, at least he was trying to help his son; at least that.

My father had taught me to hate the rich. He called them the enemies in a class war that every man, woman, and child was a part of because the division of labor was the Maginot Line between us and our destroyers.

I loved my father and so believed him. And because I believed him I hated men like Mycroft. It took me a long time to understand that I stood on both sides of the battle that every resident of the modern world faced. I was a grown man before I understood that Mycroft, in spite of his privilege, could have luck just as bad as Zella's. His money was a force to reckon with but it could not shield his soul.

"Hey, Pops."

And there Twill was. Even though I had sent him the message to meet me at the outside café I was surprised and delighted to see him.

"Have a seat."

He pulled up a chair, motioned at our waitress, and ordered a Chinotto soda.

"How'd it go?" I asked.

"I don't know, LT, I think maybe we should bow outta this one."

"Your first case and you want to let it go?"

He held out his left hand; a gesture of offering.

"Mr. Mycroft said that he thinks that his son is just caught up in something he don't get, but the way Kent tells it he's the big boss. He told me that him and his crew started out robbin' pimps and drug dealers and small gambling operations. Then, after a while, they started runnin' their own businesses. He told me that he killed two men himself."

"You believe him?"

"I believe he's crazy. Don't get me wrong, Pops. He's just another dude doin' business, as far as I'm concerned, but you the one told me that you cain't save a fish from drowning."

I laughed, and the waitress came up with the small bottle of bitter Italian soda and a chilled glass. She was short and wide, with a yard-long smile for my son.

"And that's not all," Twill said when the young woman went away.

"What else?"

"Kent told me that him and his father hated each other, that they been at each other's throats forever."

"Why's that?"

"I don't even wanna go into it, man. Just a lotta gossip, as far as I'm concerned. But we shouldn't get in it. I know that much for sure."

"Tell me something, Twill."

"What's that, Pops?"

"Why would a guy you just met give you all that?"

"He knew who I was."

"What?"

"Not that you're my father or that I'm workin' for his father," Twill said, putting up both hands and tamping them against my palpable anxiety. "I've done a few things down around the Village. They know me pretty good in his circles. That's why he had his girl tap me. He thought I was usin' his sister to meet him so that we could do some work together."

My son the gangster. I hadn't brought him in to work for me a moment too soon.

"You should let this drop, Twill. If he's running a violent crew, I don't want you to get in the crosshairs."

"That's cool. So you gonna drop it?"

"I can't do that. I promised Breland to see it through."

"So you gonna keep on workin' it?"

"Until I agree with your conclusion at least."

"Well, then . . . maybe I could get at it another way."

"What do you mean?"

"If Kent knows who I am, that means I know people that know him and his. I could ask around. I mean, if you still wanna do this thing."

"You could ask and he wouldn't know?"

"I can be as quiet as a midnight owl on a garter snake."

What kind of bedtime stories had I told my son?

33

AFTER TWILL LEFT I ordered a glass of red wine and called Gordo.

"I don't know what you said to Elsa, son, but she unpacked her bags and wouldn't even talk about leavin'. She made me a plate of meat and potatoes and said she wanted to get in the bed early."

"You deserve it, old man. She probably figure to be in your will soon so now she gonna sex you to death."

"One can only hope."

I HUNG AROUND the little café until seven. Then I followed Christopher Street over to Seventh Avenue. From there I wended my way south until coming to the Nook Petit. It was a little restaurant, hardly more than a café, on the western side of the street. It was next door to a storefront performance space that had been a makeup store six months earlier and a Thai restaurant six months before that.

Sexy Morgan, the poet, was in a window seat next to the ageless (but old) Sweet Lemon Charles. Between them sat a black-haired woman with pale skin and very beautiful eyes. I couldn't make out their color but their size and shape said that when it came to aesthetic evolutionary perfection these eyes had topped the scales. Other than that, she was plain. The blouse was a flat blue. I'd've bet even money that the skirt underneath was knee-length and black.

Lemon saw me staring, stood up, and waved me in.

When I passed through the front door a woman wearing a bejeweled purple-and-red turban approached.

"Can I help you?" she asked. Her smile was practiced but not insincere.

"My friends are at that table over there."

"LT," LEMON SAID. "Glad you could make it, brother. Here, sit, sit."

He gestured at the chair he'd occupied. There was a lot of communication in that offer. He wanted me to sit next to Tourquois, of course, but also the only other chair had its back to the window. Lemon was telling me that he understood how vulnerable I'd feel in that position and also proving, in some symbolic way, that he had left that lifestyle behind. So he sat with his back to the street while I got to sit next to the woman with the lovely eyes.

"Morgan," Lemon said. "This is the guy I was tellin' you about—Leonid McGill."

The sexpot cutie pursed her lips and held her hand out across the table.

"Stanford told me all about you, Mr. McGill," she said with assumed knowledge in her brown eyes.

"Stanford?"

"That's my real name," Lemon said. "And this is the woman I was telling you about—Tourquois."

A closer look explained why Stanford was particular about calling the teacher a woman. She was probably in her mid-forties, with pale crow's-feet at the edge of her crystal gray eyes.

She smiled and I nodded my greeting.

"Thanks for letting me crash the party," I said.

"Can I get you something to drink?" Lemon asked. "Brandy, right?"

"Cognac," I said.

"Right."

He went to the bar, merging with the mob of young Village hopefuls drinking and laughing all around.

Morgan still had her lips pursed and Tourquois was looking down at her long, delicate hands.

"Stanford told me that every policeman in New York knows your name and face," Morgan said.

"He did?"

"Do they?"

"I'm recognized from time to time. But, in my defense, often my face is familiar but not recognized. Now and then somebody might arrest me but they always let me go."

Tourquois looked up at me and for some reason I imagined her black hair going white.

"Stanford says that he's out of that life," Morgan said, her lips no longer puckered for kissing.

"That's what I say too," I replied lightly. "And I don't just say it, I mean it. And I can promise you that I have no intention of pulling your man into anything but maybe that osso buco special they got on that blackboard menu."

The kiss returned, along with a smile.

"Here you go," Lemon said.

He was carrying four drinks in his big hands. I'd forgotten about the size of his hands. They were both dexterous and strong. It was said that Lemon's fists were fearful things in his youth. I was reminded of the boxer's axiom that if a man could hit hard, he always had a slugger's chance.

"Champagne for my lady," Lemon was saying, "dirty vodka martini for Ms. Wynn, VSOP for LT, and gin with a twist for Lenore Goodwoman's favorite child."

He placed the drinks professionally and gestured for the waiter; an older white man with a bald head and a smile that wanted to be a frown.

THE MEAL CAME and talk arose, centering around poets, poetry, poetry readings, and reading in general.

"I believe that the most important book of the twentieth century is *Four Quartets* by Eliot," Morgan said with certainty.

She wasn't yet thirty but had a sharp mind and a focused intelligence.

"What do you think, Mr. McGill?" Lemon's girlfriend asked.

"About what?"

"The most important book."

The only way to explain my reaction is to say that I cast my gaze upon her. It's a heavy stare replete with violence and the ability to absorb pain. For a fraction of a second Morgan wondered if she wanted an answer to her question.

"All the religions got their books," I said. "They know for a fact that there's only one thing written that makes any difference."

"Are you religious, Mr. McGill?" Tourquois asked.

"No."

"Then what book do you nominate for most important?" Morgan insisted.

"Not one book but four," I said. "And even if they had a great impact on the twentieth century, just two of them were written in that time period."

Before that little preamble Morgan had seen me as an uneducated criminal friend of the object of her affection, the fixer-upper named Stanford "Sweet Lemon" Charles. I think that she was more than a little surprised at this street thug's pedestrian grasp of the can of worms her pronouncement opened.

"What books?" she said. It was a challenge.

"*Capital*," I said, raising up my left thumb, "*The Interpretation of Dreams*, *The Descent of Man*, and the collected essays that explain the Theory of Relativity."

"And why those books?" Tourquois asked, suddenly engaged.

"Because," I said, "those books tell us why we don't know what's happening but that it happens, and continues to happen, in spite of our necessary ignorance."

Morgan wanted to argue, to say something about poetry and the depth of its heart. But she was distracted by the possibilities that my suggestions glanced upon.

"That sounds like something Bill Williams would have said," Tourquois said.

Bull's-eye!

"Yeah," I replied. "Lemon—I mean, Stanford here—said that you knew this Williams."

"He took a class from me five years ago. I was impressed by his stories."

"What was he like?"

"An older gentleman. He was probably in his early seventies. From the little he let drop I got the idea that he had led a very political life and had turned to literature when the Revolution didn't pan out the way he expected it to."

"He was writing a novel?"

"It's said that Gogol had called his great unfinished work, *Dead Souls*, a poem. In the same way I believe that Bill's work was a prose poem in development."

"What was it about?"

"It was couched in the South American style of magical reality. The main character was a man born a slave who escaped his masters and traveled the country exhorting his brethren to either live as free men and women or to die trying to achieve it. This man, Plato Freeman, lived for many years and never aged. But, as time passed, who he was and what he knew were so roundly ignored that he became transparent to the modern world. In this ghost-like form he moved from place to place, following his descendants, primarily two great-great-grandsons that he could watch but they could not see him."

I wasn't dizzy but I doubt if I could have gotten to my feet just then.

"Why are you looking for him?" Tourquois asked.

"You know that book he was working on?"

"Yes?"

"I'm the Number One Great-Great-Son."

34

I DIDN'T GET HOME until a little after midnight.

The dinner with Lemon and his friends was unique, in my experience. I was trapped at that table like a fat and furry black fly on a sheet of old-fashioned flypaper. I wanted to bug out of there but the bait, as much as the glue, held me fast.

Tourquois Wynn had known my father for eighteen months. He took her classes and worked on his novel. She had the feeling that he never intended to finish the book; that it was more like a penance than something to be published or even read by anyone outside the workshop.

He always wore a dark suit with a collared shirt but no tie. He drank coffee continuously, and whenever he went out with the group for the end-of-semester class party he smoked real Cuban cigars.

He never said where he lived but that didn't bother me. I could always get Bug to hack the school records.

"He was always very present," Tourquois said. "You didn't need to know about where he came from or who his people were because—I don't know how to explain it, exactly—he was right there in front of you, sharing ideas and listening very closely. The usual banal questions just didn't seem to matter."

She hadn't heard from him since the class, and her phone number had changed a few times over the years. Twice during the meal Lemon had excused himself to go outside for a smoke. I went with him for the second break.

He offered me one of his Parliaments and I accepted, the first cigarette I'd had since being the cause of the young men's deaths.

"I do good, LT?" he asked.

"Yeah," I said, "like a drug dealer at the back door of a rehab program."

"He really your father?"

I took a deep hit off the cigarette before saying "Yeah" through a cloud of fumes.

"How long since you seen him?"

"Not since before Tourquois was born."

"Damn. You want me to ask around some more?"

I left him with my phone number and my apologies to the ladies.

I crushed out the cigarette and stomped the pavement as far as Forty-second Street before taking a cab the rest of the way home.

AS I WAS making certain that the security functions of the front door were activated I could hear Katrina's loud snoring.

Before finding the source of her susurrations, I went down the sleeping hall and glanced into Twill's room. That was habit. He wasn't there and I wasn't bothered by that fact. He was usually out in the world at night. Katrina was sprawled out on the daybed in my office; one foot was shod in a blue pump while the other shoe lay on its side on the floor. She was wearing an old house-dress and smelled strongly of alcohol.

Her right arm was thrown up, covering her face, and the left lolled out over the side, lifting and falling slightly with her raucous breathing. For all that was on my mind, Katrina brought a smile to my lips. There was more warmth in that knowing grin than the night of sex we'd just experienced.

She had never sought refuge in my office before—as far as I knew.

When I lifted her into my arms she stopped snoring.

"Huh?" she squeaked. "What is it?"

"I'm taking you to bed."

"Oh, Leonid. You are so strong."

There are some things that a man just likes hearing. It doesn't matter how predictable or clichéd they are. A man wants the woman in his arms to be charmed by his strength. So what if it gets him killed one day? Everybody's got to die sometime.

I TOOK OFF Katrina's clothes and then disrobed myself.

Naked under the covers, with Katrina breathing easier, I was surprised at how tired I was. Before I knew it I had passed through the veil of sleep, transformed into a little boy at the best amusement park in all the world.

There was a real spaceship and live elephants. The elephants walked under beautiful waterfalls, depositing me in front of a hall of mirrors containing half a dozen giggling naked women reflected a thousand times.

My eight-year-old heart was pounding so hard I worried that I might die before seeing all the other wonders of the park . . .

THERE CAME THREE dissonant chimes. Each was a different length and tone—and they were loud.

I recognized the sounds. I had chosen them because they were so jarring and unpleasant. The excitement of the dream helped the adrenaline work even faster.

I was up and armed in under six seconds.

As I moved toward the bedroom door I went back through the litany of every night that I came home. I checked Twill's bed because Twill needed keeping track of. He was not there. I didn't look in on Dimitri because he was gone. And what about Shelly?

THERE WERE TWO of them coming down the hall toward the master bedroom. They had gotten past the front door, with its dead bolts in the wall and floor, more quickly than I could have imagined. They were hurrying one behind the other, moving low like predators, like twin brother cheetahs on the hunt.

I shot the first one as he sensed my presence and was raising his own pistol. A tenth of a second later his rising gun hand hit mine, knocking the long-barreled .44 from my grip. This was a posthumous act because he was already dead from the bullet entering his skull.

The second killer, trying to move around the still-falling corpse, was twisting his pistol to point at my chest, but I moved, with Gordo's boxer training, grabbing the wrist of the hand holding the gun with my left and his throat with my right. He was at least four inches taller than I but still I lifted him up off the floor.

The fever returned, momentarily fueling my rage like the furnace of a hot-air balloon.

"Urk!" he yelped. One high note not unlike the feline predator he brought to mind.

Three shots fired from his pistol, his windpipe collapsed under my grip. He died almost as quickly as his comrade had.

I dropped him to the floor. My heart was beating as it had been in the dream. I stood there, naked, triumphant, and trembling. I would have been scared if it wasn't for the blood screaming through my veins.

35

"THEY KNEW EXACTLY what system you had and the tools to get around it," Carson Kitteridge was saying.

We were in the dining room. Katrina was wrapped in a plush yellow bathrobe, sitting at our hickory dining table. I was standing next to her, wearing only my blue suit trousers.

When the cops arrived I was still naked. After killing the second failed assassin I saw that his three shots had gone through the wall to Shelly's bedroom. I rushed in. Two of the bullets hit her bed but she wasn't in it. After that I called 911—the idea of getting dressed never occurred to me.

One of the uniforms answering the call told me to put on some pants. If it wasn't for her, I might have still been naked.

"They didn't know, exactly," I said. "I had a separate contractor put in the second alarm system—just bein' careful."

"Smart," Kit said, his eyes, the color of a pale afternoon, staring into mine. "Looks like they used a souped-up magnet on the electronic lock and perfectly beveled crowbars on the bolts. Real pros."

Katrina put her left elbow on the table, leaning her forehead against three extended fingers. She shook her head ever so slightly, mouthing something over and over.

"Bullets went through Shelly's wall," I said. "Two of 'em hit her bed."

"Why don't we go down to your den, LT?" Kit suggested. "Officer Palmer can stay with your wife."

Palmer was the lady cop that told me to get dressed. Her skin was milk with freckles. Even frowning, she seemed friendly.

IN THE HALLWAY there were five more cops, a coroner, and four paramedics.

Kit led me to my office, ushered me in, and closed the door. He said that we should sit. I didn't answer. I didn't sit either. I was a soldier right then; my squad had just fought off one attack and was anticipating the next.

Kit stood with me, watching closely.

While aware of the scrutiny of the insightful cop I was concentrated on the daybed where Katrina had been. I was thinking that no one had ever tried to kill me in my home before. The antithesis of that realization made me snicker.

They'd tried to kill me in a dozen other places, but that was business—nothing personal.

"You think this has to do with Zella Grisham and the heist?" Kit asked.

"If it does, I can't imagine how."

That was a grievous understatement of my imagination. Stumpy Brown had given my name to his torturers. When he saw that there was no way out he threw the dice, hoping they were telling the truth when they said that they'd let him live for just a name.

I wondered if his corpse had been recovered.

"You're the one who called me, LT," Carson said.

"I called nine-one-one. *They* called you."

"I represent the police, when it comes to you. I will protect you just as well as any innocent citizen. But you have to let me in."

A thought came to my mind, a very disturbing notion.

"Look," I said, "if this attack has anything to do with Zella or the heist, I don't know how. I mean, if I expected armed assassins in my home, do you think I'd let my wife be here?"

Among other things, Kitteridge was a human lie detector. He could quantify any emotion in his mind. That's why, even though I felt pressed to act, I chose my words carefully. In his own way the police captain was as dangerous as the hit man Hush.

"I'm going to have to take you down for a statement," he said.

"Come on, man. You've seen my wife. I can't just leave her."

"You killed two men," he said. "They'd bust my ass down to desk clerk if I didn't follow the numbers on this."

There was no way out of a trip to the police station. Most other times it wouldn't have bothered me. Part of the dance is getting close to the fire without being burned.

"Okay," I said. "All right. But give me a few minutes alone with Katrina. Let me talk to her a minute before you take me away."

Kit heard something in my tone. He knew there was more to it than what I said. But he also knew that I could be very uncooperative when feeling pressed.

"And then you come with me and give what you got?" he asked.

I nodded.

He walked me back down to the dining room and asked kind-faced Officer Palmer to come outside with him.

———

ALONE IN THE ROOM with my wife was almost a solitary experience. She was in the same position, mouthing what might well have been the same words. I was concerned about her, but there were other, more urgent things to worry about.

I called Breland Lewis on his home phone.

"Hello," he said, sleep still in his voice.

"Two men broke in my house and tried to kill me."

"How's Katrina and the kids?"

"Fine. It has to be the Rutgers thing. You are a possible target. Get your wife and the kids and go somewhere where no one will be able to track you."

"Okay."

"You still got that phone Bug sent?"

"Yes."

"Bring it with you."

MY NEXT CALL was to Twill.

"Hey, Pops," he said on the first ring.

He was wide awake, getting into mischief no doubt, but I didn't have time to question him. Instead I told him what had happened and that I wanted him to gather up his mother and take her down to Mr. Arnold's—where she would be safe.

Twill promised to call his brother and sister on the way up from wherever he was.

That settled, I pulled a chair up to Katrina's side.

"Katrina."

To my surprise she sat upright and turned toward me.

"I am not leaving my house," she said with conviction.

"But, baby, these men were pros. You need protection."

"I will not leave. This is my home and I intend to stay."

"Twill's coming to get you."

"He is welcome here but I will not go."

I had come up against this blockade before. There was no moving Katrina once her mind was made up.

So I went out into the hallway to meet my official nemesis.

"Katrina won't leave," I told him. "The kids will all be here in an hour or so. Can you put a cop on watch at least until tomorrow tonight?"

"You gonna answer my questions, right?"

"I'll try my best."

The shade of a smile across Kit's lips spoke of admiration if not friendship. I was his toughest nut but he never doubted that I'd crack one day.

"Okay," he said. "I can have guys downstairs for a few days at least."

36

WE RODE SIDE BY SIDE in Kit's unmarked dark green Ford sedan. I expected him to take me to the 20th Precinct near my home but instead he drove all the way down to the 5th on Elizabeth Street.

It was fairly empty at that hour. Kit led me to a subterranean office. When we got there I remembered that he was always on the lookout for an office where he could smoke.

This was more like a converted storeroom. There wasn't even a proper desk; just a seven-foot-long folding table and six or seven walnut chairs.

He lit up a Marlboro.

"Can I have one'a those?" I asked.

"I thought you quit."

"I did but I slipped earlier tonight, and whenever I do that I give myself twenty-four hours to quit again."

We sat on the same side of the table facing each other, puffing away. If it wasn't for the person or persons unknown trying to kill me, it would have been almost pleasant down there.

"Let's have it, LT."

"First you tell me the names of the men trying to slaughter me and my family."

"No IDs," he said. "No receipts, documents, passports, not even any scars. The cigarettes they were smoking are European but none of my people could even tell what language was on the packs. These guys were not only professional, they were expensive. Imported, probably from Eastern Europe, like smelly cheese."

Damn.

"So?" he nudged.

"You realize that I don't trust the police," I stated.

"I'm not trying to trick you," Kit replied.

"I know that. I know. But that's not what I'm sayin'. There are holes in your security. Anything I say to you is safe, but the minute it goes past you lives will be on the line."

Kit shook his pack of Marlboros at me. I took the offering.

He lit me up and tapped his left foot—slowly.

"What do you want?" he asked after a spate of silence and smoke.

"Captain Clarence is right about Zella Grisham," I said. "She doesn't know a thing about the Rutgers heist. I don't know anything about the robbery either."

"Okay."

"Somebody thinks I do, obviously. I don't know who it is. If I did, I'd tell you or else I wouldn't say a word." This last phrase meant that if I did know, I might have killed them myself.

"Okay."

"So I will cooperate with you as far as I can, but I don't have any raw data, no evidence, that's not already in your possession."

"But you think Zella getting released has caused this violence?" Kit asked.

"She's innocent and should have been set free."

"What aren't you telling me, LT?"

"There's nothing I know that could lead to an arrest," I said. "That's a fact."

"Except maybe yours."

"Come on, now, man. You know I can't sit here and incriminate myself. I did not have anything to do with the robbery. I have no idea who sent those men to kill me."

"Lethford wants to talk to you."

"I'd be happy to meet with him . . . any time you say."

Kit watched me for a few moments before saying, "That was some impressive killing you did. Naked too."

"I hope I didn't embarrass Officer Palmer."

"She said that after all she heard about you she thought your johnson would be bigger."

"Tell her that the air conditioner was on."

I LEFT the precinct with half a pack of Kit's cigarettes at about seven a.m. Before that I filled out three forms, explaining what happened, and then Kit recorded my statement on a little digital recorder. He made copies of my gun license and my PI's ticket. The whole deposition took about three hours. I didn't mind. While speaking and writing I was going over every detail for my own investigation.

I arrived at the third-floor breakfast joint a little after eight. It was right at the East River and looked up at the Brooklyn Bridge.

I was met by an offbeat waiter. He had olive skin and a few years on me. He was dressed completely in white, even his shoes, and he was ugly. There's no other way to describe his countenance. His people hailed from some part of Europe that had been conquered and raped again and again over millennia. His ears were too big and his eyes the wrong color. The index and point fingers of his right hand were huge, as if they had been cut off some giant and grafted on him. All of his teeth were edged in jagged, mangled gold.

"We don't open until nine," he said in a gruff tone. There was an accent but I couldn't place it.

"I'm here to see Clarence Lethford," I said.

Hearing this, he turned and started walking across the broad room, with its dozen or so tables. He came to a door and opened it.

I had not moved from the entryway.

When he saw this he waved impatiently.

I approached and saw that this was a small private dining room with three empty tables.

"Sit here," the ugly man said. "Lethford will come."

I stepped in and the waiter closed the door behind me.

The walls, floor, and ceiling were cut from the same dirty and reddish brown unfinished wood. The room could have been a hundred years old, cleaned daily by the man in white and his ugly ancestors.

I sat next to a small window that allowed a view of the bridge and river. It was pleasant in there. I considered resting my head against the splintery wall and taking a nap.

But instead I made a call.

"Sorkin Securities," a bright young voice answered.

"LT McGill," I said. "NY-two-six-four-four-jay."

"Just a moment."

The phone made some clicking noises and then a man's voice said, "Ron Welton, security analyst. With whom am I speaking?"

"Leonid Trotter McGill."

"Yes, Mr. McGill. What can I do for you?"

"Somebody broke through my door last night."

"There's no record on our files of your shell being broken."

"They used an electromagnet and specially made crowbars."

"That must have taken a while."

"They were in in under ten seconds."

Silence.

"Mr. Welton?"

"We will have a crew out to your house by noon today, Mr. McGill. They will replace and upgrade the system."

"I thought every configuration you had was unique."

"We will also launch an internal investigation . . . Are you and your family all right?"

"No thanks to you."

SHELLY WAS at the house when I called. Twill, she said, was having tea in the little front room with Katrina. Dimitri and Tatyana had moved into D's room. There were cops down on the street, watching the front door.

"One of them comes up every couple of hours or so to check on us," my earnest daughter reported.

"Put your brother on the line," I said. I didn't have to tell her which brother.

I told Twill about the security company. Told him that I needed any extra keys left downstairs in our mailbox.

"Something's wrong with Mom," Twill said.

"Of course there is. Armed men broke into our home."

"No, Pops, it's more than that. I don't know how to describe it but there's definitely something wrong."

"I'll sit down with her when I get home. Is there anything else?"

"One thing."

"What's that?"

"You said that you wanted me to work for you so I could be safe, right?"

"You wanna quit?"

"No, sir."

SITTING THERE in the dowdy but private dining room, listening to traffic from the street and the clinking clanging of the restaurant workers getting ready for their clientele, I wondered about Velvet, crouching over her spent works.

Maybe I was being punished for breaking my oath and covering up yet another crime . . .

Try as I might I could not muster up any faith in superstition. I laughed and looked up.

At just that moment big, brutal Clarence Lethford banged into the room.

37

"WHAT YOU LAUGHIN' AT?" he asked, a lion addressing an unruly hyena.

"You wanna go back out that door and start over? Or should I just leave now?"

"You better watch out, son. I'm not the kinda man you can fuck with." Lethford took three steps and was standing over me.

"I already killed two men today," I replied easily, "and it's still only morning. So bring it on, mothahfuckah, bring it on."

The huge cop stared down at me. I was ready for the fight, actually welcomed the chance.

But instead he pulled back an ancient spindly chair and lowered his bulk onto it.

"You don't want me for an enemy, McGill."

"Kit said you wanted a meet," I replied. "Here I am."

Rage was a regular part of the policeman's makeup. But he was disciplined.

"Zella Grisham had nothing to do with that Rutgers heist," he told me.

"I know that."

"How do you know?"

"What does the color red look like?" I replied.

"Huh?"

"Go on, man. What else you want from me?"

"Where is Grisham?"

"Safe."

"Safe where?"

"You know I'm not gonna tell you that."

"I could throw your ass in jail."

"Throw all you want. I bounce."

That brought the wisp of a smile to the rough customer's lips.

"Let me tell you something, Captain Lethford."

"What?"

"After this meeting you're going to write a note, saying what we said and what your impressions were."

"Uh-huh."

"Five minutes after you file that note I could get it delivered on the fax machine of my choosing." If looks could kill . . .

"So," I continued, "if I tell you where Zella is, I know that she will be dead in the time it takes for one phone to talk to another. I don't know you. I can't trust you. But I will say that Zella is safe and she'll stay that way."

After swallowing a little more wrath he said, "There's only two reasons that I'm not sweating you in an interrogation room right now. The least is that word came down from on high to lay off Leonid Trotter McGill . . ."

This wasn't the first time I'd been told that officialdom in the NYPD had put a shield around me.

". . . the greater," he continued, "is that the most respected man on the force, Carson Kitteridge, says that if anybody will find an answer to these killings, it's you."

"Kit said that?"

"Question is, what do you have to say?"

"I know you think I'm seven kinds of guilty, Captain. That I either stole millions or that I'm trying to get at the money now. I'm innocent of your suspicions regardless of how much you doubt me. But now you're here, talking about killings, and last night two men tried to murder me and my family—real professionals. That said, I'm listening to you."

I took out a cigarette and lit it. The policeman didn't try to enforce the smoking ban.

"Bingo Haman," he began, "Mick Brawn, and Simon Willoughby. That's the heart of the most successful heist crew in the whole country. I was pretty sure that it was them that did the Rutgers job."

"So why didn't you arrest them?"

"Somebody called the DA and said that Zella Grisham had written in a diary about her plans to kill Harry Tangelo. They said that the journal was in her storage unit. Some overzealous cop snipped off the locks. He found no confession but he did uncover fifty thousand dollars in counterfeit Rutgers wrappers.

"I was taken off the case and they sentenced Zella as hard as they could."

"Haman, Brawn, and Willoughby," I said. "That was the crew?"

Lethford bobbed his long, angry head.

I remembered Sweet Lemon talking about the deaths of the henchmen.

"What about the point man?"

Lethford's aspect became suddenly still.

All those years ago, when Gordo put me in the ring with the heavyweight named Biggie, I got in a lucky punch in the seventh round of an eight-round fight. It was an unorthodox roundhouse right, landed flush on the tip of the big man's chin. Biggie's face froze like Lethford's did in that private dining room. Biggie had stopped moving forward for a good three seconds. If my left side hadn't hurt so much, I might have been able to make some kind of combination and change the tide of the one-sided fight. As it was, I was able to survive to the bell. I was on my feet at the end of round eight too but the judges liked Biggie for the contest.

"You know you'll never get as deep into this shit as I can," I said to Lethford. My side didn't hurt that morning.

When the cop was still quiet I asked, "Is the point man dead too?"

The point man is a counterstrategist who might also gather information for the heist crew. As a rule this man works only with the leader of the crew and offers not only information but also a second pair of seasoned eyes on The Plan.

This armchair tactician never goes out on a job. He simply advises and supplements intelligence. When it's all over this passive partner receives a modest percentage of the take.

"No," Lethford said. "I don't think so."

"You don't think so? Either he's dead or he's not."

"Bingo was good. We thought we knew who his adviser was but we were never sure. The person we suspected is still alive but . . ."

"You don't know for sure if he ever worked on the job."

Lethford nodded.

"Let me talk to the man. I might be able to make headway where a legal inquiry would not."

"Why should I trust you?"

"Because the best cop in New York told you to."

Clarence blinked twice and then squinted. He stayed that

way for quite a few seconds; much longer than it took me to kill two men.

"Miss Nova Algren," he said at last.

"A woman?"

"The best in the business. She retired two months after the Rutgers thing. Living in a retirement home near Saratoga Springs."

38

BEFORE I LEFT the Ugly Man's diner Lethford gave me an envelope with photographs and details of the deaths of the Haman crew. I shuffled through the file in the taxi on the way up to a parking garage near my apartment.

When I was at the entrance I decided to hoof my way back home.

The door was still broken on its hinges. But when I tried to push it open I found that it held fast.

"Anybody home?" I called through the crack.

"Here, Daddy," Shelly piped.

I heard something on the other side and then the heavy door was dragged open.

Seeing my daughter made me swallow hard. She was wearing an off-white dress that was broad at the hem and close fitting above the waist. I grabbed her up in my arms and squeezed tight.

"Daddy, you're hurting me."

"I'm sorry, baby girl. I'm so sorry." I put her down.

"It's not your fault and I wasn't there."

"No," I said, "you weren't."

Her smile was a little crooked, probably because my gaze was so hard.

"What's that I smell?"

"Mama's cooking."

IN THE KITCHEN Katrina was standing over her great-grandmother's stewpot mixing with a big wooden spoon that was older than any of her children. Tatyana was sitting at the kitchen table, mincing onions.

There was nothing right about that scene.

"Hey, babe."

It took Katrina a moment to stop what she was doing and turn to me but when she did her smile was resplendent. She was wearing the pink dress that buttoned up the front and a floral apron that I hadn't seen in years.

"Leonid, I didn't expect you so early."

"You guys gettin' along?" I had to ask.

"Tatyana is a wonderful cook," my wife of too many years said. "She has the touch."

The Belarusian Mata Hari looked up at me and smiled. She was in T-shirt and jeans. I could see that she had already cut up mushrooms, green and red peppers, garlic, and leeks.

The head and claws of a kosher hen lay on a plate to her left.

"Are you all right, Katrina?"

"Yes. Of course."

"That was pretty bad this morning."

"I cleaned up all the blood. My mother once showed me how to do it with baking soda."

I could see what Twill meant. Her eyes were clear but vacant. Her tone was so matter-of-fact as to inspire fear.

"Do you need me to do anything?" I asked.

"No. Will you want lunch?"

"No, honey. I'm going up to Saratoga Springs. I have to talk to somebody."

"Will you be home for dinner?"

"I hope so."

"Yes," Katrina said. "It would be so nice. All my children will be here."

I FOUND TWILL and Dimitri playing chess in Twill's room. Whenever I watched them play I got the feeling that Twill let his older brother win most of the time.

"Hey, boys."

Dimitri looked up but Twill kept his eye on the board—it was hard to lose and make a good showing of it at the same time.

"Pops," Twill said.

"Did you find out why they did it, Dad?" Dimitri asked. His tone was one of deference. It had been a long time since Dimitri had shown me such respect.

"Not yet. But I sure will, and soon."

"Check," Twill said. "Hey, Pop, can I talk to you a minute?"

IN THE HALL Twill closed the door to his room and stood close.

"I know a guy who knows a guy who knows somebody in Kent's crew."

"You talk to him?"

"Is the president of the United States a black man?"

"And what did he say?"

"No question that Kent's the boss. On top of rip-offs and dealing they're running protection now too. They killed this one dude in the West Village to make an example."

"You sure?"

"Pretty much. He called me."

"Who?"

"Kent."

"What did he say?"

"That if I wanted to do business south of Fourteenth Street, I had to work with him."

"Okay, T. Let it lay for a bit. I need to talk to Breland about this."

AFTER CLEARING the Whitestone Bridge and wending through various highways you come into the vast forest that makes up most of New York State. Leaving the city always makes me wonder about the wilderness and the hatred it must have for the edifices of humanity.

The day was clear and bright blue over the senseless green of the surrounding woods. I was listening to Joni Mitchell playing on my MP3 on the speaker system of the car. Her high-pitched complaints found a resonance in my heart and I sang along in an off-tune, gravelly way.

WINDSONG ESTATES was a rambling property on the north side of Saratoga Springs. It abutted a dense pine forest and was comprised of a huge old mansion, various bungalows, and modern-looking residence buildings.

The parking lot was red clay. I walked from my classic '57 white-and-green Pontiac across a broad lawn to the terrace-like veranda that went all the way around the front of the white-washed house.

No one was on the green, well-trimmed lawn.

No one was on the porch until I put a foot on the first stair.

Then a short Japanese woman in full-length baby blue nurse's garb came out the screened door. Behind her ambled a huge white orderly with a bald head and porcine eyes. He was pale and heavy, but the fat was held in place by a goodly amount of muscle.

"May I help you?" the woman said with a perfect American accent.

"Nova Algren."

"And you are?"

"Tell her that Leonid McGill brings her greetings from Bingo Haman."

"And your business?"

"Is with Ms. Algren."

The orderly's shoulders raised a quarter inch.

The Japanese nurse was in her fifties, on the short side and the color of dark honey. She was fit and serious.

"Salesman?" she asked.

"No."

"Insurance?"

I shook my head this time.

"I have to tell her your business."

"Leonid McGill with greetings from Bingo Haman and his crew. That's all you need."

"This Haman is a sailor?"

"No."

"What kind of crew, then?"

I was tired of negativity and so did not answer at all.

The orderly's squinty eyes were getting restless.

The nurse turned, made an impatient gesture at the big man, and they both disappeared into the dark maw beyond the screen door.

No one invited me in so I leaned against a white column, which had once been a tree, on the left side of the staircase.

I thought about lighting a cigarette and decided against it. There were four left in the pack. I had to finish them off before the next morning but the need would most likely be greater later on.

I had discovered after many years of trial and error that if I smoked for only twenty-four hours the withdrawal symptoms were negligible. It was like a GET OUT OF JAIL FREE card, if I was disciplined about the slip.

"Mr. McGill," a wispy gentlewoman's voice said.

She was standing behind the gray haze of the screen door, tall in a dark green pantsuit, her gray hair coiffed, with glasses hanging from a string of natural freshwater pearls around her neck.

"That's me," I said, pushing myself to an erect posture.

The elderly woman smiled and pushed open the door. Her steps had an extra oomph to them, a little more energy to make sure her feet didn't stumble. The older you are, the harder you have to work.

"You're here for Bingo?" she asked.

"In a manner of speaking."

"I thought he had died."

"The dead often leave messages behind."

"Mysterious." She must have been a beautiful woman in her youth. She was handsome at seventy-something.

"Shall we go over to the side of the building?" she suggested.

I followed her well-metered gait around the porch to the side of the house. There we came upon an iron table attended by four iron chairs, all painted pale pink.

"The staff doesn't like us to be in view of the public," she said as we both sat. "They feel an onus, to go out there to make sure we aren't kidnapped or mugged."

I liked this lady very much.

"You were saying something about Bingo?" she asked.

"You knew him?"

"I knew a man named Aaron Sadler," she said.

AARON SADLER. The police were after him for a string of extortions where the threats were always shams; kind of a soft-porn crook. He found rich kids that didn't mind fooling their parents for a twenty-five percent cut of the take. Aaron used his own name but had a stand-in, Poland Jarvis, as the contact for his youthful confederates. It all went along swimmingly until Jarvis got arrested for DWI and Sadler had to make contact with one of the kids in person.

Aaron's luck worsened when the cops tumbled on the conspiracy and put pressure on the young heir to a Midwestern dairy empire, Robert Fleiner.

It fell to me to gather evidence that young Mr. Fleiner was involved in the death of a prostitute some years before. Faced with a life sentence versus the possibility of getting cut out of a healthy will, Bob decided to forget what the real Aaron Sadler looked like.

"Bingo is dead," I said, "as you've heard."

Nova's eyes were blue-gray and had the mien of matronly kindness. There was no change in them.

"I thought so."

"So are Mick Brawn and Simon Willoughby."

"Really?" The slightest bit of concern gathered around her light-colored orbs.

I handed her the rather graphic photographs of the dead men.

She flipped through them like a grandmother pretending to be interested in another old woman's family album.

Handing the pictures back to me, she said, "Horrible."

"A police captain named Lethford told me that these deaths were connected to the Rutgers heist."

"How is Clarence?"

"Mad at the world and proud of it."

She laughed pleasantly.

"He came up here a few times, thinking that an old woman like me would have anything to do with thugs and thieves. But he always brought me chocolates."

"Why are you here, Mr. McGill?"

"Two men broke into my home and tried to murder me."

"Tried?"

"I killed them."

Without missing a beat she said, "I killed my stepfather, Charles Clement, when I was only eleven years old. No doubt the men after you made the same underestimation that Mr. Clement did."

We were on equal footing. I wondered if she had a derringer somewhere on her person; the best assumption would be that she did.

"The people that sent those men after me, if they become aware of you, might send a visitor to Windsong."

Nova's smile was wan and unconcerned.

"I want to know who it is," I said, "for obvious reasons."

"Yes, I can see that."

"Can you help me?"

"I'm not sure. I'll have to think about it."

"As I said—your life could be in danger too."

"My death is already a foregone conclusion, Mr. McGill. Thank you for your concern but I have never relied upon the good graces of another to protect me."

"So you have to think about it?"

"Yes."

"When will you know?"

"When I know." She stood up and began walking toward the front of the building.

I followed her to the screen door and even opened it for her.

"Thank you, Mr. McGill. I don't need the help but I do appreciate good manners."

39

THE TRAFFIC WAS pretty good and I made Lower Manhattan somewhere between two-thirty and three.

That afternoon I told the first-line security desk at Rutgers Assurance that I was there to speak to Johann Brighton. That request altered the mode of access. I was guided to an elevator at the front of the building that took me to the twenty-seventh floor, leaving me at what can only be called a large glass cage where a young receptionist sat behind a bright blue desk.

The carpet surrounding the desk was black, and across from it, against a glass wall, was a row of seven padded yellow chairs.

Beyond the transparent walls were many doorways. For a moment I imagined that I was in a theater where the audience sat center stage and the actors performed on the periphery.

In this flight of fancy I had arrived, no doubt, at intermission.

The nameplate for the lovely café au lait receptionist read KINESHA MOTUTO. She looked up at me and smiled.

"Have a seat and someone will be with you," she said.

"Do you know how long it will be?"

"I'm sure it will be soon," she said, returning her gaze to the papers on her blue desk.

"What section is this?"

Kinesha looked up at me pleasantly and said, "Just have a seat, sir. Someone will be with you soon."

I took the center chair and laced my fingers, prepared for a long wait. But less than a minute later a door behind and to the left of Kinesha swung inward and Alton Plimpton appeared. That day the slight manager wore a dark green suit and a bruised-banana tie. He stared at me a moment from behind the doubtful protection of the glass barrier. Then he rapped on the glass.

Kinesha turned, saw who it was, and touched something on her desk. An invisible panel began rising from the floor, forming a gap large enough for a man to pass through.

Alton walked up as I stood to meet him.

Before he could speak I said, "I'm here to see Johann Brighton."

"I had your name associated with mine in the visitors' database," he replied.

"Funny, there's a captain in the NYPD that's done the same kind of thing with me."

"What is your business here, Mr. McGill?"

"Mr. Brighton," I answered.

"Mr. Harlow does not want you on the premises."

"Who's that?"

"It's enough for you to know that he doesn't appreciate your presence."

"Then why did you let me up?"

"We have a security team standing by."

"And do you think that they could grab me before I broke your neck?" I hadn't had much sleep in more than thirty-six hours. The spark on my fuse was entering the body of the bomb.

Kinesha stood up. I wondered if she was part of the security team.

A tall man in a dark suit passed through the space in the glass wall.

"Mr. Plimpton?" the man said.

Alton turned, giving me the opportunity to scrutinize the new corporate player. This man was tall, black-haired, and fit. Either he was wearing a blue suit or I was; we couldn't both be because our clothes were different species in the capitalist jungle.

"Mr. Brighton," Plimpton said with a deference that no doubt tore at his nerdy self-esteem.

"What are you doing here?" the VP asked the manager-at-large.

"Mr. Harlow asked me to inform Mr. McGill that he was not to come here."

"I don't remember asking Mr. Harlow to take that action."

Ah . . . the chain of command.

"Well, I, we didn't think that you needed to be bothered."

Brighton turned his attention from Alton to me.

"Johann Brighton," he said, extending a hand.

"Leonid McGill."

Brighton was handsome and charismatic. Mentally, I had to bear down a little not to start liking him.

"Your name has been all over my desk of late, Mr. McGill. I was happy when my secretary told me that you were here."

"Mr. Brighton," Alton Plimpton said.

"Come with me, Mr. McGill," Johann Brighton said, ignoring the underling. "We'll go up to my office to talk."

40

WE PASSED THROUGH the glass wall and entered a door that opened onto a long slender hallway. We followed that vascular path to a cylindrical room with four elevator doors placed at ninety-degree intervals. Brighton held a thick card in front of a crystal green panel and one of the doors slid open.

Inside the chamber a voice said, "Hello, Mr. Brighton, sixty-sixth floor?"

"Yes," he said.

I was impressed.

"Mr. Plimpton doesn't seem to like me," I said, just making conversation.

"Alton has worked for Rutgers thirty-three years. He started in the mailroom."

". . . and," I said, "has only recently realized that coming in at the bottom almost always precludes reaching the top."

The VP turned his head to regard me. His eyes were green and his aspect somewhere between that of a fox and a wolf; the one creature preying on smaller animals, and the other, with his pack, used to taking down creatures much larger than himself.

Which one, he was wondering, was I?

The elevator door slid open and we were presented with a

triple-wide hallway that was tiled in emerald and gold. On the walls hung large still-life oil paintings, mostly landscapes, with the occasional study.

There were no offices on this half-block journey, not until we came to the dead end. There the double walnut doors we encountered swung open automatically and we entered the antechamber to his office.

Not for the first time in my life I had made it to the top. For some reason this made me hanker for a chili dog with chopped onions under a blanket of processed American cheese.

The reception room for Brighton was large and well appointed. There was a window looking out over the Statue of Liberty. The kidney-shaped desk was clean, and the woman behind it—the woman known as Claudia Burns—looked up, attentive to her charming boss's any need.

She saw me but was unconcerned and unimpressed.

I saw her and was reminded of a photograph I had seen years ago. The hair was shorter and another color, now she wore glasses, but I was sure that the woman sitting there was Harry Tangelo's lover—Minnie Lesser.

"Hold my calls, C," the perfectly attired captain of industry said to the woman going under the false name.

"Yes, sir."

BRIGHTON'S OFFICE WAS the same as many rich and powerful businessmen and -women I'd known in Manhattan. Lots of window space looking out across his domain, good carpeting, and an imposing black desk that wasn't exactly rectangular. In one corner sat a love seat and a good-sized stuffed chair, both black, both looking to contain more comfort than the average working stiff has ever experienced.

"Have a seat, Mr. McGill." Johann waved toward the chair.

I took the love seat.

Without missing a beat he sat in the chair meant for me. There he leaned back comfortably.

I put my left forearm on my left knee and the heel of my right palm on the other leg joint.

Brighton smiled and nodded slightly.

"How can I help you, Mr. McGill?"

I sat up and back, crossed my legs and frowned.

"How much did your suit cost?" I asked.

"It was made for me by the personal tailor of a Saudi prince. So I guess you could say that it was either free or priceless."

"Huh. The only thing anybody ever gave me was grief . . . the most they ever took was blood."

"That's very dramatic," the VP said.

"You think so? Then try this: Last night two assassins broke into my home. They came to kill me while I was up in the bed with my wife, in the same apartment where my children sleep." My head jerked, releasing an iota of the deep-seated tension in my body and soul.

"They, they actually came into your apartment?"

"They were halfway down the hall before I killed them in their tracks."

"Oh." It was Brighton's turn to lean forward. "You shot them?"

"One," I said. "I crushed the other's windpipe with my hand."

I was sure that Johann Brighton had forgotten the name of the Saudi tailor but I could see in his face that he would never forget mine.

"What did the police have to say about this?" he asked.

"What they always say—fill out form twenty-two AB, write an account of the circumstances, and then answer a battery of verbal questions that are recorded and filed away so that one day they can come back and incriminate you."

"I mean," Johann said, "what did they say about the killers? Who were they?"

"European. Probably East European. Men who traveled six thousand miles or more just to see me die."

Brighton was hard to read. He didn't make it to that lofty perch with his heart dangling from his sleeve.

"Maybe your dramatic flair is earned," he said.

"Fuck that. I'm here to ask you why."

"What could Rutgers Assurance have to do with assassins in the night?"

"Not Rutgers," I said. "You."

"You've lost me, Mr. McGill."

"Oh? Aren't you the one who said that my name was all over your desk?"

"Yes, but—"

"And doesn't my place on your blotter have to do with Zella Grisham, Antoinette Lowry, and fifty-eight million dollars that went away during the biggest heist in Wall Street history?"

"What does any of that have to do with men trying to kill you?"

"You don't know?"

He shook his head and held my stare the way your opponent does before the first round of a fight that he just knows he's going to win.

"Zella Grisham," I began, "was arrested for shooting her boy-friend."

"If you say so."

"I do and she was. This boyfriend, Harry Tangelo, was in the bed with Zella's friend Minnie Lesser." I stopped there to see the cracks appear in the VP's façade and also because a thrum of rage was rising up somewhere below my heart just above the diaphragm. I don't think I had ever been so close to violence without perpetrating an actual physical attack.

"I'm not familiar with Grisham's arrest before the money was found in her possession," he said. If he could see the rage in me, he didn't respond.

Maybe he felt secure in physical superiority. Maybe he had a black belt in some Eastern defense art. Whatever he felt he was wrong.

I took a deep breath and held it thrice as long as usual.

Exhaling, I let flow out "How long has your assistant been working for you?"

"What does that have to do with anything?"

"Was she in this office when the heist went down?"

"I don't remember." If he was nervous, he sure didn't show it.

"Maybe she knows more about you than you think."

Words, for the moment, had abandoned the handsome millionaire. His left eye almost closed and I was allowed a glimpse of the man behind the corporate veneer. This momentary bout of speechlessness was the first indication I had that my predicament was even more complex than I had thought.

He raised his hands in a gesture of confusion. "Is there anything else, Mr. McGill?"

"Whoever sent those men into my home is going to pay," I said. "I might not wear the same species of suit that you got but all men bleed and all men die."

Brighton stood up and I followed suit.

"Mr. McGill, you have to believe me when I tell you that I, nor anyone else at Rutgers, would consider using paid assassins to solve our problems."

I WAS ALLOWED to find my way back down the wide hallway to the elevator. The door was open. All I had to do was step in and I was delivered to the twenty-seventh floor. From there I made my way to the outskirts of the glass cage.

The receptionist did her panel-sliding routine and I found myself with her and a dusky-skinned Caucasian man of medium height and middle age, wearing a tan suit with a few dozen scarlet threads shooting through.

"Mr. McGill?" the man said. His face was a pinched isosceles triangle, standing on its pointy chin.

"Yes?"

"My name is Harlow."

"Yes, Mr. Harlow?"

"You will not be allowed admittance to these premises again."

"Does that come from you or Mr. Brighton?"

"I am the one speaking, am I not?"

There are few times in a human's life when the choice is clear and obvious. But there's always another way, another approach. That's why most people like a job where there's a boss and a set of rules written down; a time to arrive and a dollar amount on every hour you toil.

The workingman believes that he has no choice, my long-gone father used to say. *He believes that his whole life has been planned out for him. He's right about the plan but wrong about the destination.*

At that moment, in that glass cage, I knew that the only action to take was a solid one-two to the man Harlow's rib cage and head. I wanted to hit him even though I knew that the act would buy me a prison sentence of interminable length because the rage I felt would certainly kill this stranger.

My action and his death were foregone conclusions.

And then I remembered "Bartleby, the Scrivener," and Melville spoke out from his moldering grave, telling me that fate was not inescapable and that this man Harlow would live at least one more day.

41

I TOOK A SUBWAY toward midtown and my office. The second-to-the-last car of the A train was empty enough that I could sit on the end, next to the sliding doors. I put in earbuds connected to an ultra-thin MP3 player and listened to the seventies album, *Below the Salt*, by Steeleye Span, the English folk band. Nasally and dark, mystical and mysterious, the tones seemed to fit my predicament, telling me that the path of my life had been traveled for centuries and who was I to feel so special?

WARREN OH WAS at his post behind the high podium at the front of the Tesla Building.

"Warren."

"Mr. McGill."

"How's the family?" I asked the Chinese-and-black Jamaican man.

"Mother's coming to live with us."

"She is?" I stopped.

"She's too frail to take care of herself and my aunt died in the spring."

Our eyes met. Understanding, sympathy, and acceptance of

our fates were transmitted without words. He gave me a wan Island smile and I nodded—the perennial New York pessimist.

WHEN THE ELECTRIC LOCK clicked I pushed open the office door expecting to see Mardi, her pale expression of devotion providing a moment of respite from the jagged threat of the streets of New York, encroaching old age, and innate negativity.

Young Ms. Bitterman was there behind her white ash desk but her expression was one of helplessness instead of welcome. Turning my head thirty degrees to the right, I saw the cause of her mild despair. Seated next to each other on my client's bench was Aura, the woman I loved, and Antoinette, newest leader of a wild pack that had been on my trail for decades.

Aura stood up immediately, taking the two steps needed to reach me.

"Mr. McGill," Antoinette complained.

"You'll have to wait a moment, Ms. Lowry." I took Aura's hand and led her out into the hallway.

"Bad time?" were the first words she uttered when the door to my office closed behind us.

"If that was all, I wouldn't need three days."

"How bad?"

"Baby, I love you. You know that, right?"

When she smiled my heart trilled a high note.

When she kissed me I understood that love is always and only here and now.

"Okay," she said. "I'll give you your three days."

I took her hand and said, "It's a really hard time, baby."

"It always is," she said to my heart.

As Aura walked away I took a moment to breathe before going back into the heavy atmosphere that surrounded my natural enemy and her mindless instinct.

I MOTIONED to Antoinette when I returned to the reception space. She followed me down the aisle to my office. On the way we passed Twill, sitting at his desk, talking on a cell phone.

"Pops," he said, then nodded at the private agent of industry.

I grunted at my son and plodded toward the back office.

Once Rutgers's predator was seated I settled in.

"I was informed of the attempt on your life," she said. She wasn't impressed by the view or the size of my work space compared to hers.

"Bad news . . ." I said, feeling no compunction to finish the timeworn saying.

"Maybe now you'll see how it is in your own best interest to cooperate with me."

I laughed.

"Are you a fool?" Antoinette Lowry wanted to know.

"Lady, I killed two professional assassins while buck naked ten seconds after I'd woken up from a deep sleep. One I shot and the other I ended with my bare hands. Now you tell me what the fuck you could have done but get in my goddamned way?"

"Maybe if you shared information with me the attempt would have never been made."

"Are you saying that Rutgers had something to do with those men?"

"No," she said in a tone that revealed much more.

"But maybe somebody else?" I suggested. "Maybe Johann Brighton?"

"No." This time she was much more certain.

"But there are some shadows up in there. You do business in places where the laws of man are different, sometimes virtually nonexistent."

That was the beginning of our real conversation. I had shown that I was both capable and wise to the ways of her world. I could tell by the intensity in her gaze that she suddenly saw me as a worthy opponent—or ally.

"What do you know about your attackers?" she asked.

I covered the important details, as blasé as I could manage.

Antoinette listened closely, trying her best not to show how deeply the particulars of the attempt impacted her.

"Does any of what I say sound familiar?" I asked after cutting off the tale at the interrogation imposed on me at the Elizabeth Street Precinct.

"Why would it?"

"I don't know. You're the one investigating the robbery."

"From the sounds of it, Mr. McGill, you have called this contract on yourself. For all I know this attempt on your life might have nothing to do with my business."

"Com'on, girl," I said. "Don't be coy with me. Does this shit sound like some street-level thug or even some kinda upscale mobster? Foreign assassins don't only take a lot of money. You got to have serious connections to make something like that happen."

"Maybe," she conceded.

"Anybody hire me is already on a level way below that kind of action. And you know if they're trying to kill me, I have to be getting close to that fifty-eight million."

"Maybe you already have it," Antoinette offered. "Maybe you ripped off your confederates in the crime."

"Darling," I said, "you know my history probably better than I do. You know how many times my life has been on the line and the limits of my lifestyle. Do you think I'd be here in New York if I had all those millions? No, I'd be in some country with no extradition treaty with the U.S., buying judges beach condos and bedding the local hotties."

This long-held fantasy seemed to go halfway to convincing my current nemesis.

"Then why?" she asked.

"Lewis and I got Zella out of prison. That has to put a strain on the real thieves' exit plan. They want to destroy anything having to do with Zella and her possible innocence."

"But why come after you? If you didn't have anything to do with the heist, then you pose no threat."

She had brainpower to spare.

"Scorched earth," I explained. "Kill the principals when releasing Zella and the crime comes back to her. I mean, why else would she and her supporters get killed?"

"Maybe." She still wasn't completely convinced.

"What else could it be?"

"Maybe it's just the fallout between former partners."

"Do you think for one moment that if I knew who was after me that they would still be breathing?"

Antoinette had my police files. She knew that I knew Hush.

"So what do you suggest?" she asked.

"Give me a number where I can get to you when I need to. I promise that if I crack this nut, I'll share the meat with you."

WE TRADED INFORMATION and I walked her past Twill and then the reception desk to the front door of my suite.

After she'd gone I asked Mardi, "What does your third eye tell you about her?"

"You were better off with the fever, boss."

It was at that moment I realized that Mardi would one day inherit my business.

42

DECIDING NOT TO GO back to my desk, I took the elevator down to the street.

Meandering in a westerly direction, I realized that I was not only angry but also confused. I wanted to gather up Hush and declare war on my enemies only I wasn't sure just who the enemy was.

Minnie Lesser had something to do with it—though that made no logical sense. Johann Brighton was involved. And then there was Antoinette Lowry; was that child of the South trying to kill me too?

In the back of a yellow cab, headed for home, I sent a text to Bug Bateman in what felt like a vain attempt to keep moving forward.

WHEN I GOT to our place I found a new key in the mailbox; it worked perfectly on the repaired and replaced front door.

Tatyana and Katrina were sitting side by side in the little front room, chatting in soft tones. My wife was smiling almost ruefully while Tatyana paid close attention to her every word.

"Ladies," I said.

I went to the pink padded chair beside the maroon sofa and Tatyana moved to rise. Katrina put out a hand and the Belarusian sat back down. This interaction alone told a full story—albeit in a language foreign to me.

"How are you, Katrina?"

"Fine." The soft smile was not reassuring. "I've made lasagna for you and the children."

"I'm so sorry about what happened."

"No, Leonid," she said, "it is I who should be apologizing. Most men support their families with safe jobs at insurance companies and auto garages. I've been cruel to you and every day you're out there with your life in the balance. If one night that danger spills into this house, I cannot blame you. I should have been working, taking some of the weight off of your shoulders."

"I never asked for that," I said.

"But I should have taken the initiative. I can see now that it is as much my fault as yours what has happened."

"Katrina . . ."

"Tatyana has been supporting her family for years and she is so young," my wife said. "When I was her age I expected men to buy me things and here she is doing for others."

This was definitely not the woman I had married. Her words indicated a change so profound that I had no idea how to respond. I was a lone Crusader washed up on the shore of the New World after my ship had foundered, taking with it all hands but me.

"Can I make you a drink?" I asked. Old standards are always the best.

"Cognac," my wife said.

I looked inquiringly at Tatyana. She shook her head almost imperceptibly.

———

IN THE DINING ROOM I found Dimitri reading a hardback book.

"What you readin'?" I asked.

"Technics and Civilization," he said, "by Lewis Mumford."

"I once read a book by him. *The City in History*, or something like that."

I took a seat next to my boy.

Dimitri closed the book, turning his attention to me.

"It's my fault, right?" he said.

"What?"

"That Mom almost got killed."

"Of course not. Those men were after me. And it's not even my fault. I didn't do anything to them."

My phone chirped, telling me that it contained a message. I resisted the lure.

"But I wasn't here," Dimitri said.

"I was."

"Yeah . . . You know, I was thinking, Pops . . . maybe I should start goin' to Uncle Gordo's gym."

"You got the build for it," I said, "that's for sure. But you can't protect everybody you meet."

"Just Mom and Taty, is all I care about."

"What about school?"

"I'll go back after Tatyana gets her degree. You know I love history and science. But she'll be able to get a better job quicker than I can."

I put my hand on D's right forearm. He put his left hand over my fingers. We hadn't been so close since he was an infant but still our levels of experience placed us miles and miles apart.

———

THE MESSAGE was a forwarded e-mail from Bug. Once you help a man with his love life he responds with alacrity. I went to my den and downloaded the pages of data he'd sent.

What he found wasn't an answer to my problems, not exactly, but it indicated a path I might take.

"HELLO?" she said on the fourth ring.

"Ms. Lowry?"

"I didn't expect you to call so soon."

"We should meet."

"About what?"

"Considering the clout of my enemies, I'd rather not say on the phone."

"Enemies?"

"Anybody who sends cutthroats to my door is an enemy."

"Do you know the Pink Lady?" she asked.

"Yeah." I hadn't been there in years.

"I'm busy right now but I can get there in a few hours, let's say eleven?"

I POURED COGNAC into a chilled snifter and grenadine and sparkling water into a tall tapering glass. These I delivered to Katrina and Dimitri's girlfriend before going back out on the street— where I belonged.

43

CENTRAL PARK is glorious after dark. City lights glow in the distance, making the shadows between the trees even deeper. Many a night when I was on the run from child services and the police I'd slept in the hidden recesses of that man-made wilderness.

It might have been dangerous for some but I was armed and angry. The .25 in my pocket looked like a toy when in my big hand but it could still rip through flesh and bone, spill any man's blood who wanted to do me harm.

I strolled around the dark paths with impunity, maybe even hoping a little that some poor miscreant wanted to confront the short and fat middle-aged park walker.

Lucky for the unnamed troublemaker, he didn't see me or was wise enough to keep his distance.

THE PINK LADY was the only classical music nightclub in all New York—maybe even in the entire world. That evening a woodwind quintet was playing eighteenth-century sonatas and chamber music.

There were fifteen or so round tables set in a semicircle around the dais where the musicians performed. There was also a bar. People sat and drank, spoke in soft tones, and appreciated the European precursor to jazz.

Lowry sat alone at a table set farthest away from the players. She was sipping at a bright pink drink of sloe gin and strawberries—the signature cocktail of the club.

"Hey," I said, taking the seat next to her.

"You found it okay?"

"I used to come here with a friend a long time ago."

"Really? I wouldn't expect you to know a place like this."

"Why not?"

"What did you want with me, Mr. McGill?"

"You were born Dwalla, Iché Dwalla. The name might be from Africa but your people were in Alabama for generations all the way back to the seventeen hundreds. They were Tellfords and Mintons, Mummers and Daltons before becoming Afrocentrists. But you rebelled against that—renamed yourself and went on to Harvard, then Stanford. Your education might seem to some to be at odds with the decision to join the army but I see that as the continued rebuke of your parents' politics."

"Impressive," she said. "You know how to get information. But I don't have anything to hide. I'm not afraid of your knowledge."

"I'm not trying to frighten you. I'm just explaining why I wanted to meet."

"And why is that?"

"I don't know who's trying to kill me, Ms. Lowry. I don't have any millions of dollars. Zella Grisham is innocent. So I figure that it's either the heist men or Rutgers after me—either of them or both.

"You've only been with Rutgers for twenty months. When the heist went down you were entering the armed services as an intelligence trainee."

A light slowly rose in the dark woman's eyes.

"Why would you suspect the company that was robbed?" she asked. "Why would they do something like that and put me on your trail too?"

"Maybe not the whole company," I ruminated. "Maybe just a few parties who set up the robbery. Clay Thorn might not have acted alone."

"And you think because the hit men were exotics that only someone with power could have set it up," she said.

"The top heist men could set up a hit like that but these guys didn't."

"Oh?"

I told her about Clarence Lethford's tale of Bingo, and his men. I didn't say anything about Nova Algren.

"I didn't know that," Antoinette said. "I knew that Lethford had been in charge of the investigation but he refused to talk to me. Now I can see why."

"Yeah," I agreed, "he probably suspects you guys too. So the only question is, would you follow the bread crumbs if they led you back to your own masters?"

"That's my job," Antoinette Lowry said solemnly. "But I have no reason to think that the guard Thorn had anything to do with the upper echelons of Rutgers. The internal investigation after the heist revealed that he had a cousin doing time for armed robbery. We believed that his cousin's contacts got him to set up the job."

"Have you proven that?"

"No."

"Have you at least interrogated the cousin?"

"Steven Billings died of lung cancer three years after the robbery."

"But if you suspect Thorn and Billings, why believe that Zella had anything to do with it?"

"There was proof in her storage space. Do you have proof that any other employees of Rutgers are involved?"

"Not ironclad—no."

"Then why are we here?" Antoinette asked.

Instead of answering I gestured toward a young waitress. Like all of the servers she was white and blond, wearing a little black dress.

"Yes, sir?"

"Cognac," I said, "as close to twenty-five dollars a glass as you can get."

She smiled at the ordering technique and went away.

"The corporate flowchart indicates that you don't report to Johann Brighton," I said to Antoinette.

"I could have you arrested for just knowing that."

"Is that chart telling it like it is or is it just a fiction?"

"I don't report to him."

"Did you know that Minnie Lesser, the girlfriend of the man that Zella Grisham shot, is now Brighton's personal secretary? She changed her name to Claudia Burns."

The slip of a waitress brought me my snifter. I took a sip and savored the burn.

"But you claim that Grisham is not involved," Antoinette said when the waitress was gone again.

"Somebody had to set her up."

I was on shaky ground. I knew that Minnie couldn't have been involved with the crime before it was committed but that didn't mean she wasn't pulled in after. And even if it was some big co-incidence I still needed Antoinette working with me.

By any means necessary, as my father and Malcolm X were known to say.

The quintet was playing something from the Romantic period. It sounded like Brahms without the piano. Lowry turned her attention to the music while taking small mouthfuls of her pink drink. I allowed her to savor and listen, knowing that I had brought a bitter taste and a sour note to her investigations.

She was in a tight spot. If someone from the upper crust of Rutgers was involved, the solution of the crime might have been beyond her pay grade. She could get fired or even follow in the footsteps of Bingo and his friends.

She put down the glass and returned her full attention to me.

"I'm not afraid of a fight, Mr. McGill."

"You should be."

"Tell me something."

"What's that?"

"The person you came here with, were they white?"

"She was a black woman," I said. "As a matter of fact you remind me of her in many ways."

"What happened to her?"

"She was murdered." A muscle in my diaphragm twitched.

"You loved her?"

"Not enough."

"I've given up on black men," Antoinette said as if this was somehow a logical continuance of our conversation.

"You don't like us?"

"No, it's not that. I find black men infinitely attractive and interesting. But they take me to a place that I don't want to revisit."

"Maybe down in Alabama," I said. "In New York we might take you to the Romantic era."

"I'll consider what you said . . . about the robbery. I'll look into it a little and get back if I find you're being straight with me."

44

TWO BLOCKS from my house, at nearly one in the morning, my cell phone hit a dour note.

"Hello?" I said as if I didn't know the caller.

"I read about you in the newspaper today."

"We all get our fifteen minutes," I said.

"That's okay if it's not the last minutes of your life."

"They were from Eastern Europe," I told Hush, "serious as a motherfucker."

"You want me to get involved?"

"Hold that thought."

THE APARTMENT was dark and silent when I got in. The only light I saw came from the three bullet holes in Shelly's wall.

Her door was open and she was asleep, a paperback book lying next to her on the bed. I flipped the wall switch and moved back into the hall. That's when I noticed the faint glow coming from the little front room.

TATYANA WAS CURLED at the far corner of the sofa, reading a huge tome.

I walked in and she looked up, a little drowsy-eyed.

"What you readin'?" I asked.

She tilted the book up so I could read the dust cover: *Historical Aspects of Globalization*.

"Okay, I'll bite. How old is globalization?" I asked.

"Ever since there was a river with people on, either side," she said, revealing a much older soul than she seemed.

"What side are you on, Tatyana?"

The smile my question elicited was clear evidence why I feared for Dimitri's heart, both physical and metaphysical.

"He came for me when I was in trouble," she said. "He used everything he had and never blamed me for what I am. He did that once here and then again when I went away."

I took the space next to her on the sofa.

"You know I don't make judgments on people, right?" I said.

"How could you?"

"People like us don't get to say what we think very often. What we know is too close to the bone for that."

"This is true." She closed the book.

"So when I tell you that there have probably been quite a few men who have come for you, saved you, that wouldn't be a lie now would it?"

"I have always looked for powerful men like you and your wife's son—Twill. Powerful men are what a woman needs—that's what I believed."

"And now?" I asked.

"Dimitri loves me."

"Yeah."

"Before I met him I thought that love was like money, that even it was money. I give you and you give me. But then I take away from D and he comes for me anyway. He wasn't strong enough or rich enough but there he was. He looked so silly in his cargo pants and white T-shirt that I almost laughed when I saw him. It was like seeing a silly magic creature from a child's book."

"And what does all that mean for my son?"

"I will stay until the magic is gone."

My cell phone sounded, punctuating her hard truth.

"Excuse me," I said, rising to my feet. I was tired, very much so.

"Hello?" I said out in the hallway that led to the foyer of our large prewar apartment.

"Have you found Harry or my daughter, Mr. McGill?" Zella Grisham asked.

"I already told you that I got the names of the people that adopted your baby."

"I want to see them."

"I know you do. But the law does not recognize the relationship and so I need to go talk to them before I try to put you together."

"Then talk to them."

"First I have to get Rutgers off your ass and the cops off mine."

"I don't care about them."

"So then you're lucky I do. And as long as I have you on the phone can you tell me something?"

"What?"

"Your ex-friend, Minnie Lesser, what kind of woman was she?"

"I don't want to talk about her," Zella said.

"You want me to find Harry and then you're gonna tie my hands?"

"What does she have to do with him?"

"Neither one testified at your trial. That puts them together in more than just the bed."

"She was just a girl like me," Zella said. "Nothing special."

"What did she do for work?"

"She was a secretary."

"What kind of secretary?"

"I don't remember. She worked in a midtown office. Before that she was a temp. That's how I met her. She temped at my law office. I was the one who introduced her to Harry. We all had dinner one night."

"Was she bent?"

"What do you mean?"

"She seem like the women in prison with you? Like she would steal from her employers?"

"She and my boyfriend cheated on me."

A rumbling voice sounded in the background over the line.

"Hold on," Zella said.

A moment later a man's voice addressed me.

"LT," Johnny Nightly said.

"Hey, Johnny," I said, looking at my watch. It was way past two in the morning. That math said more than any male braggadocio.

"What happened at your place the other day?" he asked.

I told him.

"Is this some other case?" he asked.

"No. It's straight up Rutgers. You should pull up stakes and take her someplace that I never heard of before."

"That bad?"

"They broke down my front door, man. I came closer to death than I ever have."

———

LOVELY AND SYLPH-LIKE, Tatyana sat on the sofa next to her big book. She was pensive and somber.

"Tell me something, Tatyana."

"Yes, Leonid?"

I stopped for a moment, a little stunned to hear my first name coming from her lips.

"You said 'my wife's son.'" I continued the question. "What did you mean by that?"

"It is obvious that Dimitri is your only, how do you say, your only blood child in this house."

No outsider had ever spoken about it before. I had lived a whole life telling my children that they were mine. Living a lie you begin to think that everyone is fooled but maybe, I thought, the only fool was me.

Tatyana stood up and kissed me on the cheek.

"Good night," she said.

Watching her leave, I began to think that maybe she would be all right and that Dimitri would too.

BY THE TIME I was back in the foyer Taty was gone and Katrina's snoring could once again be heard throughout the lower quarters of the apartment. I imagined that she had turned in her sleep, ushering forth the heavy breathing.

Instead of joining her I dragged a hickory chair into the front hall and sat there, leaning against the wall, napping and standing guard in turns.

45

IT WAS MORE SLEEP than watchfulness by four fifty-four that morning. I know the time because that's what my phone read when I answered it.

"Leonid," the caller said when I grunted, too groggy even to say hello.

"Breland?"

"What the hell is going on?"

"Are you safe?"

"Yeah. Yeah, I am. But I got up early and called my service. There was a message from Shelby Mycroft."

"What did he say?"

"You don't even know?"

"I ain't gonna play twenty questions with you, man. Either say something or hang the fuck up."

"Kent has been arrested."

"Charged with what?"

"Conspiracy, murder, racketeering, and about a dozen other crimes."

"So, what's that got to do with me?"

"The chief arresting officer was Carson Kitteridge."

"Oh."

"So I'm going to ask you again—what's going on?"

"I'm . . . not sure. I haven't talked to Kit about this. Not at all."

"It can't be coincidence."

"Maybe it is. But I promise you that I'll look into it. Just as soon as the sun comes up."

"Mycroft wants to see me. He wants me at his house."

"Don't go and don't answer him."

"I have to do something."

"I'll take care of it."

"Leonid, Shelby is a powerful man. I can't just ignore him."

"You want to make your wife a widow, your children fatherless?"

Silence.

Exhaustion hovered over me like a demon bear. I think for a moment I nodded off even with all that was on my mind.

"I'll get to the bottom of this arrest and get back in touch with you. But you and the family stay away. If you could see me right now, you'd know why."

"How's your family, LT?" the lawyer asked in a conciliatory tone.

"Breathing," I said. "Sleeping too."

TWILL'S ROOM was empty.

I removed my blue clothes, took an ice-cold shower in place of eight hours' sleep, and donned an identical suit. After downing a press pot of French roast coffee I was on the street in front of my building by six.

THERE'S A COFFEE SHOP near Ninety-third and Broadway, Shep's Schleps. It's just a counter with a kitchen behind it that makes deliveries from six to six. There Shep's wife, Nina, served me an egg-and-bacon sandwich with yellow mustard and raw onion while I read the sports pages of that morning's *Post*. Baseball was in full swing. The Yankees had beaten the Mets, two games to one, in a Subway Series. Wladimir Klitschko failed to knock out David Haye but retained his heavyweight crown.

By six minutes after seven my anger had lowered to a reasonable level. I called Twill's cell phone and got his answering service.

"This is Twill," his voice said. "Leave a message."

"Make sure you're in the office at one," I told the mechanism. "You already know what this is about."

THE BROWN BRICK apartment building was on Ninety-fourth a little east of Broadway. I searched the legend and pressed a little green button.

"Yes?" a woman said.

"Leonid McGill for Seldon Arvinil."

"What is this about?"

"College business. I work for the security department."

"What happened?"

"Is Mr. Arvinil at home?"

"I'll get him."

———

"MR. McGILL?" a man asked over the speaker maybe two minutes later.

"Mr. Arvinil."

"I'll be right there."

I backed down the stairs to the middle of the sidewalk, wondering if Seldon owned a pistol. He might have. How many times had the jealous man been killed by the object of his rage? As I pondered this question a white man of slight build appeared at the front door of the brown stack of apartments. He was wearing a square-cut red-and-cream leisure shirt and blue jeans. His hands were empty so I waved instead of drawing my own gun.

"Mr. McGill?" he asked.

I pursed my lips and nodded.

"What is it?"

"Come on down here, man."

Arvinil had tanned skin, bushy brown hair crusted a little with gray, and brown eyes. He listed back a bit and then, finding the courage somewhere, walked down the stairs without stumbling.

He faced me eye to eye.

He was three inches taller than I. I had forty pounds on him.

"Yes?" he asked.

"You know why I'm here?"

He winced in answer.

"She's a child," I said.

"No."

"No what?"

"She's young," he stammered, "a young woman who is better than I deserve. But she's a woman, not a child."

"Just because a girl can have sex doesn't make her a woman."

"Why are you here, Mr. McGill?"

"Your daughter is only a couple of years younger than Shelly," I said. When he remained silent I added, "What would she and your wife have to say about what you're doing?"

"From what Shelly has told me about you that would be letting me off easy," he said.

I preferred assassins in the night. Them I could fight and kill. Seldon was brave with no muscle, innocent with no excuse.

"Why?" I asked him.

"Has a young woman never made your heart sing?"

I suppose he expected me to think of the women I'd known, young and older. But what I thought about was the lie I'd let Shelly live with, the bullet holes in her wall. If she wasn't out rutting with this graying history professor, she'd be wounded or dead and I'd be to blame.

The biceps in both my arms ached with violence and exhaustion. I realized that I couldn't speak without attacking, so I turned and walked away, heading farther east.

46

WHEN I REACHED the park it was not yet eight.

Somewhere above 101st Street, a few hundred yards in, there's a huge pile of boulders that come together forming a grotto of stone. I climbed up the man-made hill and was happy to see that no one had been there for a while.

It was going to be a hot day but the morning air still held the chill of night. I hunkered down in the rocky crevice and closed my eyes. Sleep came on in an instant and I was transported to the comparatively peaceful time of my homeless, directionless adolescence.

My dreams were not indecipherable mysteries wrought from unconscious material. Instead they were of people I knew or wanted to know. Zella and Antoinette were there, also Johann Brighton and someone else, someone that might have sent killers to my paper-thin front door.

The path of my life appeared before me—hard and clear. I could, in the dream, turn around and take everything back. I could pass through time and decide not to help Zella or lie to Shelly. I could travel all the way back to the womb and be another person or no one at all. But I was too comfortable on that quartz plinth under the summer's sun. As I was lying there my life seemed to have enough meaning to engender nostalgia—the greatest enemy of human logic.

I found comfort in that old hiding place. There I had temporarily escaped the evil machinations of an enemy set into motion by my own foolish acts.

My heart was a tin drum; my breath the sighs of a forlorn, slightly out-of-tune cello. But music, no matter how sad it becomes, is still a solace for the soul.

My dreams became incomprehensible and I smiled. New York faded from consciousness. I was all alone in a wilderness before Eden, before good or evil . . .

. . . and when I awoke I was completely refreshed. The medicine had worked. The fever, along with whatever infection that caused it, was gone from my body. Men were trying to kill me, but so what? I was reborn. A born-again agnostic risen from the ashes of faith.

I GOT TO A CAB on Central Park West and made it to the office by twelve fifty-eight.

"Twill in there?" I asked Mardi.

"Yes, he is," she said. There was gleam in her eye. We, Twill and I, were her favorite men and she was happy to have us together behind the door where she stood guard.

Twill was at his desk. He stood up when I approached.

"Hey, Pops," he said.

That morning my son was clad in grays. From his light ash jacket to the coal-colored shoes on his bare feet. His pants were a misty seaside morning, the lead-hued shirt threatened to become blue.

"Call this number," I said, reciting the digits for the special cell phone Bug Bateman had long ago given my lawyer. "Put it on speakerphone."

"Sure. Who is it?"

"You'll see."

"Hello?" Breland said after four rings.

"I got Twill here with me," I said, then nodded at my favorite son.

"Mr. Lewis?" Twill uttered, the slightest twinge of discomfort showing around his mouth.

"Yes, Twilliam?"

"Breland called me this morning," I said. "He wanted to know about how Carson got involved with Kent Mycroft."

"Look, man," Twill said to the omnidirectional phone receiver. "I don't know what Kent did while he was gone from New York but whatever it was he learned how to be a gangster. His crew got their fingers in gambling, drugs, prostitution, and insurance scams. In between they do burglaries. Just about the only thing they don't do is mugging. But they for sure killed this one guy. Kent and one of his men both say that he did that himself. There might be another one, and there's other stuff too."

"You don't know any of that for sure," Breland the lawyer argued. "Maybe it's just a kid trying to make himself look important."

"I know the difference, Mr. Lewis," Twill said, managing to get both confidence and deference in his tone. "Kent is crazy and the people working with him are scared of him too."

"How did the bust come about?" Breland asked.

"You got to understand, man," Twill said. "I had to make a choice."

"What choice?" I said.

"A guy named Lucia had a gift shop on Greenwich Street. He made a deal with Kent to do a torch job on the place. The cops tumbled to the arson and because there was no break-in they arrested Mr. Lucia. But then they let him go the same day. Kent thought he was gonna talk and they were supposed to kill him last night."

"How could you possibly know all that, Twill?" Breland asked.

I wondered too.

"I met with one of his guys," Twill admitted. "You know, Kent is smart about business but not people. The guys he works with aren't all that tough. This one dude was so nervous that it was easy to get him talkin'.

"I called Captain Kitteridge and told him about where Kent and his guys meet. They got contraband in there and merchandise from their burglaries."

"You turned in your own client?" Breland asked. "Did you know about this, LT?"

"I had to act fast, man," Twill answered. "Kitteridge said that he'd give the guys worked with Kent deals if they cooperated. That was the best I could do."

"LT?"

"I didn't know, Breland," I said, "but I might have done the same thing. I mean, this kid Kent seems like a bad seed."

"What am I supposed to tell his father?"

"Why tell him anything? He doesn't know that we know Kitteridge. Maybe when he sees how bad his son is he'll accept what's come down."

"I don't know. I mean, this is his only son."

"A son who was planning murder, Breland. You couldn't expect Twill to let that pass."

"I have to think about this," my mostly honest lawyer said. "I have to go."

When the call was over Twill and I sat there—me on his desk and him in the chair.

"Is there any more to this, Twill?"

"What you mean, Pops?"

"I'm not sure. You should have called me. I mean, if you want to climb in bed with Carson Kitteridge, there's a lot you need to know about him and me."

"Okay. I mean, it just seemed so straightforward. Like you said, I couldn't turn my back on a murder like that."

There was more that Twill wasn't telling me but that fire seemed to be out for the moment so I moved on to the next flare-up.

47

I REACHED an address in Bayside, Queens, a little after four. There were children moving about the streets and sidewalks on skateboards and bicycles, in-line skates, and even on foot. It was summer and everyone was home except those parents who were still at work, trying to make the rent or mortgage.

The house I had come to visit was small and yellowy with a large yard all around it. Surrounded by bushes and trees, it was the perfect setup for a burglary. But I wasn't there to commit a crime; not even to investigate one, not really.

I knocked on the front door. It opened immediately, a small redheaded girl child, barely in grade school, standing there behind the screen. The image made me think of Nova Algren; she had once been a child—still was one when she committed her first homicide.

The little girl in front of me wore an orange-and-blue swimsuit.

"Hi," she said, looking up in stunned surprise.

"Is it Mrs. Braxton, honey?" a man called from inside the house somewhere.

"Uh-uh," the little girl said.

I was prepared with a story. My name was Farthing, Mr.

S. Farthing, and I worked for the adoption agency that helped
Sydney and Rhianon Quick get the little red-haired girl standing
behind the screen door.

I smiled at the child while footsteps sounded on a carpeted
floor behind her.

When the man appeared behind his daughter my lie faded
away.

"Yes?" he said. "Can I help you?"

"Hello, Harry," I replied. "I'm here for Zella."

"That's me," the little girl said a little dismayed.

"Not you," I said to allay this fear. "It's somebody else with the
same name."

Harry Tangelo, aka Sydney Quick, exhibited the same surprised stare that plastered his daughter's face.

"What do you want?" he asked.

"I need to talk to you about the other Zella."

"I don't understand. How did you find me?"

"I'm a detective. Finding people is what we do."

"Um."

"Can I come in?"

"What do you want?"

"My client, the woman with the same name as your daughter,
has gotten her sentence overturned."

"She's out?"

"And very sorry for the things she's done."

Harry Tangelo's mouth gaped open. His eyes were looking far
beyond me.

"Daddy, can I go swimming?" the child asked, already bored
with adult gibberish.

"Um, uh . . . Sure, honey. Sure. What was your name again, mister?"

"McGill. Leonid McGill."

"Would you like to come out in the backyard, Mr. McGill? I was just filling the little pool for Zell."

IT WAS JUST an inflated red rubber tub, fed by a green hose, with water cascading over the side.

Screaming Zella the Second ran and jumped into the man-made puddle with a great splash.

It felt like I had just jumped into the deep end myself. While Harry went to the spigot at the side of the house, to turn off the hose, I watched and wondered what to do next.

"Have a seat, Mr. McGill," Harry said, waving at two redwood chairs that were set in permanently reclined positions.

I lowered into one and he took the other.

We were both a little wary, like boxers in the first round of an out-of-town fight.

Tangelo would have been called cute if he'd been a woman. He had black hair, heavy lips, and eyes that seemed in turn sympathetic, then sad.

"Look at me, Daddy!"

"What does Zella want?" the adoptive blood father asked.

"To see her daughter and apologize for what she did."

"The heist or the shooting?"

"She's been exonerated for the Rutgers thing," I said. "The DA admitted that he would have let her off on the shooting for diminished capacity."

"I thought they found part of the money in her storage unit?"

There was a huge elm standing at the corner of the pine fence that separated the Quicks from their neighbors. The shadow that tree threw was like a stain across the green lawn. This darkness seemed appropriate.

"Hello," a woman called.

"Mrs. Braxton!" the child screamed.

She jumped from the pool and tore out toward the back of the house. There, emerging from the sliding glass door, was a middle-aged woman wearing a violet dress and a white sweater in spite of the heat.

Harry stood up, following the girl toward the house. He spoke to the gray-haired white woman, gesturing toward me.

"Nooooo!" the child complained.

Then little Zella lowered her head and followed the babysitter into the house.

When Harry returned I was ready to engage him in our awkward contest.

"I don't understand what Zella wants, exactly," he said.

"I was hired by an attorney named Lewis to investigate the evidence in her conviction," I said. "What I found proved that she had nothing to do with the robbery. We got her out of prison and the only thing she wanted was to find her daughter and make amends to you. But honestly, I came here today expecting to meet Sydney and Rhianon—not you."

My words had the ring of truth to them. Harry grimaced and bit his lower lip.

"I changed my name after getting out of the hospital," he said. "You know, I was adopted and so it wasn't my real name, my birth name anyway. And because I was adopted I paid a lot of money to get little Zella. She's my blood and I won't have her be a ward of the state like I was."

"Her mother would love to see her."

"Her mother shot me three times."

"That's over with, Harry," I said.

It felt good to be involved with a clear-cut element of the case. Zella wanted to see her child. The father had said child and was raising her in comfort and safety.

"Hi, honey," a woman called from the glass door.

"Hey, babe," the man known as Sydney Quick said.

I looked up and there, walking across the lawn toward us, was Claudia Burns, aka Minnie Lesser, now aka Rhianon Quick.

I stood up.

She stopped in her tracks, glowering at me.

"What?" Harry/Sydney asked.

The woman wanted to turn around and run—I could see that clearly.

"I'm already in your house, Minnie," I said. "I'm already here."

If epilepsy was in her DNA, she would have succumbed at that moment. She took in a deep breath and approached us.

"You two know each other?" Harry asked.

"Mr. McGill was at the office today," she said. "He was talking to Mr. Brighton."

"What for?"

"Even though the courts exonerated your ex-girlfriend it seems that Rutgers is not so easily convinced," I said. "They're hounding my client and I was there to try to get them to lay off."

"I don't understand," Harry muttered. "Are you here looking for Zella's daughter or because of the robbery?"

"I want you out of this house," Minnie said to me.

"And I will leave just as soon as I'm satisfied that you and Harry here don't have anything to do with Brighton, the heist, and the people who tried to kill me a few nights ago."

"Kill you?" Harry said.

"Give me fifteen minutes and I will be happy to leave."

48

HARRY AND MINNIE shared the redwood chair next to mine. He had a confused expression on his cute mug while she exuded cold anger.

"Why would you think that these people trying to kill you would have anything to do with Zella?" Harry asked.

"It's my only active case," I said, "and the police think that at least three men have already died behind it."

"What could we have to do with that?" Minnie asked.

"You're working for Rutgers," I said. "That's enough right there."

"But . . ." She was about to rebut my claim but then a thought occurred before the words could come out. She turned to Harry and he looked down at the lawn.

"Harry?" she said.

He looked up at me.

Harry/Sydney was not a stupid man but neither did he have a strong character. The look on his face told of how he was smart enough to get into trouble but too weak to fight his way back out again.

"A man came to me," he said.

"Your friend Stumpy Brown," Minnie put in.

"I didn't really know him before then, honey," Harry said. Then to me, "He offered me money and a way to get out from under all the publicity. He also helped me when I wanted to adopt Zella."

"Stumpy?" I said. "What kind of name is that?"

"I never knew another name. He said that he worked freelance for Rutgers and that they needed to know about the heist. He offered me some money and a job for Minnie."

"Didn't he think that someone at Rutgers might know who she was?"

"What money?" Minnie asked.

"She wasn't in the papers when the shooting happened," he said. "That was the week of those big tornadoes in the Midwest. After that she stayed at her mother's and never came out. All they had were high school pictures without her in glasses and with dark hair."

I wondered then where Gert had gotten the more current pictures of the girl.

"What money?" Minnie asked again.

"He gave me thirty-three thousand and told me to stay low," Harry said.

"You said that you were doing telephone sales."

"Yeah."

"Why would Stumpy do all that for you?" I asked.

"He wanted me to stay in touch with Zella, to get her to tell me where the money was."

But, I thought, Stumpy knew that Zella was framed. He was the one that set her up.

"And why get Minnie here a job at Rutgers?"

"He was working for them," Harry said. "That's the place where he could get her a job. After that he helped me adopt little Zella."

"Big Zella says that you never got in touch with her again after she shot you. That's why she had me looking for you—so she could apologize."

"That bitch has got no rights in this house," Minnie said.

"I told Stumpy that I'd try to get the information out of Zell but I just couldn't," Harry told me. "She'd already shot me and there was a guy murdered in the robbery. I only went up to the prison one time—"

"You did?" Minnie said.

"—but I didn't even go in. After Zella shot me my nerve was gone."

Not one thing he said made even the least sense. Zella didn't commit the robbery, she knew nothing about it. Stumpy knew better than I who did do the job. It was Bingo and his crew. Wasn't it?

"What do you have on Brighton?" I asked the incognito couple.

"What do you mean?" Minnie asked.

"He did have something to do with the heist, right?"

"Not that we know of," Harry answered. "He was just the job that Stumpy's contact got her hooked up with."

"And who was Stumpy working for?" I asked. "What was his name?"

"I don't know. He never said."

"So it could have been Brighton."

"Maybe," Harry said a little helplessly. "But why pretend?"

"You were pretending to talk to Zella."

"I tried but I just didn't have the nerve."

"So what did you tell Stumpy?"

"The first few times I talked to him I said that she still said that she was innocent. And then, after a while, Mr. Brown just stopped calling."

"He stopped calling and you didn't get suspicious?"

"About what? He got Minnie a good job. I had the money he promised me. We got, we got little Zella. There was nothing to worry about."

I sat back in the slanted chair perplexed by the muddle the maybe innocent couple sitting before me presented.

"You said that you had a friend at Rutgers," Minnie said to her husband, "that it was just a coincidence about the robbery."

"I was half right."

"Why didn't you tell me?"

"Because you wouldn't have let me go see Zella, and then later, when I never went, it was already too late."

"Why would Stumpy help you adopt Zella's child?" I asked.

"It's my baby too."

"But what did Stumpy get out of that?"

"You sound like you know him," Minnie said suspiciously.

"What do you want me to call him—Suspect X?"

Her resultant frown was, for me, like that piece of cake that Proust ate before writing his major opus.

> *There comes a time in the lives of ducks*
> *When a window opens and the hatchling looks up*
> *To see his fat mama bump and sway*
> *Through blades and branches . . .*

That was the beginning of a poem my father used to recite to my brother and me to illustrate the power of instinct. That duck's mama might have been a rolling wheelbarrow or a crafty crow. The duckling will imprint on anything leading forward.

"That's what people do, boys," my father would say. "They will follow the leader out of instinct all the while believing that they're exerting free will."

I had been following down the wrong trail. The path was set out there in front of me and I was just like that duck, brain-washed by instinct.

"Did Stumpy give you a way to get in touch with him?" I asked Harry.

"No."

"Do you have an Internet connection?" I asked the executive secretary, Claudia Burns-Quick.

"Yes."

"The crew that the police think robbed Rutgers was made up of three men," I said, giving her the names of Bingo and his gang. "While you're looking do a search on my name over the last few days. I think you'll see that I'm not lying."

WHILE SHE was gone Harry and I tried to have a conversation.

"I don't understand any of this," he said. "I mean, did Zell have something to do with the robbery or not?"

"The courts let her go."

"That might be on some kind of technicality."

"Might be," I said, "but isn't."

"But you think Mr. Brown did?"

"Did what?"

"Had something to do with the robbery?"

"Maybe," I said, "maybe not. But the people he was working for most definitely did. Zella was framed and then your wife was hired by the company that got robbed. That's just too much co-incidence."

"But it's been years."

"Yeah," I said, "it has."

Harry twisted on the lawn chair, trying to contort his body into some kind of understanding.

"What was it with you and Minnie?" I asked, if only to keep him from breaking his spine.

"What do you mean?"

"You were living with Zella. She was Zella's friend. How long were you fooling around behind her back?"

"The day she shot me was the first time," he said, suddenly sober and still. "We were planning to give her a surprise birthday party. Minnie came over and things just got out of hand."

"All the way to the chapel," I agreed.

"I know it sounds strange but getting shot like that brought Minnie and me closer. She called at the hospital every day and took me to her mother's house when I got out. She blamed herself for what happened and I just needed somebody to care."

There are as many kinds of love as there are flowers and bugs put together, my father used to say, *but men and women and their needs are all the same.*

Zella the Second wailed piteously. She was standing at the glass door, staring after the only mother she ever knew. Mrs. Braxton was holding the child's arm, keeping her from running after Minnie.

At any other time the stand-in mother's heart would have melted, I'm sure. But Minnie was on a mission at that moment. She didn't even hear the girl's cries.

"What is it?" Harry asked Minnie.

"All dead, right?" I said.

"A man named Durleth 'Stumpy' Brown was found dead this morning in his apartment in Coney Island," she said.

The stink had finally brought the law into that laundry room.

I looked around the manicured backyard. It seemed so cookie-cutter, so anonymous. For years Minnie, Harry, and Zella's daughter Zella had been hiding from the wrong thing in that yard. But that day they were visited by the Truth wearing an inexpensive blue suit.

"I don't understand," Minnie said.

"You got to get outta here," I explained. "I don't know what it is exactly but somebody is killing anyone who had anything to do with that robbery."

"But we weren't involved in that," Harry said.

"You are now."

49

TRAUMA CHANGES the way a brain works. If Harry had never been shot by a woman who claimed to love him, he might have decided to go to the police when given the information I provided. But he knew that the law couldn't help, that he had no proof anyone was after him. He knew that a man could be shot again and again and that no amount of logic or indignation could stop it.

"You should leave this house," I told them. "Drive to the airport or a bus station and disappear in the night. The people that tried to kill me are professional and connected. They'll know your license plates and credit card numbers, Teresa Lesser's address over on Hobart Street, and all the friends that the Quicks, Lessers, Tangelos, and Burnses have ever known."

"Why should we trust you?" Minnie Lesser asked.

"Did you look me up like I asked?"

She stared, giving a wordless response.

"Then you know that men broke into my house and tried to kill me. You know that I know what I'm talkin' about. If I wanted to hurt you, that would already have happened."

"We could call the police," Minnie argued. "We should call them."

"Maybe so," I said. "Call them. Tell them about your changed names and Stumpy Brown, about the heist and why you're working at Rutgers. That would be better than waiting here for the people who tried to kill me."

I was trying to scare them.

From the looks on their faces I had succeeded.

"We don't have any money," Harry said to his wife.

"What do you want, Mr. McGill?" Minnie asked me.

Minnie was a pretty woman. Not as cute as her husband but sexier. Her features were petite and clear-cut. When she got older she'd seem severe, but not yet.

"I don't want anything from you, Minnie," I said. "My trip out here was for Zella. I got the names of the people that adopted her daughter and I was going to ask them to meet her."

"But you found something else," she said.

"And I gave you my best advice. Four men are dead. They tried to kill me and my family. You were helped by a man working for whoever did the killings, you can bet on that. Take your husband and your daughter and run. I'll tell Zella what happened. She will have to understand."

"Where can we go?" she asked. "What can we do? How can we even make a living if these men know everything about us?"

"Fifteen minutes ago you were telling me that you wanted me to leave," I said. "Now you want my help?"

"Yes, we do." She took her husband's hand and held it to her breast. He nodded as I felt he must have often done, acquiescing to his bride's decision.

The sky was still light but the day was becoming evening. The onset of night made me sensitive to my surroundings.

"I can call somebody," I said. "He will come and he will hide you for the time it takes me to either follow this thing down or die trying. But if I do this, you have to promise to meet with Zella. She deserves to know her daughter."

Harry looked to Minnie. She finally nodded.

"HELLO," Johnny Nightly said, answering his cell.

I explained as much as I could over the phone, asking him to come, without the elder Zella, and bring the Quicks and their adopted blood daughter to a safe haven.

"Okay, LT," he said. "I'll do it. Luke said that he wanted to teach Zell how to play pool anyway. But I need to tell you something, man."

"What's that, Johnny?"

"I've gotten to like your client. I wouldn't want anything bad to happen to her."

"We're on the same page, then," I said.

JUST BEFORE DARK the Quick family and I put a hole in the pine fence at the back of their yard. We walked through the next yard, down the driveway, and out to the street one block over. Nobody questioned us but, even if they did, what could they say?

A dark blue van with no windows was parked at the corner. Johnny Nightly, the deadly handsome coal black killer, was seated behind the wheel. He smiled at me and I nodded politely.

"This here is Johnny," I said to the Quicks. "Do what he tells you and you'll have a ninety-nine percent survival rate."

I would have said a hundred percent except for the time when

Johnny made that minor slip. That mistake cost him a serious stint in the hospital and had nearly caused his death and mine.

Harry, Minnie, and Zella the Second climbed into the back of the van. I slid the door shut and slapped it.

Johnny drove off to parts unknown.

BACK IN the Quick residence I turned off the lights and made sure that all the windows were closed and locked—all except one. A solitary window at the side of the house, where the bushes were thickest, I left unlocked and partly open.

That window opened into the dining room. I put a chair in the little hallway that led from there out to the kitchen. Then I sat back comfortably, doing what PIs do best—waiting in darkness.

I had the whole night ahead of me. If nothing happened by morning, I'd go to Kitteridge and tell him what I knew. He'd probably tell Clarence Lethford. That'd be okay with me.

There was a faintly sweet floral scent on the air, in the darkness. I liked sitting there inhaling that flavor. Many times I had considered getting out of the PI business. As long as I did that kind of work I was vulnerable to my criminal past. But I didn't want a regular job, a boss, or a business telling me what to do. All I wanted was an unfamiliar shadow that slowly blended with my own.

AT ELEVEN FORTY-SEVEN my cell phone vibrated in its pocket. A few seconds later I took it out to see who had called. It was a 917 area code but the number was unfamiliar.

"My dear and dead friend was instructed to hire Mr. B to cover his tracks," Miss Nova Algren's recorded voice said. "And the number he garnered was twelve, not fifty-eight."

Bingo hired Stumpy. That meant that he also arranged for Minnie to work for Brighton.

AT ONE TWENTY-NINE I was still in the dark, still wondering where the other forty-six million had gone. The phone throbbed again. This time it was an unknown number. I didn't answer and there was no message.

At two thirty-seven I saw a brief flash of light near the open window at the side of the dining room.

I stood up from my chair.

There came the slightest rustle from the bushes and then the window slowly opened wide. I held my breath with the kind of excitement that had some distant connection to fear. At that moment I was fatherless, childless, and wholly alone in a life that existed only right then and was oddly perfect.

The man who came in was maybe five-seven.

The fever returned in an instant and I welcomed its reckless burn.

Just before the professional killer could begin his late-night prowl I lunged forward with a precision I'd practiced in Gordo's gym for decades.

He reacted to my presence half a second too late. By the time he'd reached for whatever weapon he carried I cracked his jaw like Barry Bonds hitting a fastball. But, even falling backward, his right foot jutted out in a nearly perfect shotokan sidekick.

I was thrown backward, landing on my ass.

Swiveling on the floor, I rose up moving toward the home invader. I expected that man to be out, but bad men like myself spend endless hours going through the scenarios of street fighting. We have to be ready for adversity.

My opponent had been stunned. He was staggering in shadow, reaching for something on his person. I grabbed a maple chair and swung it at him. I followed the chair, falling upon the man as he grunted in pain.

I hit him more times than necessary but by then my actions were mostly chemical, like a soldier ant or a teenager in love.

50

FROM THE TRUNK of my car I had retrieved the tools needed for the confrontation. I had plastic ties for my prisoner's wrists and ankles, thick black electric tape for his mouth.

In the light I could see that he was white with dark hair. His hairline was receding but I put him at thirty—maybe even younger. I used nylon rope to lash him to a dining room chair.

My hands were shaking from the rush of battle. I took one of the pills that Dr. Bancroft had given me and sat in front of the unconscious assassin while letting the logic of polite society reestablish itself in my heart and mind.

The transition was like one of the old black-and-white movies where Mr. Hyde slowly turns back into Dr. Jekyll. The physics of the change were all internal. The killer in my chest slowly ebbing, leaving its human husk spent and exhausted on the shores of civilization.

THE WOULD-BE and has-been killer was still unconscious. I took out my cell, found a number I'd called not long before, and pressed enter. After saying as few words as possible I disengaged the call and sat back in a chair, wondering what kind of fool takes on an unknown quantity in the dark without benefit of a weapon or a friend.

There could have been two or more killers assigned to the Quick family. How would I have fared against those kind of odds?

The answer to that question was quite simple. I had already killed two men, and even though that act provided ugly satisfaction in my heart it didn't help me to figure out my client's problems or my own. Anyway—if I had hefted a gun and pointed it at the killer, he would have probably relied on his reflexes rather than raise his hands in surrender—that's what I would have done.

When I looked up I saw that the assassin's eyes were open. His jaw was swollen and the left eye was almost closed but he wasn't complaining. He was using that lopsided stare in a vain attempt to intimidate me.

I considered killing him but then decided to wait a little while more.

AT THREE FORTY-FOUR I was wondering about the phone call I had missed—the unknown number that left no message. It was late for a call that wasn't an emergency. I worried that I'd missed something important.

Just then the doorbell rang.

The assassin looked up attentively. I shrugged at him and lumbered off to the front door.

The navy dress blended almost perfectly with her dark skin. And she was wearing coral-colored lipstick. The makeup was probably my biggest surprise that night.

"If I didn't know better, I'd think that you were looking for excuses to call me" were Antoinette Lowry's first words.

"I like seeing you," I admitted. "But that's because when you're not there in front of me I have to wonder what you're doing behind my back."

She smiled, saying with that fleeting exhibition of humor that, just possibly, I could be the first black man in a very long time that she might give a second look.

"Come on," I said. "Let me show you something."

I led her into the living room.

She came in and stood beside me, looking at my human package and exhibiting no surprise whatsoever.

"Who is he?" she asked.

I went into the long explanation of how I came to that little house in Queens. I mentioned Minnie and Harry, with all their names, and Johann Brighton too. I talked about Bingo and his dead men and my conviction that the hit list had expanded to include a primarily innocent family of three.

"Parlez-vous français?" she asked the prisoner.

He nodded and then shot a glance at me. I tried my best to look as dull and brutish as I could; this because Antoinette did not first ask the man if he could speak English.

She reached into her nylon bag and came out with a good-sized blackjack. She showed him the bludgeon, they came to a tacit understanding, and then she ripped the tape from his mouth.

"What are you doing here?" she asked in French. Her accent could have come from a Parisian's lips.

"Rien," he said—nothing.

"You are in a tight situation, my friend," she continued in the foreign tongue. "This man has already killed two who tried to get at him. If you want to go home, you have to give."

"What promise can you offer me?" he said. The French he spoke was from farther south, maybe as far down as Algiers.

Antoinette smiled while I stared stupidly off into space.

"The men I work for are more frightening than you," the man said.

"Fine," Antoinette told him.

She stood up and put the blackjack back in her bag. Before she could turn away he said, "Wait."

"What?"

"I don't know anything. They gave me my orders in a meeting in Berlin. Passports, papers . . . a phone. I only got the address of this house today."

"You were supposed to kill these people?"

He didn't answer. He didn't need to.

Antoinette turned to me. "He doesn't know anything," she said.

"What was all that he said, then?"

"He's worried about you."

"Me?"

"He thinks you'll kill him."

"Where'd he get that idea?"

Antoinette gave me a knowing, lying smile.

The problem with people like Antoinette, people who have only partly comprehended that race is no longer the primary defining factor of American life, is that they, her and her kind, unknowingly keep watch over the masters' wealth; and that the power of that wealth maintains all the ignorance of centuries of classism, racism, and the hierarchy that ignorance demands.

Antoinette knew that my brother and I were homeschooled by

a father, a man descended from Southern sharecroppers. She knew that I was an orphan before my thirteenth year. Armed with this partial knowledge, she assumed that I was not versant in any foreign language, especially not one as important and inaccessible as French. But indeed I am conversant in French and Spanish—German too. We spoke all those languages in my house and at the radical meetings my father dragged us to.

"What do we do now?" I asked, sounding as innocent and ignorant as any beast of burden.

"What do you suggest?"

I unrolled more tape and moved to cover our prisoner's mouth again. He avoided me so I socked him, taking out the anger I felt toward Lowry. I hit him harder than I planned, because the chair fell over and he went to sleep.

I set him upright, put the tape on his mouth, and turned back to the question at hand.

"What do you know about Brighton?" I asked.

"He's a very rich man," she said. "They say he's in line for CEO. I can't believe that he'd be involved in this."

"Then explain Claudia Burns."

"I can't," she said and I believed her.

"What about this guy?"

She sighed and said, "It's rumored that sometimes our international arm makes connections with mercenaries outside of the U.S. These resources are usually there for protective services. But they do perform other jobs for governments and the like."

"Assassinations?"

"I have no firsthand knowledge of that but it is assumed."

"International arm," I said speculatively. "Alton Plimpton was sent after me by a guy named Harlow . . ."

"Leonard Harlow. He used to be in charge of the international arm before he was transferred to domestic affairs."

"What about him?"

"I don't know. I suppose it's possible. Nine years ago he would have been involved with monies held. He has connections in places where the mercenary armies work."

"How much money was taken in the robbery?"

"Fifty-eight million."

"You're sure?"

"Yes. Why?"

"What's the reward on that?"

"Like I told you, one and a half percent on all funds recovered."

"That's fifteen thousand per million, right?"

"Yes."

"If I lead you to it, you'll put my name up?"

"If you do."

"What about this guy?"

"I have some connections at the State Department," she said. "From my military days. I'll call them."

"And what will they do?"

"What they do."

51

WE LEFT THE HOUSE with the would-be assassin still in his tape-and-nylon restraints. I didn't like the idea but there were places to go and lives to save—not least of all, my own.

At a little after five I walked Antoinette to her vintage pink Jaguar. She stood in the way women pose when they expect you to try to kiss them and they haven't yet made up their mind on how they might respond to the attempt.

I had no intention of failing or succeeding at said kiss. Antoinette thought I was stupid in spite of the progress I'd made on her case. This was an insult not deserving of any expression of desire.

I held out a hand. She took it, wondering, I believe, if I'd try to pull her into an embrace. But I just shook and released.

"Will your State Department friends launch an investigation?" I asked.

"I'll tell you what they've told me by early afternoon," she said.

"Okay. You got my number."

IN THE CAR on the way back to Manhattan I called the landline in my home. It was not yet six a.m. but I was concerned about my family and their safety.

"Hello?" She sounded awake and sober, if a little airy.

"Hey, Katrina," I said. "I expected one of the kids to answer."

"They are all asleep," she said. "Is something wrong?"

"They still got cops on the door downstairs?"

"Mmmm, Twill said so. They are all here taking such good care of me."

"Are you okay, Katrina?"

"Oh yes. I've been thinking of how lucky I've been. To be loved, to have my health, and to be able to make mistakes and not lose everything."

"You sound like it's all over."

"What is?"

"Life. Like you been beaten or something."

"No. It's just that I spent so long blaming you, Leonid. Blaming you and never questioning myself. And I can see now that I came so close to keeping Dimitri from becoming a man. He is a man, you know."

"Yeah. I know."

"When will you be coming home?"

"Don't know yet. I want to make sure that we're all safe."

"Thank you, Leonid."

"For what?"

"For guarding over me," she said, "for saving me from myself when I didn't deserve it."

I WAS DISTURBED after the talk with Katrina. She'd rarely exhibited such friendliness and certainly not any appreciable degree of self-awareness. She was the kind of woman who men loved for their inaccessibility. For her myriad lovers she was a trophy like the head of a saber-toothed tiger mounted on a wall that no one else knew existed. For me she had always been the woman who could never be satisfied.

I didn't even consider the next call before I made it.

"Hello?" Aura Ullman answered.

"Want to meet me for breakfast at the new restaurant?"

"They don't serve breakfast."

"Not for you?"

After a brief pause she said, "I'll call Maurice and see if anyone's up there. Take elevator eleven all the way up."

THE MUSTACHE was on the ninety-seventh floor of the Tesla Building, just below the Observation Deck. It was a French restaurant that served lunch and dinner, but the cooks came in early, and the owner, Maurice Denouve, owed a lot to Aura for getting him in. There was a huge bidding war over the space, but Aura liked the Frenchman and paved the way for him receiving preferential treatment by the owners.

By the time I got there they were just serving our fruit-filled crepes and French roast coffee.

Aura was wearing a peach-colored summer dress and a shell-shaped white hat on the side of her head.

"Never seen you wearing a hat before," I said, taking the seat across from her.

I took her hand and kissed it.

"You look kind of beat-up, Leonid," she replied.

"You should see the other guy."

"We have found some bacon, mademoiselle," a skinny black-haired, white-shirted waiter said. He wasn't wearing a jacket; a silent complaint at the fact of being forced to work before the place was open to the public.

"No thank you," Aura said.

"*Mais lardons pour moi, monsieur,*" I said in my subpar version of his lingo.

He frowned and went away.

"You speak French?" Aura asked.

"There's some things I have to tell you," I said.

"In French?"

"In the language of fools but not love."

Her smile made me happy in spite of the exhaustion and feelings of inadequacy.

"What is it, Leonid?"

"I know I asked you to wait three days, Aura, but I don't want you to think that I've changed or anything. I mean, I want to be with you in the worst way. I want you in my life, every day. But, but things aren't getting any easier . . ."

I told her about Zella and alluded to how I had framed and then freed her. I explained that the men coming to kill me were probably there because of my actions with Zella. I laid the whole thing out there in front of her.

Before she could answer the bacon came and then my phone sounded.

I looked at the little panel and said, "I have to take this."

She nodded.

"What you got for me, Ms. Lowry?" I said into the phone.

"The man who broke into the Quicks' house has been taken into federal custody," she began. "He'll probably be deported, seeing that there's no proof that he intended to kill anyone. He'll be questioned but I don't think that he knows anyone connected to the crimes from this end. He had a pay-as-you-go cell phone and never met with anyone here in the States."

"That doesn't do much. What about Claudia?"

"She filled out an application for her job two weeks after she was put on the payroll. All earlier contact has been either altered or eradicated. I'll have to talk to her myself if you want any more information."

"That's not gonna happen."

"Don't you trust me?"

"I just ordered my breakfast," I said, "in French."

I disconnected that call and turned back to the woman I loved.

"Don't worry about it, Leonid," she said.

"About what?"

"Theda's going away to college this year," she said. "Brown. With her out of the house I won't have to worry about anyone's safety but my own."

"But what kind of asshole would I be to put you in danger like that?" I asked. I meant it. "I've done some terrible things, Aura. There's no getting away from that. And even when I try to make it right I only bring on more trouble."

She took a mouthful of strawberry crepe and chewed it lightly. The window behind her looked up Central Park all the way to Harlem, almost to Yonkers.

"I joined an executive Internet dating site about nine months ago," she said.

"Really?"

"Every other week I go out with some lawyer, banker, or entrepreneur."

"Nice guys?"

"Most of them work out but not like you do. As a rule they

have money and success. I've met at least three men who are tough-minded and equal to me in every way."

"I see."

"Twill and Theda had lunch yesterday," she said. It seemed as if she was intent on keeping me off balance.

"Yeah?"

"He told her how you killed the men who broke into your house. He said that you wanted Katrina to go into hiding but she refused."

I threw half a strip of the thick maple-infused bacon into my mouth and chewed.

"So?"

"Don't you see, Leonid?" Aura asked.

"That Katrina's gone off the deep end?"

"That you did not try to force her. That's the difference between you and the men I've met."

"What's that?"

"They've all become rich and powerful because they're afraid of the world; they need to feel like they're conquering everything and everyone in order to feel safe. You just face the problems and stand strong. Ever since I met you I've known that you are what I want in a man." She paused a few seconds and then added, "In my life."

52

AURA AND I talked for quite a while in that empty restaurant. The temporary wall that we'd thrown up over the past few years fell down and we were lovers again.

She talked about problems with some tenants and I told her that Twill had taken unwanted initiative on the first job I'd given him.

"He's just like you," she said of my son.

"We aren't even related."

"Neither are we," she said, "but you're my man just like he's your blood."

FOR A CHANGE I was in the office before Mardi and Twill. I sat behind her ash desk, flipping through the notes she wrote in light purple ink.

She kept detailed handwritten records of every case I'd had since she'd been with me. She also had some more sketchy coverage gleaned from audiotapes I kept from previous jobs.

Mardi had a deeper understanding of human nature than did I. I could see, often, what people were trying to hide. But Mardi saw what was hidden beyond vain attempts.

Her take on a job I'd done three months before was especially enlightening.

A woman had come to me worried about what was going to happen with her ex-husband. He had been sending her threatening e-mails and leaving certain disturbing items at her doorstep. A thug named Lassiter had appeared at various places she frequented; her job, the supermarket, and sometimes he drove by her on the highway and would ring her cell.

This woman, Laverne Sails, had left the husband, Benjamin Lott, a decade earlier, taking with her their two children. He was a rich man and she was from a working-class background. The courts had granted him custody and she and the children, now nineteen and twenty-one, had run from Connecticut to New York. There she managed, with a women's legal group, to fend off Ben's attempt to strip her of her children.

Laverne Sails said that Benjamin hated her for what she'd done and the children for not wanting to come back to him. She thought he meant them all harm.

I investigated Laverne for five weeks trying to find a break in her story. But I couldn't.

The thug Lassiter and I had a physical altercation that put him out of the picture for the eight weeks it took him to heal.

Ben was an egotistical freak who had used his money and power to break Laverne down and bend the local law to his will. His attitude toward the world came from the same place his wealth did—his father, Lincoln Lott.

The elder Lott had used his self-confidence to build an empire; his son used a similar force to destroy whatever displeased him.

I took what evidence I could amass to Lincoln and asked him what he thought a man like me should do about someone like his son. No more than a few dozen words passed between us.

The next day Laverne called and said that Ben had been transferred to a glass-manufacturing factory that the family owned in southern India and that she and the children had been invited to come live at the Lott family compound in Connecticut.

Lincoln's will was rewritten. Laverne didn't elaborate on the details but I was pretty sure that bodily harm against Ben's family would end up with him being out on his ear.

These results were satisfactory for me. I'd played Laverne's hand with just the right amount of risk.

Mardi had written down the essentials of the case with insight but it was her note at the end that impressed me most.

Mr. McGill realized that his client was in real danger and he went out of his way to resolve the issue because he knew that he had to either stop Benjamin Lott or end him, she wrote.

She was right. I don't think that I was completely aware of the conundrum while in the middle of it but my receptionist knew.

"Good morning, boss," she said.

I was so deep in her files that I hadn't heard her turn the locks.

I stood up like a kid being found out while going through his father's *Playboy*s.

"Um," I uttered. "I wasn't snooping."

The pale young thing smiled and shook her head. "It's your office, Mr. M. Everything in my desk belongs to you."

I suppressed the desire to say thank you and moved to the side, allowing the brilliant child to get behind her desk.

"People have been trying to kill everyone involved in this Zella Grisham thing," I said.

All Mardi did was look at me and nod. She'd experienced worse fears in her short life.

"So keep the door locked until you know exactly who's out there," I continued.

"Okay."

ABOUT AN HOUR LATER Twill knocked on my office door.

When he was seated before me I asked, "What else is it about this Kent kid?"

"What you mean, Pops? He was gonna kill that dude. Ain't that enough?"

"It is but that's not all of it."

"What's that supposed to mean?"

"There's something personal about this, something that got to you. I mean, if it was just that store owner's life, you would have come to me."

Twill grinned and looked away, then back at me.

"Whatever," he said.

I held the young man's gaze a moment and then said, "All right. But I expect you to share with me in here."

"It's nuthin', Pops. Really."

ALONE IN MY OFFICE, with the reinforced door locked and cops on the job back at my home, I was almost comfortable. Antoinette Lowry found me attractive but unintelligent. Katrina believed that, after all these years of discord, she had been unfair to me. I was in love with Aura and she returned the emotion. Putting all that together, I irrationally figured that it was time for a break in the case.

"Call on line six, Mr. M," Mardi said over the intercom.

"Who is it?"

"He said his name is Plimpton."

"MR. PLIMPTON?" I said into the phone.

"I got a call from Ms. Lowry this morning," he said.

"That Antoinette gets around."

"She wanted to know how Mr. Brighton's assistant, Claudia Burns, got hired and by whom."

"I don't have the answer to that question. Maybe you wanna try HR."

"Lowry said that you believe Miss Burns has something to do with the heist eight years ago."

"That's going a little far. I said that someone believes that she was involved. Or maybe they want us to think so."

"And who would that be?"

"Why are you calling me, Alton?"

"What do you know about Miss Burns?"

"She married a man named Quick," I said.

"Do they have anything to do with the robbery?"

"Some people think so. I doubt if they do."

"What is that supposed to mean?"

"Why are we talking, man?"

"Do you believe that Claudia Burns was involved in the robbery?"

"And murder," I added.

"What?"

"One of your guards was murdered. That's a crime too."

"And do you believe Miss Burns or Quick or whatever was involved?"

"I think that the person who hired her was involved."

"But not her?" he asked.

"I doubt it."

"Why?"

"What are all these questions about, Mr. Plimpton? Does Rutgers want to hire me?"

"Are you available?"

"I have a job right now but no one is paying me. If you have the same interests as my client I could possibly bring you in on a twofer."

"Can you prove that the person who hired Claudia was involved in the robbery?"

"If I'm given proper access, I believe that I can—yes."

"What if I were to hire you?"

"Out of your own pocket?"

"This theft is the worst single event that has ever happened to Rutgers," Alton Plimpton said with deep gravity. "It is a perpetual thorn in the side of the corporation. If I could solve the crime, maybe even recover some of the money, I would assure a promotion and maybe even a bonus."

"You might even get that one-point-five percent reward," I suggested.

"No. No. Employees aren't allowed to get any reward offered by the firm."

"But I could get it and split it with you on the side."

"I never considered that."

"No?"

"No."

Silence descended on our electronic connection. Maybe Alton was considering the possibility of sharing the reward with me. Maybe he'd just run out of words.

"Why did you call me, Mr. Plimpton?"

"I think I know how Claudia Burns got hired."

"Tell Ms. Lowry."

"I don't trust her."

"You think she's involved somehow?"

"No. But she works for the higher-ups. I don't believe that she will have my best interests at heart."

"You think that she'll take all the glory for herself."

"Can I hire you, Mr. McGill?"

"Sure you can. But it'll cost ten thousand dollars."

"Ten thousand!"

"That's my corporate rate."

"I don't have that kind of money."

"Can you borrow it?"

"I'm not a rich man, Mr. McGill. I've worked for Rutgers my entire life but I have an ex-wife and two children near the end of high school. If I put out that much money, I'd have to have guarantees that you will produce."

"Guarantees come with washing machines, Alton, and even they have time limits."

"Are you sure that the man who hired Miss Burns was involved with the heist?"

"I can't see it any other way."

"Why?"

"Am I hired?"

The floor manager didn't answer immediately.

For that moment I fell into a waking daydream; in that reverie I was set upon by a boa constrictor. I was fast. I'd grabbed its head but it'd looped its tail around my left leg. With my free hand I got it by the tip of that tail but then it encircled my neck with the central bulk of its slithering scales.

That snake was my unwanted case. It was both my telephone cord and my fault.

Fault: Responsibility, and also a natural material flaw. I was wrong no matter what way you looked at it.

"All right, Mr. McGill," Alton Plimpton said. I'd almost forgotten that he was there. "I'll pay you. But it'll take me a few days to come up with the money. I'll have to borrow it."

"Great. Come by my office with the cashier's check or the cash and I'll get right on it."

"We can't wait on this, Mr. McGill," Plimpton said. His voice had become brittle.

"You expect me to help you without some kind of assurance?" I smiled at my use of the last word.

"You could, you could start to investigate and only turn the information over after I paid," he suggested.

"Okay," I said. I shouldn't have agreed. If I were advising Twill about the business, I would have said that people don't call you on the phone and throw information at you like that. As a matter of fact, if I was anyone else instructing my son, I'd have never suggested PI work.

"Okay," I said again. "Who is it that hired Claudia?"

"That's a difficult question."

"With a two-word answer."

"Johann Brighton is the reason she was hired but it was Seth Marryman that completed the paperwork."

"Not Harlow?"

"No. Leonard has nothing to do with it."

"How can you be so sure?"

"Seth died three months ago," Alton said. "It was a heart attack, completely unexpected. I knew his family and was asked by Human Resources to help with anything they needed. I've been with the company for so long that I've done that with other unexpected deaths. Seth's wife, Virginia, told me that he had papers from the company in a trunk in their attic. Removing any information from the workplace is strictly forbidden. I should have told somebody but that might have affected the monies his family received so I took them to my place and asked her not to tell anybody else."

"Okay," I said, "I'll bite."

"He had a file on Claudia Burns. It was her employment assignment and a letter he'd signed recommending her. He was very specific in stipulating that she be assigned to Brighton. He even had Brighton's previous assistant promoted to make the job available."

"That's not much to go on," I said, "him being dead and all."

"There was also a document detailing a Swiss account with eight hundred and eighty-two thousand dollars in it. It's a numbered account. Seth made less than I did. There's no way he saved up that much. The deposit goes back eight years, just nine months after the robbery."

"Explain something to me, Alton," I said.

"What's that?"

"Why didn't you tell anybody about this?"

"If I turned those files in, his wife might have lost that money and maybe his retirement too."

"But the timing."

"When I discovered it I had no reason to think that Claudia and the money had anything to do with each other. It's not enough to have come from the heist; I mean, that would be millions. There were no other accounts. It's only when Agent Lowry asked about Claudia that I became suspicious in a larger sense."

"But you still aren't going to the company," I said.

After a significant pause Plimpton said, "It's a lot of money."

"Yes," I said, "it is."

"The man you want is Johann Brighton," he said then.

"How did you come to that conclusion?"

"There's a request from Brighton for Seth to hire Burns. It's just a note with the words *personal* and *confidential* written in red across the bottom."

"You're sure about that?"

"Yes, I am."

"But what could any of that have to do with the robbery? I mean, if Zella is innocent, and I believe that she is, what could Zella's boyfriend's girlfriend have to do with anything?"

"What are you talking about?"

"Claudia Burns is Minnie Lesser."

"Who?"

"The woman that was with Zella's boyfriend when she shot him."

"Oh." He sounded really surprised.

"So how could she be involved with the heist if Zella wasn't?"

"I don't know," Alton said, "maybe this Burns woman found out something about the evidence, proving that Grisham had been framed. All I do know is that Seth received nearly nine hundred thousand directly after Claudia was hired."

"Okay," I said. "I'll accept your argument for the moment. But even if that's all true, what can we do but tell Antoinette and her bosses?"

"You get Brighton to confess to you," he said. "Maybe you can even get him to pay you off. Then you can tell the higher-ups that I hired you because I suspected something I couldn't prove and I was afraid that if I brought it in-house that Brighton would find out."

"So you just want me to go to his office with Marryman's name and see what he does?"

"No. No. They won't let you in the building now. Harlow has made sure of that. But Brighton has a meeting with a man named Furrows this afternoon at an apartment we own in Tribeca. I'll cancel Furrows and you can go instead. Confront him with the information and get him to confess and maybe pay you off."

"You can do that?" I asked. "Cancel a private appointment for a VP like Johann?"

"It's all computerized," he said. "You just have to know what codes to enter."

53

I'D NEVER HAD a case like that one: a looping snake looking you in the face and attacking from below and behind at the same time.

Leaning way back in my office chair, I closed my eyes and tried to imagine the interconnections.

There had been two thefts committed, Nova Algren attested to that. Bingo and his men were blamed for taking fifty-eight million but they only got twelve. There was at least one inside man, Clay Thorn, the guard. He and someone—Brighton or maybe this Seth Marryman—had removed forty-six million before the robbery went down. Clay was double-crossed by his inside confederate. Bingo killed Clay and then hired Stumpy to find a fall guy, Zella. Then Stumpy goes to Harry and gets him to drop out of sight and connect his girlfriend with a job at Rutgers.

Why?

Maybe Seth Marryman wanted to set up Brighton in case an internal investigation found that Thorn wasn't working alone. That was just stupid enough to make sense.

On the other hand Brighton could have been setting up Marryman.

Zella was innocent. I knew that much. Or did I?

Gert was the contact point on the job, not I. She was the one that told me Stumpy wanted to frame someone. She also pointed me at Zella. That was why I had switched the wrappers and used counterfeit locks on the storage unit. It wasn't that I didn't trust Gert. But I wanted to make sure that Stumpy couldn't come back and pull a trick on her—and me. I didn't trust anybody in those days.

What if Harry and Zella were involved somehow? No. She would have turned him over . . .

I spent more than an hour going over the possible scenarios. None of them made much sense. The only thing I could come up with was that no one and nothing could be trusted—not even my own memories of events.

In the middle of this morass I took out a moment to make an insurance call. There are times when the only people you can trust are your proven enemies.

AT TWELVE FIFTY-SEVEN the buzzer to the outer office sounded. Mardi was at her post so I left that up to her. A few seconds later she spoke to me through the intercom.

"There's a man I don't know at the front door," she said.

I pulled open the bottom drawer of my desk, revealing four video monitors attached to the same number of hidden cameras recording my front door from various angles. When I saw who it was I pressed the intercom button and said, "Get Twill to answer it and to bring our guest down here to me."

YOU KNOW that it's bad when you welcome in one trouble just so that you can ignore another.

There came a knock at the door and I said, "Come in."

Twill pushed the door open and ushered Shelby Mycroft over the threshold.

"You come in too, boy," I said when it looked as if my son were going to leave. "Have a seat, Mr. Mycroft."

Twill waited for our client to pick his chair and then he settled in the other. This was a new experience; on-the-job training for my son while being reamed out by an irate client.

"I'm not happy with you, Mr. McGill," Shelby said.

"I can understand that."

"Is that all you have to say?" There was a threat in the timbre of his question.

"Your son is a criminal," I said. "The police arrested him. You can't hold me responsible for his crimes."

"Mirabelle tells me that your man Mathers here is actually your son, Twilliam."

I shot Twill a look and he shook his head, denying having given up that information.

"Where'd she get that?" I asked.

"From Kent. He recognized the boy."

"Yes," I said. "He is my son. So what?"

"He's a criminal himself," Shelby said, trying to attain some kind of moral parity.

"What is it you want exactly, Mr. Mycroft?"

"Your son is a free man," he said. He paused then, expecting me to connect his dots.

"This is not your boardroom, brother," I replied, the man of the streets rising under my skin. "Spell out what you mean or walk away."

"I've asked around about you," he said. "It's said that you're specialty is altering evidence in order to contaminate criminal investigations."

Glancing at Twill again, I saw a kind of boredom glazing his eyes.

"I have an appointment, Mr. Mycroft."

"Cancel it."

"You got two minutes to say something to me or I'm gonna come around this desk and kick your ass . . . hard."

I put my hands on the desk. I have big scarred hands.

This physical display impressed the billionaire.

"Okay," he said. "I'll tell you. Either my son finds his way out of this predicament or you make me and all of my money and influence your enemy."

I won't lie. I considered shooting him. I did. But Twill was sitting there and I knew my anger came from other sources.

"Excuse me," Twill said.

"Shut up," Shelby Mycroft said to my son.

That got me to my feet.

"Stand up, man," I said.

"Pops," Twill said in a most diplomatic way.

"What?"

"Mr. Mycroft don't wanna hear from me but I could still tell you what I got to say. He can listen or he can leave."

"Go on," I said, sitting down again.

"The problem starts in the womb but the story begins with a eighteen-year-old girl named Velvet," he said. His words reminded me of the way I often spoke. "This girl Velvet was wild and kinda confused. She used to kiss Kent in the laundry room and then fuck his father on a yacht on the Hudson."

"I'm not listening to this," Shelby Mycroft said. He made to stand.

"No?" Twill asked. "Where you think I heard all that? Mirabelle don't know it. But when Velvet had her baby and told Kent that you were the father he ran away from home."

Shelby got a stunned look on his face. The sportsman's tan started to pale.

"Th-that has nothing to do with my business here," he stammered.

"What if I said that on Thursdays you still go out on the yacht with another teenage girl and do the humpity-monkey from nine to midnight? What if I also said that the code for the gate to your gangplank is twenty-seven fifteen? The one to the entrance to the boat is seventy-five twenty-one."

"How could you possibly know that?"

"Not only that, man," my son added. "You got a red lacquer lamp at the edge'a your bed on that boat has some kind of signature at the bottom only somebody in your family would know about. Kent told his crew that if you turned up dead on that boat, he would give any man who handed him that lamp twenty thousand dollars. He got the money in cash in a safe in his apartment."

Shelby's lips moved but no sound came out.

"Now, say again how you want my pops to free him," Twill said.

I was surprised at the sudden aggression in my son's attitude. I suppose I shouldn't have been.

"Kent told you this?" he asked.

"It's common knowledge among his crew. The only reason you

aren't dead already is that he got a bunch'a pussies workin' for him. That and they were a little nervous about killin' the girl too."

Shelby looked to me. All I could do was shrug.

Now I understood why Twill had taken such swift and certain action. He was outraged that a son would go against his father like that. That was probably one of the worst crimes his young mind could imagine.

"So?" I asked Mycroft.

"He said a red lacquer lamp?" Shelby asked Twill.

"With a signature on the bottom that only somebody from your family would know."

The rich man sat there looking for the flaw in Twill's presentation. But it was of perfect geometric design.

"You hired us to do a job and we did you one better," I said after a while. "He would have gotten himself caught sooner or later but you might not have survived that long."

"How did he get my codes?" Shelby asked. "I change them every three months."

"Probably Mirabelle, right?" Twill said. "No reason for her to think that he was out to get you. Maybe he told her that he wanted to take Luscious out there for a night. That way she wouldn't have told you."

It's a wonderful thing to see a billionaire, a captain of industry, reduced to his human parts. His brow creased and his jaw went slack. If he were my opponent in the ring, I'd have known that he was about to go down.

"Are we done here, Mr. Mycroft?" I asked.

"I have to check this out," he said, "look into, into these allegations."

"Be my guest. But if it turns out that Twill here is right, you still need to pay us."

Mycroft got to his feet.

"And one more thing," I said.

"What?"

"The arresting officer, Carson Kitteridge, is a friend of the family. Twill and I will tell him about your romps with teenagers. Take that as fair warning from your son."

54

TWILL RETURNED to my office after seeing Mycroft to the door.

"He's busted up," Twill said as he lowered into the seat Mycroft had taken before. "I don't blame him. Must be hard to have your own blood treat you like that."

"Why didn't you tell me?" I asked the old soul in the young man's body.

"I didn't wanna say it out loud, Pops. You know it hurt me just thinkin' about that mess."

"Kent's man could have made all that shit up."

"Uh-uh."

"Why don't you think so?"

"I went down there and checked it out," Twill said.

"Down where?"

"I got on the boat and found the red lacquer lamp. The signature on the bottom was made by Kent when he was a child—*Winnie-ther-Pooh*. Everything my boy told me was true."

"And why would he tell you anyway?"

"He probably thought that I'd do the deed, you know. I told him that if I did do it, I'd split the money with him."

"Did you give Kit all that?"

"Naw. I just told him the names of the dead men and said he

might wanna ask about that store owner who had his store torched."

I let that part of our conversation settle for a bit. Then I said, "You got anything you want to know?"

"No."

"Nothing?"

"Not that I can think of."

"Not even what Mycroft said about me covering for crimes?"

"Hey, Pops. You the boss here. I'm not supposed to be questioning you."

A QUARTER HOUR later I was in a cab headed down to Greenwich Street in Tribeca. Twill was on my mind. I'd brought him into the business to keep him out of a life of crime. But he'd turned out so much like me I had to wonder if anyone or anything, outside of death, could save him from himself.

My phone vibrated. There was a text message there that read "In place."

Before I could put it away the phone sounded with three chimes.

It was another unknown number, maybe the same one that called while I was waiting for the assassin in Queens.

"Hello?"

"Trot?"

I believed that I was beyond shock or surprise that deep into the case. A terrorist attack wouldn't have kept me from my mission. A diagnosis of pancreatic cancer would not have stopped me from finding the people that had sent assassins into my home.

But that voice on the phone nearly managed to derail me.

"Dad?"

"You recognize my voice?"

I began to tremble. Anger, love, rage, and a deep, deep wound opened up in me. I closed my eyes but it made little difference; even with them open I couldn't distinguish images—only light and dark.

"Son?"

"Where are you?"

"On a bench in Prospect Park. Can you hear the Congo line playing?"

Yes, in the background there was the sound of African drums.

"What . . . why are you calling?"

"Tourquois got your number from that friend Lemon. She said you seemed to want to find me, that you knew I was in New York."

"It's been forty-four years," I said. "Mom died because she couldn't live without you."

"I wasn't in the country the first eight," he said. "I was in the jungle fighting for three and then in prison for three more. It took me two years to make my way back. By then you and Nicky had become men. Your mother was dead already."

"Why didn't you get in touch with us? Why did you hide?"

"It's hard to explain, son. The Revolution changed me or, I should say, it changed me again. Maybe it even destroyed me. I knew where you were and what you were doing but I . . ."

"You what?"

"I'd like to talk to you face-to-face."

"Nikita's in prison," I said.

"I know."

"I'm married with three children."

"We should meet, son."

I hadn't expected the depth of feeling. I hadn't believed that I'd ever see my father again. Less than an hour before I'd seen the truth dismantle a rich and powerful man. This demolition made me feel superior. But now I saw that I was no better, that life conspired against all of us, eroding everything—even the ground beneath our feet.

"There's that restaurant you like going to," my father, Tolstoy McGill, was saying. "The steak house at Columbus Circle. We could meet there for a late dinner, maybe ten or so."

"How, how do you know where I like to eat?"

"Meet me at the steak house at ten, Trot. I'll be there. If you want to see me, you'll be there too."

"Why haven't you tried to get together with me before now?"

"I'll see you at ten, son."

The call clicked off in my ear but I didn't put the phone down, not immediately. The chance to hear my father's voice had been the single most powerful desire in my life. I missed him terribly, hungered for his attention and his survival. I hated him too but the deep sense of loss drowned out any antipathy like a nuclear bomb detonated over an angry hornets' nest.

"Here you go," somebody said.

The cab had come to a stop after a forty-four-year journey. The modern façade of the building was glass and shiny steel. It rose fifteen or sixteen slender floors above its dour brick neighbors like a silver pin jabbed into a concrete fingernail.

Looking up, I wondered if this was the day I'd die. I'd always associated my father with death. Before she passed on, my mother told Nikita and me that she was going to meet my father in the place people go after breath leaves their body.

"That'll be twelve sixty-five," the cabbie said.

I handed him a twenty and shambled out of the taxi.

Standing on the broad sidewalk in front of the glass doors, I wondered again about mortality. I had a wife somewhere and grown children that I loved. There was my lover, whose kisses I couldn't imagine right then. There was a life that had been lived sideways and backward, and hopes that had lost their meaning.

My mind felt empty—the Buddhist ideal. That thought brought a smile to lips. I took a deep breath and headed for the door.

55

"**FURROWS FOR** a four-thirty meeting," I said to the sour-looking man at the front desk, "suite twelve-oh-three-A."

"State-issued ID," he replied.

"Don't have it."

"I can't let you in without ID." The guard wore a black jacket that had the look of something military. He was a black man of the gray-brown persuasion and my age. He was big but loose, strong but probably slow.

"I wasn't told about any ID," I told him. "Just Furrows, twelve-oh-three-A."

The guard didn't like me. But he opened up a big ledger on the slender ledge in front him and ran a thick finger down the page. He found something that soured his mouth and then said, "Take the third elevator on your right."

SUITE 1203A WAS a solitary room furnished with a floor-to-ceiling window that looked down on Greenwich. There were no curtains or window shade. The sun shone in but central air kept the room cold. There were only two chairs in the small room and

I took one of them, feeling exposed and vulnerable but not timid or afraid.

It was three forty-seven and I was prepared for the wait. I was ready to die too. It had been a long run and the return of my father signaled an ending to the race.

Sitting there in the exposed room, I thought about my children. They were all damaged and beautiful, expecting the best and dealing with what they had. I wasn't a failure in my life or theirs but I lacked agency, and this deficiency, I believed, also limited the range of my heirs. I was a counterpuncher by nature and so I'd lived a life of blundering out into the fray, expecting to meet my challenges as they came.

These thoughts were not very complex but it took me a long time to come to them. Before I knew it it was four-thirty and Johann Brighton was coming through the unlocked door.

I stood to meet the handsome CEO-in-waiting.

"Mr. McGill? This is a surprise."

"It is?"

"Yes."

"Completely?"

"Absolutely. What are you doing here?"

"I know that Seth Marryman hired Claudia Burns and had her come to work for you."

"Mr. Marryman died three months ago."

"He still hired Claudia."

"So? What could an executive assistant have to do with anything?"

"Why don't you tell me?"

"I don't have time for this, McGill. How did you even get here? And where is the man I was supposed to meet, Mr. Furrows?"

"Alton Plimpton canceled your meeting and slotted me in."

"Alton? He doesn't . . ." Brighton stopped there in the middle of his sentence, putting together thoughts and notions that I would have liked to share.

"What do you have to do with Alton?" he asked.

"He called and asked who I thought was the inside mastermind behind the heist eight years ago. I told him that it was the man who hired Claudia Burns."

"Why would you say that?"

"Because Claudia is actually Minnie Lesser. Minnie Lesser was the girlfriend of the man Zella Grisham shot."

Brighton took in these claims, wondering about them like a housewife gauging the ripeness of fresh fruits.

"Even if that's true," he said. "What does it have to do with Seth?"

The door behind us swung open then. Through it came the sour-faced guard followed by Clarence Lethford, Antoinette Lowry, and Carson Kitteridge. After that came the assassin with the receding hairline from the Quick house in Queens. He was in handcuffs again and shepherded by two uniformed cops. One of them was holding a high-powered rifle fitted with a telescopic sight.

The expression on Lethford's face would have been perceived as a glowering frown on most men but I knew him well enough by then to see it for what it was—a triumphant smile.

"You were right," he said to me. "It was a setup. This guy was going to kill you both."

"How'd he get out of federal custody?" I asked Antoinette.

She shrugged and gave me an apologetic look.

"Plimpton provided him with a good lawyer," she said. "We

picked up Alton boarding a chartered jet headed for the United Emirates. He had sixteen suitcases with forty-one million dollars in them."

"What is this all about?" Johann Brighton asked.

Kitteridge spoke up then. "Mr. Plimpton told us that he was working for you, Mr. Brighton. But we have the calls he made to this man. He was setting you and Mr. McGill up for an assassination."

"And you let me walk into the trap?"

"LT didn't tell us that you were on the guest list."

"Hey," I said, "I didn't know if you weren't a part of this. I still don't, for that matter."

"Would you mind coming down to the station with us, Mr. Brighton?" Lethford asked.

The captain of industry was temporarily out of his depth. He nodded weakly and walked out of the room with the prisoner and police escort.

"We'll need you to come down and make a statement, LT," Carson told me.

"What do you think it is, Kit?" I replied.

"The money speaks for itself. From the circumstances I'd say it was all this Plimpton guy. He's blaming everybody else but he had the money and he called the man with the gun."

"What about Harlow?"

"Plimpton had been training under Leonard for a few years a while back," Antoinette said. "He could have figured out the foreign arm, made the contacts he'd need."

"And how about taking the money from the vault before the heist?" I asked.

"He could have managed that with the help of Clay Thorn,"

she said. "That was back before the new security procedures were put into practice. The way Rutgers works with short-term assurances is to put them in storage and use them for credit advances."

"If they were connected, we'll find it," Kitteridge promised. He was not a man to make idle assurances. "Will you come down to the offices at Elizabeth Street this afternoon?"

"In the morning," I said. "I got a big night in front of me. I'm supposed to have dinner with my father."

Kit frowned at that. He knew my past better than anyone outside of Aura. He'd studied me the way a wild dog did the skat of his prey.

"I'll be there at nine," I said.

Kit didn't like it but he knew enough to lay off.

"Nine," he said, pointing at me. Then he walked out of the cold, sunny room.

Antoinette and I were left in the room by ourselves.

"Cutting it pretty close to the bone, weren't you?" she asked.

"I was thinkin' about that before your boss walked in."

"Shall we have a seat?"

56

THERE WAS ELECTRICITY coming from Antoinette's side of our face-to-face. I could tell by the way she looked at me that I had passed some kind of unconscious test that her id gave every black man.

I'm a twenty-first-century New Yorker and therefore have little time to contemplate race. It's not that racism doesn't exist. Lots of people in New York, and elsewhere, hate because of color and gender, religion and national origin. It's just that I rarely worry about those things because there's a real world underneath all that nonsense; a world that demands my attention almost every moment of every day.

Racism is a luxury in a world where resources are scarce, where economic competition is an armed sport, in a world where even the atmosphere is plotting against you. In an arena like that racism is more a halftime entertainment, a favorite sitcom when the day is done.

That said, Antoinette was one of the racists. She hated her own people because they didn't see her for what she was. She felt betrayed by black men and then I came along. I brought out a thrill in her heart, and maybe her nether regions. That was all good and well; she was a handsome, brave, and intelligent woman, but I was preoccupied with pain so profound that I could barely tell if it was mine alone.

"Why did you call the cops and me at the last moment?" she asked. There was a queer friendliness to the question.

"I called you right after Alton called me."

"You didn't believe him?"

"He didn't strike me as the kind of man who makes snap decisions," I said. "He'd never betray a VP like Brighton unless it was a sure thing. I thought that they must be working together or maybe that Alton was Johann's dupe."

"You were wrong."

"Yeah. I was and will be again. I've spent nearly my whole life in the penalty box but that don't mean I'm not in the game."

Antoinette Lowry smiled. I don't think she was aware of it. She'd been looking for a man like me for her entire life. She hadn't known that either.

"I'm willing to advance your name for the reward," she said; a queen offering her throne to a brash, conquering barbarian.

"Six hundred and fifteen thousand," I said.

"Unless we find more."

"You won't. Not that you'll be able to prove anyway."

"How can you be so sure?"

"Alton probably spent twenty years working on this plan. I bet you'll find that Harlow will have connections planted between him and Brighton. Maybe he'll have a numbered account somewhere. You won't be able to tie it to Plimpton. He wanted to kick up enough dust that he could make his getaway in the sandstorm. If Zella hadn't got out of jail and the police weren't looking into the heist again, he might have made it. I'll tell you what though. Let's break up the reward between me and Zella Grisham. I'll take seventy-five thousand and leave the rest for her."

"Really?"

"She spent all those years in prison. Somebody should pay for it."

"Why you?"

"Why not?"

"There has to be more to it than that."

"Maybe." I gazed across the short space between us, thinking that everything we see and experience is always in the past: the light from stars, a brief expression of love.

"You're an intriguing man, Mr. McGill."

"Most of the time I wish I had become a dull plumber. What are you gonna do, Annie?"

"What do you mean?" She didn't balk at the pet name.

"You can't stay at Rutgers. They need to bury this as soon as possible. You won't be able to stomach the changes they'll put you through."

This was a new thought in the security officer's mind. I put it there because the passion growing in her was too much for me to deal with right then. I needed time to go over my entire life and put it in order. I might even have to murder somebody before the night was through.

"I got to go," I said.

"To meet your father."

"Yeah. To meet my old man."

"Are you close?"

"I'll drop by your office sometime tomorrow," I said. "We can see about this reward thing then."

"Maybe we can have lunch."

"Yeah. I'd like that."

THE RESOLUTION of criminal cases was often like that—anticlimactic. A little guy with big ideas crushed by the pressures cultivated in his own mind. He'd robbed his own company, had his confederate murdered, and then used the ill-gotten resources to cover his crimes.

I wondered why his wife had left him. Maybe if she had stayed he might never have gone bad.

I'd been walking for nearly an hour before I was even aware of it. I couldn't remember green lights or anyone I'd passed.

I came to the entrance of the C train at Twenty-third Street. I even went down to the turnstiles with a MetroCard in hand. But I couldn't go through. The world was closing in on me. Every misstep I'd ever taken had brought me to that hole in the ground. I scurried up the concrete stairs like a coal miner running from an underground collapse.

Most of the men who died at Plimpton's behest had been condemned because of my actions. Alton Plimpton was my pawn before I ever knew his name. I was a virulent pathogen loosed on the world, wreaking carnage merely by my existence. I had evolved from my father, another deadly virus that rode invisibly and silently on the air—looking for a home in the lungs of children.

AFTER ANOTHER HOUR of walking I decided to take a bus up the West Side, reaching my building sometime after seven. Walking up the stairs, I wondered about the plan in Alton's mind. He had set up Zella and wanted to keep that subterfuge going. Maybe he'd always planned to destroy Brighton. The police would never get enough evidence to try him for murder but Rutgers would make sure that he paid for his crimes.

THERE WAS MUSIC coming from down the hall of bedrooms, emanating from Dimitri's room. He was in there with his femme fatale unafraid, and probably unaware, of the dangers she engendered.

Twill's room and Shelly's were empty. I was happy not to have to see either of them. Maybe they'd both be better off if I had disappeared like my father had . . .

It was then I noticed that there was no scent in the air.

When Katrina was on her game she cooked every night. And she had gotten better. There should have been a meal in the making.

"Katrina?" I called down the hall.

Dimitri came to the door of his room.

"You seen your mother, Bulldog?" I asked him.

"She's down in the bedroom," he said.

"How's it goin'?" I asked him.

Tatyana came out from behind him, wearing one of his yellow dress shirts—and nothing else. She was a gorgeous woman. I noted that fact about every third time I saw her.

"Fine," Dimitri said, answering my question.

I walked past the young lovers.

"Katrina?" I called again.

———

OUR BED was unmade. That was a more severe warning than the three chimes of the late-night alarm to my mind. Katrina never left an unmade bed. She tucked the blankets in at hotels and other peoples' houses. She'd dust a waiting room if you gave her the rag.

HER SKIN was white to begin with but add to that the deep red of the tepid bathwater, from the blood she'd lost, and my wife looked like a dead swan in the darkening waters of her suicide.

"Dimitri!" I shouted.

I had already gotten my arms under her body. I was lifting her from the tub, staining our turquoise tiles to an approximate violet.

"Dimitri!"

I heard the first thump of his heavy foot on the wooden floor.

I felt for her pulse but my own heart was beating too fast to feel what little her vein might be giving.

"Dimitri!"

"Mom!" he yelled, coming through the bathroom door.

With the strength of despair he shouldered me aside, reaching for the comatose woman. I went with the push, going to the cabinet for bandages and maybe an anticoagulant.

"Dimitri!" Tatyana shouted. She had jumped on his back, hooking her forearm across his throat. She yoked him while saying, "Let your father take care of her. She needs him to help stop the bleeding."

As my son fell back he went down on his knees. I used bath towels to dry the skin around the deep wounds on her wrists.

"Call nine-one-one," I said to the Belarusian.

She darted from the room.

"Mom!" Dimitri bellowed. "Mom!"

I slathered the salve on the wounds and tied the bandages first around the cuts themselves and then as tourniquets applied just below the elbows.

"Hold these," I said to Dimitri, indicating the bandages on her wrists. "Hold them tight."

He lurched forward, his knees slipping on bloody water, and did what I asked.

Tatyana ran back in. She didn't say anything. She didn't need to. While Dimitri held her arms I huddled around Katrina's alabaster body in an attempt to keep her warm.

"Did you leave the front door open?" I asked Tatyana.

She nodded, staring hard at the maybe dead woman in my arms.

57

THE WAIT was oddly peaceful. Tatyana moved up next to me and pressed her fingers against Katrina's throat.

"I think I can feel a pulse," she said to Dimitri. "She is living."

My son's cheeks were shaking. He was still on his knees, holding his mother's wrists. I might have been worried about him if I hadn't slipped into a fugue state in which the only reality was my body's warmth and the transference of the heat from me to her.

After what seemed like many hours there were banging sounds from the hall.

If there were more assassins coming, me and my family were dead.

"Down here!" Tatyana shouted. "We're down here!"

THE HOSPITAL we were brought to was called the Sisters of the Consecrated Heart. It was little more than an infirmary on 112th Street but the staff was professional and they seemed equipped for the emergency.

Helen Bancroft arrived at the same time we did. Tatyana had called her. I never asked how she came across the name.

Helen told us that it was a double waiting game.

"First she has to survive the night," she said, "and then we have to hope that the damage is not permanent."

Dimitri sat in a chair at the foot of the bed, his big hand clutching a metal rod that was part of the frame. Tatyana stood behind her man. She had her hands on his big shoulders, her chin perched on the top of his head.

I could see the pain in my son. For the first time I realized that his dour disposition was due to an extraordinary sensitivity. As big and brutish-looking as he was, Dimitri was delicate, even fragile. The frail ex-prostitute who caressed him was the strength he needed to survive this world.

"Daddy," Shelly whined as she came into the single room. She was wearing a rainbow-colored dress that showed off her slim figure.

I stepped to the side so that she could see her mother.

"Oh no," she cried, rushing past me to Katrina's side.

"Hey, Pops," Twill said.

He had on an emerald linen suit over a silken orange shirt. He looked serious and mature.

He put an arm around my shoulders and asked, "How you doin'?"

Twill was very nearly the only person who was concerned with my well-being; the only one who expected nothing in return.

"It's bad, Twilliam," I said. "Dr. Bancroft says she might not make it."

"I knew something was wrong," he said. "She just wasn't actin' right."

"You told me. I should have listened closer."

"You couldn'ta stopped this, Pops. Moms always been in

charge'a her business. You know she cross the street when she wants to. Fuck the lights."

I laughed for the first time that evening.

Twill went to his brother and actually kissed him. He patted Tatyana's arm and then moved to sit with his sister.

My son the Godfather.

THE WAIT was hours. Somewhere around midnight Dimitri passed out. Helen gave him a sedative after that and found a bed for him on another floor. Tatyana followed him up there, afraid, I'm sure, of what he might do if left to his own devices.

At seven minutes after two Twill told me, "I'm goin' home to get some rest. I figure you'll be here tomorrow and somebody should cover the fort. Soon as Mardi finds out you know she'll be here, so that only leaves me."

I took his hand and asked, "How are you, boy?"

He held my gaze and smiled.

SOME TIME AFTER FOUR Shelly was napping in her chair. If the machine next to Katrina was right, her vital signs had improved.

"Seldon told me that you came to his house," Shelly said. Her eyes were barely open.

"Sorry about that."

"Why'd you go there?"

"Lookin' for a fight, I guess."

"I love him, Daddy. He wanted to come here with me but I told him you wouldn't like it."

"No, I wouldn't. But that doesn't matter."

"Why not?"

"If you hadn't been with him, that gunman's bullets would have found you in the bed. His desire for you saved your life. That's a natural fact."

I took a deep breath and remembered something. The memory must have shown on my face.

"What is it?" Shelly asked.

"I was supposed to meet somebody for a late dinner. I completely forgot."

"You can call them tomorrow."

"I don't have his number."

W&N

blog and newsletter

For exclusive short stories, poems, extracts, essays, articles, interviews, trailers, competitions and much more visit the Weidenfeld & Nicolson blog and sign up for the newsletter at:

www.wnblog.co.uk

Follow us on

 and **twitter**

Or scan the code to access the website*

*Requires a compatible smartphone with QR reader. Mobile network and/or wi-fi charges apply.
Contact your network provider for details.